Berkley Prime Crime titles by Kate Kingsbury

Manor House Mysteries

A BICYCLE BUILT FOR MURDER
DEATH IS IN THE AIR
FOR WHOM DEATH TOLLS
DIG DEEP FOR MURDER
PAINT BY MURDER
BERRIED ALIVE
FIRE WHEN READY
WEDDING ROWS
AN UNMENTIONABLE MURDER

Pennyfoot Hotel Mysteries

ROOM WITH A CLUE
DO NOT DISTURB
SERVICE FOR TWO
EAT, DRINK, AND BE BURIED
CHECK-OUT TIME
GROUNDS FOR MURDER
PAY THE PIPER
CHIVALRY IS DEAD
RING FOR TOMB SERVICE
DEATH WITH RESERVATIONS
DYING ROOM ONLY
MAID TO MURDER

Holiday Pennyfoot Hotel Mysteries

NO CLUE AT THE INN
SLAY BELLS
SHROUDS OF HOLLY
RINGING IN MURDER
DECKED WITH FOLLY
MISTLETOE AND MAYHEM

Titles by Kate Kingsbury writing as Rebecca Kent

HIGH MARKS FOR MURDER
FINISHED OFF
MURDER HAS NO CLASS

MISTLETOE AND MAYHEM

KATE KINGSBURY

BERKLEY PRIME CRIME, NEW YORK

THE BERKLEY PUBLISHING GROUP
Published by the Penguin Group
Penguin Group (USA) Inc.
375 Hudson Street, New York, New York 10014, USA
Penguin Group (Canada), 90 Eglinton Avenue East, Suite 700, Toronto, Ontario M4P 2Y3, Canada
(a division of Pearson Penguin Canada Inc.)
Penguin Books Ltd., 80 Strand, London WC2R 0RL, England
Penguin Group Ireland, 25 St. Stephen's Green, Dublin 2, Ireland (a division of Penguin Books Ltd.)
Penguin Group (Australia), 250 Camberwell Road, Camberwell, Victoria 3124, Australia
(a division of Pearson Australia Group Pty. Ltd.)
Penguin Books India Pvt. Ltd., 11 Community Centre, Panchsheel Park, New Delhi—110 017, India
Penguin Group (NZ), 67 Apollo Drive, Rosedale, North Shore 0632, New Zealand
(a division of Pearson New Zealand Ltd.)
Penguin Books (South Africa) (Pty.) Ltd., 24 Sturdee Avenue, Rosebank, Johannesburg 2196,
South Africa

Penguin Books Ltd., Registered Offices: 80 Strand, London WC2R 0RL, England

This book is an original publication of The Berkley Publishing Group.

FIRST EDITION: November 2010

Library of Congress Cataloging-in-Publication Data

Kingsbury, Kate.
    Mistletoe and mayhem / Kate Kingsbury. — 1st ed.
        p.   cm.
    ISBN 978-0-425-23690-1
    1. Baxter, Cecily Sinclair (Fictitious character)—Fiction. 2. Pennyfoot Hotel (England : Imaginary place)—Fiction. 3. Murder—Investigation—Fiction. 4. Christmas stories. I. Title.
    PR9199.3.K44228M57   2010
    813'.6—dc22   2010017096

PRINTED IN THE UNITED STATES OF AMERICA

10 9 8 7 6 5 4 3 2 1

To Bill, for being the love of my life.

ACKNOWLEDGMENTS

I have been so fortunate with my editors, all of whom have been supportive, understanding, and encouraging. My new editor, Faith Black, is no exception. Thank you for making the transition so smooth and enjoyable, and for so quickly accommodating the inhabitants of Badgers End. They appreciate it as much as I do.

Grateful thanks to my agent, Paige Wheeler, for all your support and understanding in a difficult year. Your efforts on my behalf are so greatly appreciated.

Again I'm blessed with yet another incredible cover from Judith Murello and her talented team in the art department. I've loved each and every one of my covers, and I can't thank you enough for all your hard work.

Thanks to my lifelong friend, Ann Wraight, who keeps me in touch with my homeland and helps me keep my facts straight.

My deepest thanks to all my wonderful fans. Your e-mails mean so much, and I hope you all know how very much I enjoy them. By the time you read this, another year will have passed. None of us know what the future holds, and this year promises to be an even more uncertain one for me. I hope this isn't the last of the Pennyfoot books, but just in case it is, I want to tell you all that writing for you has been one of the greatest joys of my

Acknowledgments

life. Thank you for letting me know how much you have enjoyed the lives of the staff and guests at the Pennyfoot Hotel.

Lastly, as always, my thanks to my dear husband, Bill. I could not have done any of it without you.

MISTLETOE AND MAYHEM

CHAPTER
1

The chill wind from the ocean had brought gray skies and the threat of rain earlier that morning. In fact, the Pennyfoot's chief housemaid thought she smelled snow in the salty air as she stepped out into the kitchen yard.

Above Gertie McBride's head, seagulls circled in search of food, their shrill cries echoing across the smoking chimneys. It wasn't the hungry gulls that caught her attention, however. It was the sound of raised voices, one shrill, the other harsh and grating.

Gertie recognized them both. The high-pitched voice belonged to the new maid, Ellie. Gertie didn't like Ellie. She was the sort that acted sweet and innocent in front of Mrs. Chubb, but behind her back was as saucy as a concubine.

Gertie, on the other hand, believed in saying what she

thought, no matter who could hear her. All that putting on airs and graces was nothing better than lying, and Gertie couldn't stand a liar.

The other voice, even harsher now, Gertie knew belonged to the coal man, Stan Whittle. She'd recognize his Scottish accent anywhere. She'd been married to a Scot, and knew what one sounded like. From the sound of it, Stan was really angry with Ellie, for some reason.

The maid, however, seemed more than capable of holding her own. Her voice rising, she shouted words that made even Gertie blush. Deciding that the last thing she wanted to do was get in the middle of an argument, Gertie determined that the wine cellar could wait. They wouldn't need the sherry for another two hours. She'd come back later.

Leaving the two voices to their battle, she turned around and went back inside the kitchen.

No one would ever guess, when first glimpsing the red roofs of the Pennyfoot Country Club, that the sparkling white walls hid a dark and menacing secret. Indeed, upon first sight, the tastefully decorated foyer offered a warm welcome to all who ventured inside.

Met with bright crimson ribbons, boughs of holly, and wreaths of lush green fir adorning the staircase, not to mention the graceful Christmas tree glowing with white lace angels and silver balls, one was immediately engulfed in the best of the Edwardian Christmas spirit.

A tantalizing aroma of spicy boiled Christmas puddings, tangy mince pies, and roasting chestnuts lured the visitor even deeper into the hallways, where anxious staff members, eager to please, extended a guiding hand.

Since long before the turn of the century, the Christmas season at the Pennyfoot had offered its visitors an enjoyable week or so of appetizing food, warm hospitality, and exciting entertainment.

Perhaps too much excitement for some, as a few previous guests might have attested. For all who entered the Pennyfoot's walls in December did so at the risk of falling prey to the infamous Christmas curse.

Not that such misfortunes were ever advertised, of course. In fact, everyone employed at the club looked forward to the Christmas season with the firm belief that this year would prove to be the exception.

Cecily Sinclair Baxter was especially determined that no misfortune should mar the festivities, regardless of the Christmas curse. Having once owned the Pennyfoot when it was a hotel, she had sold it to her cousin who had then turned it into the country club.

Cecily had taken over the management and now it was her job to see that each and every guest enjoyed a pleasant and rewarding visit and returned home with many happy memories that would last a lifetime.

She would allow no forbidding thoughts to surface, in the hopes that an optimistic outlook would bring positive results. Nevertheless, her resolve was somewhat shaken when her husband arrived home that evening from his office in London with an ominous declaration.

"He has struck again," Baxter announced, throwing his homburg onto the bed in the boudoir.

Seated at her dressing table, Cecily stared at his image in the mirror. "Who has struck what, darling?"

"Not what. Whom." Baxter pulled off his cravat and ran a finger around his starched collar. "Another young girl, brutally slain. It's disgusting. You'd think Scotland Yard could have caught the scoundrel by now."

Cecily felt a shiver of fear. "Oh, dear. You're talking about London's latest serial killer."

"I am, indeed." Baxter sank heavily onto the bed. "He's got most of the city terrified out of their wits."

"Are they so sure it's a serial killer? Couldn't it just be more than one murderer?"

"Unlikely. The victims are all young women and all similar in appearance. The trademark of a serial killer. Not only that, with each victim the murderer has left a memento behind."

"Memento?"

"Yes. You know, the sort of badge that distinguishes him as the perpetrator of the crime."

Cecily shuddered. "As if he's proud of his gruesome handiwork."

"He usually is," Baxter muttered darkly.

"So what kind of memento is he leaving?"

"No one knows. Scotland Yard refuses to disclose a description. They call him the Mayfair Murderer. Apparently all the bodies have been found on or close by Savile Row."

"Good heavens." She sat up. "That is a very nice part of town. Whatever is the city coming to, harboring a murderer in such a respectable area?"

"Which makes one wonder what it was about that place the killer hated so much." The clip-clop of horses' hooves

4

and the rumble of carriage wheels outside caught his attention. He rose and walked over to the window. "Looks as if some more guests are arriving."

"Most of them are here now." Cecily leaned forward and dabbed at her nose with her powder puff. "The honeymoon couple arrived first. Geoffrey and Caroline Danville. They are such a precious couple and so obviously in love. The very first thing they did was kiss under the kissing bough. Just so adorable."

Baxter raised his eyebrows. "Kissing bough?"

"Yes, dear. That big round ball of greenery hanging in the foyer. Surely you must have seen it? It's enormous!"

Baxter merely grunted. "Another of Madeline's works of art, I presume."

"You presume right, dear." Cecily decided to ignore the hint of derision in her husband's tone. Madeline Pengrath Prestwick was one of Cecily's best friends.

Tall and slim, Madeline resembled a woodland nymph rather than a doctor's wife. Her frocks were of the finest linen, but flowed to her bare feet without any of the confining tucks and seams that fashion demanded. With great disregard to protocol, she often left her black hair unbound, allowing it to fall to her waist. It pained Cecily that not one hint of gray appeared in the gleaming locks. In fact, Madeline had not seemed to age at all in the years Cecily had known her.

That her perpetual youth was due to her mysterious powers with herbs and wild flowers was never in question, and Cecily had often been tempted to ask for a bottle of whatever magical potion kept her friend looking twenty years younger than her age.

Only pride had kept her tongue still. Pride and the knowledge that if Baxter were to ever find out, she would never hear the last of it. Madeline was considered a witch and feared by many of the inhabitants of Badgers End. Baxter shared in that belief. He tolerated the woman solely because she was a beloved friend of his wife's.

Cecily leaned forward and studied her face in the mirror. No matter how much cold cream she smeared on her skin at night, the little lines at the sides of her eyes seemed to grow deeper every day. Just a few short years now until her fiftieth birthday, and the closer she got, the less she liked it.

She glanced at her husband's image again. Baxter looked no older than the day she'd met him. Drat the man. Why was it that men appeared better looking with age, while women just became old and decrepit?

"Isn't that in questionable taste?"

Having forgotten the point of their discussion, Cecily blinked. "I beg your pardon?"

"The kissing ball thing. Do you really want people to put on a public exhibition in the foyer? Don't you think that might give the Pennyfoot a somewhat unsavory image?"

Cecily swung around on her stool. "Bax! How terribly unromantic of you! The kissing bough has been an English Christmas tradition for hundreds of years. Besides, we've always had a sprig of mistletoe hanging in the foyer. You've never found that unsavory."

Baxter shrugged. "Maybe because it wasn't quite so obvious as a monstrous ball of the stuff. I have visions of our guests fighting to slobber all over each other in full view of the front door. I can't imagine that would enhance our reputation."

"In case you haven't noticed, the Pennyfoot's reputation has never been exactly pristine. It's common knowledge that the aristocracy use our facilities for illicit relationships, and may I remind you that it's only recently that we have had a license to conduct card games. Until then, if you remember, we were forced to keep our illegal card rooms underground. I hardly think a kissing bough compares to any of that."

He must have heard the resentment in her voice, as he moved over to her and laid a warm hand on her shoulder. "Forgive me, my dear. I'm being overly critical."

"Yes, you are." She peered up at him. "Are you, perhaps, not well?"

Shaking his head, Baxter walked over to the wardrobe and opened it. "I am disturbed, that is all. I happened to see a picture this morning of the Mayfair Murderer's latest unfortunate victim."

Cecily was surprised to see her husband visibly shudder. Baxter was usually complacent in the face of adversity, and it troubled her to see him so upset. "That must have been quite horrifying."

"It was." Pulling a black dress coat from the wardrobe, Baxter muttered, "Diabolical. I hope they catch the wretch before he butchers someone else."

Cecily ignored her little flutter of apprehension. "Well, thank goodness we are far from the city. We have no such worries here."

"Not that far. After all, most of our guests have traveled here from London."

Cecily managed a nervous laugh. "Well, I'm sure we won't be offering hospitality to a serial killer."

"I sincerely hope not." Baxter moved closer and reached

7

for the white bow tie lying on the dresser. "I don't know why you insist we join the guests for the welcome banquet. All those introductions, small talk, and hand shaking—not to mention that fussy little photographer getting in everyone's way. By the time we're done with it the food will have grown cold."

Cecily rose from her seat to assist her husband with his tie. "Hush, dear. You know quite well that we always personally greet our guests at the welcome banquet and that you always enjoy conversing with the ladies. As for the photographer, just think of the memories we'll have to look back on when we are too old to manage the country club anymore."

Baxter grunted again and dropped a light kiss on his wife's forehead. "If you say so, my dear."

"You'll enjoy meeting Sir Walter and Lady Hayesbury. He's a baronet and such a charming man. He was most understanding when I explained about the roof."

"The roof?"

"Yes, dear. Ellie, the new maid, noticed the bed in room four was quite damp. When Mrs. Chubb went up to inspect it she saw the roof had been leaking. She summoned the roofers, and they arrived this afternoon. I had to explain to Sir Walter that there might be some noise while the repairs are going on, and he was most accommodating. A very engaging man."

"Hmmph. Not too engaging, I hope."

Cecily smiled. "Never fear, my dear one. No one will ever take your place in my heart."

"I'm happy to hear it." He peered in the mirror to inspect her handiwork. "Who else do I have to worry might steal my wife's affections?"

She laughed out loud. "Well, there is one particular gentleman. Mr. Mortimer. He will be spending Christmas here alone, so I feel rather sorry for him."

Baxter straightened. "It always amazes me how some people can run away to a strange place to be alone, especially at Christmastime."

"Sometimes it's easier than being surrounded by the familiar." Cecily frowned. "I can't help feeling that this gentleman has suffered some kind of tragedy. He barely speaks and keeps his face hidden by one of those awful slouch hats that painters wear. He didn't even sign his first name, just an initial, J. Mortimer. A very unhappy man, I would say."

"I do hope you are not going to spend the entire Christmas season worrying over a complete stranger who might simply be suffering from a bilious stomach."

"No, dear. Of course not. I shall be far too busy." She held up the two ends of a string of pearls. "Would you be an angel and fasten these for me, please?"

His fingers fumbled at the back of her neck, sending delicious little tingles down her spine. "It sounds as if we have a mixed bag of guests as usual."

"We also have two children staying with us. Lord and Lady Millshire have brought their son, Wilfred, and their daughter, Adelaide. Rather rambunctious, I'm afraid. "

His hands stilled. "There goes the peace and quiet. Young children?"

"About the same age as Gertie's twins. It's too bad the twins are in London until Christmas Eve. They could have played together."

"I hardly think our guests would allow their children to associate with the offspring of a housemaid."

"Chief housemaid." Once more Cecily gave her husband a worried look. "Good heavens, Hugh, the twins are your god-children. You didn't have to sound so derisive. Gertie has been with us since she was a child herself. She's part of our family, as is all our staff. You're not usually so contemptuous. You really must be out of sorts." She rarely called her husband by his first name, and usually did so when she was annoyed with him.

Apparently acknowledging this, Baxter was immediately contrite. "I'm sorry, dearest. I shall make no more comments, I promise, until I'm in a better frame of mind."

"That would be wise." She pulled open a dresser drawer to retrieve a white lace-edged handkerchief. Tucking it into her sleeve, she murmured, "Perhaps we should join our guests for dinner. Maybe they can improve your disposition."

She led him from the room, feeling a deep sense of fore-boding. Something had greatly upset her husband. If it were indeed the picture of the slain girl that had generated such concern, then she shuddered to think what the poor woman had suffered at the hands of such a beast. In light of that, it was difficult to hold forbidding thoughts at bay.

Descending the gaily decorated staircase, she sent up a silent prayer that the Christmas curse be forever banished from the Pennyfoot Country Club. May this be the first year they could escape such tragedy and simply enjoy the happiest season of all.

Mrs. Chubb, the Pennyfoot's industrious housekeeper, was in a particularly good mood. She had received news that her daughter was expecting an addition to the family, and she was already planning her summer visit.

Much as she loved living in the tiny village on England's southeast coast, there were times when she missed her daughter dreadfully, and lived for the excuse to make the long journey north.

So it was that when Ellie, the new maid hired for the busy holidays, had alerted her that one of the ceilings on the top floor had sprouted a leak, soaking the bed beneath it, Mrs. Chubb had viewed the calamity with less concern than she might have done normally. After all, what was a wet bed compared to a new life on the way? She had simply rung the roofing company and demanded they start work that very afternoon.

Even when her chief housemaid, Gertie, charged into the kitchen with her usual lack of grace and decorum, cap askew and strands of dark hair flying, Mrs. Chubb resisted the temptation to scold her and made do with a loud sigh instead. "One of these days, Gertie, my girl, you'll rush in here like that and do some real damage. Then you'll be sorry, mark my words."

Gertie grinned. "Sorry, Chubby. I was in a hurry. Pansy forgot to bring the shakers up to the dining room." She rushed over to the dresser and grabbed up the tray of silver salt and pepper shakers. "She'll forget her bloody head one day, that girl."

"How many times do I have to tell you? Don't call me Chubby." The housekeeper wagged a finger at her unrepentant maid. "I don't know what you and Pansy get up to in that dining room, but you were both supposed to be back here half an hour ago. Michel will be in any minute and you know he throws a fit if his potatoes aren't peeled."

Gertie wrinkled her nose. "Michel throws a bleeding fit

11

over nothing. All that crashing and banging around gives me a headache. You'd think he was the king of England instead of a blinking chef. I don't know why madam ever hired him. He's nothing but a big baby with a bad temper."

"Gertie Brown McBride!" Mrs. Chubb dug her fists into her ample hips. "Hold your tongue! Calling people such names, indeed."

"All right, all right. Keep your bloomin' hair on." Gertie stomped over to the door with the tray. "I've got to get back to the dining room with the shakers, or we'll never have the tables ready for the welcome banquet."

Mrs. Chubb held up her hand. "Just a minute! As soon as you've finished up there, tell Pansy she's to boil up some water for hot water bottles."

Gertie raised her eyebrows. "We already aired all the beds."

"Yes, well, one of them's soaking wet, so we're going to need hot water bottles and warming pans to get it dry."

"Someone wet the bed? How could they? We haven't had any guests until this afternoon." Gertie widened her eyes. "It weren't Mr. Baxter, was it?"

All of Mrs. Chubb's patience evaporated. It was one thing to insult the chef, but to cast aspersions on madam's husband was something she simply would not tolerate. Raising her voice, she barked, "No, it wasn't Mr. Baxter! It was a leak in the roof. Get up there right now so you can both get back here and get that water boiled and the warming pans filled with coals."

"All right, all right. I'm going." Gertie bashed the door open with her knee and disappeared, though she could be heard muttering to herself all the way down the corridor.

12

Letting out her breath, Mrs. Chubb turned to Ellie, who had been cowering in the pantry throughout the exchange. "What are you doing in there? Come on out here. I need you to get the hot water bottles and warming pans from the laundry cupboard. Right this minute."

Ellie scurried to the door and pushed it open. "Yes, Mrs. Chubb. Right away, Mrs. Chubb."

The housekeeper watched the door swing to, behind her. If only Gertie and Pansy were half as obedient and respectful. This new maid was such a polite little thing. Maybe a bit too jumpy and nervous at times, but always willing to please. With that flaxen hair and blue eyes, at times she looked like a little angel.

Mrs. Chubb's lips twitched. There was no possible way Gertie could ever look like an angel. Not only was she as dark haired and dark eyed as the devil, she had the build and constitution of a bull. And every bit as stubborn.

Still, she had to admit, the Pennyfoot would be a dull place without Gertie McBride and her runaway tongue. Not that working in the club was ever dull. Especially at Christmastime. Her stomach gave a little flip. No, not this year. This year there would be no nasty business. This year was going to be different. She'd bet her best bonnet on it.

CHAPTER

❀ 2 ❀

Upstairs in the dining room, Gertie dumped the tray of condiment sets onto a white-clothed table. Madeline Prestwick had decorated the walls with colorful paper chains and fluffy white cotton balls that made it look like it was snowing.

Hanging from the ceiling were green and red paper balls that twirled every time someone walked beneath them. Gertie thought the balls were a bit gaudy, but who was she to say. Mrs. Prestwick had been decorating the Pennyfoot for Christmas ever since Gertie had worked there, and every year people would praise her handiwork. As far as madam was concerned, Mrs. Prestwick could do no wrong.

On the other side of the room, a young girl stood by the tall, narrow windows, gazing out onto the bowling greens. At the sound of the shakers rattling, she spun around.

"You made me jump! I didn't hear you come in."

Gertie frowned. No matter how little she ate, she'd never be as skinny as Pansy. She tried not to let it bother her, but she couldn't help a little twinge of envy every time she looked at the slender maid. "What the blinking heck are you doing, standing there in a trance? You were supposed to have all the serviettes in their rings by now." Gertie snatched up a silver embossed ring and waved it at her. "Does this look like it's got a bloody serviette in it?"

Pansy shrugged and wandered back to the tables. "Sorry. I was thinking about something."

"Not still mooning over that Samuel, are you?" Gertie placed a salt and pepper shaker in the middle of the lace tablecloth, then moved on to the next table. When Pansy didn't answer right away, Gertie looked up, searching her friend's face. "What's he gone and done now?"

Pansy's face puckered up, as if she was about to cry. "I think he fancies Ellie."

Gertie laughed. "What, that little twerp? Our Samuel wouldn't look at her twice. You know him, he'd rather be doing his job looking after the horses and motorcars than chasing after a bit of fluff like Ellie. Besides, I happen to know she's sweet on one of the footmen."

Pansy brightened. "Which one?"

"Charlie, the dark-haired one with a mustache."

"Oh, the nice-looking one. How do you know?"

"I saw them kissing under the kissing bough."

Pansy squealed. "Ooh, go on! I love that kissing bough. Mrs. Prestwick is so clever. She always has something different every Christmas, and this is the best one yet. I'm hoping to get Samuel under there to kiss me."

Gertie snorted. "I can think of better places to kiss someone."

"Who cares where it is as long as it happens."

"Well, obviously Ellie didn't seem to mind when she kissed Charlie." Gertie studied a salt shaker for a moment, then polished it with the corner of her apron. "Mrs. Chubb may think Ellie's all pure and innocent, but I could tell her a thing or two."

Obviously enthralled, Pansy's eyes widened. "Like what? Do tell me!"

Gertie shrugged. "I heard her this morning shouting at Stan Whittle."

"The coal man? I heard her, too, but I couldn't tell what she was saying. What was she shouting at him for?"

"I dunno, but she sounded really, really angry. I tell you, she was using words I never heard of, and I thought I knew 'em all."

"Go on! What did she say then?"

"I wouldn't repeat what she said to no one. Chubby thinks she's such a goody-goody, but she don't know her. Chubby told me Ellie used to work in London, but she didn't like living in the city, so she came home to Badgers End. I reckon she learned a lot about men while she was up there. Them city girls are too bloody bold for their own good."

"She certainly likes to lead Samuel on." Pansy poked a serviette through a ring with a little more force than needed. "She was laughing and giggling and carrying on something awful."

"Ah, but was Samuel laughing with her?"

Pansy shrugged. "I didn't stay around long enough to find out."

"That's where you made your mistake." Gertie sighed

17

and moved on to the next table. "Like me. I think I must be getting old."

Pansy laughed. "How can you be old when you're not yet thirty?"

"I feel old." She straightened a place setting on the table, then placed the shakers above it. "I've been seeing Dan forever, it seems, and yet he still hasn't asked me to marry him."

"He will. Some blokes like to take their time with things like that."

Gertie pulled a face. "Some blokes don't want to get tied down, neither. Can't say as I blame him, what with me having the twins and all. They can be a bit of a handful."

"Well, they're with their nanny in London right now, aren't they?"

Gertie nodded. "Daisy took them up there to see her sister, Doris, perform in a pantomime. They'll be staying with Doris until they come back Christmas Eve."

Pansy grinned. "Well, now's your chance. You got some free time on your hands. Make the most of it. Go romancing with your Dan and make him propose."

"It's all right for you." Gertie stomped over to the next table. "You're skinny and pretty and not yet twenty-one. I'm big and clumsy and the mother of twins. What chance do I have of getting a man to marry me?"

"Go on with you. Any man would be lucky to have you for a wife. You're funny and clever and you like taking care of people. A man likes that in a woman."

Gertie had to smile. "You want to tell Dan that?"

"I will. The very next time he comes over."

If he comes over, Gertie thought, as she carried the empty tray back to the dresser. He'd been making excuses lately, and it worried her. Everything seemed to bother her lately. Maybe she was just missing the twins. Or maybe she was seeing her chances of getting married again slipping away.

"Come on, cheer up," Pansy said behind her. "It's Christmas. Where's your Christmas spirit?"

"In London with my twins," Gertie muttered. "I'll be glad when this one is over."

"Well, let's at least hope we don't get clobbered with the Christmas curse again."

Gertie swung around. "Shshh! You know we're not supposed to say anything about that."

Pansy grinned. "There's no one here to hear me, except you."

"Yeah, well." Feeling a cold tingle down her back, Gertie glanced around. "Just mentioning it is bad luck. So just keep your trap shut. We don't want no more horrible things happening around here, do we. Now, let's get these tables finished before Chubby comes up here with her rolling pin."

Gazing around the dining room later, Cecily felt a little rush of warm pleasure. The festivities had begun, and she could feel the anticipation in the room. The ladies were simply enchanting in gorgeous evening gowns, while the gentlemen in their black frock coats and white bow ties added to the elegance of the scene.

Even the maids looked resplendent in black dresses and frothy lace aprons, as they hurried back and forth bearing silver platters of food. In the corner of the room a string quartet played discreet melodies, barely heard above the chatter and laughter of the guests.

19

Leaning back in her chair, Cecily uttered a satisfied sigh. It was worth all the hard work and headaches. Madeline had achieved miracles as usual with her deft hand and eye for color.

The room positively sparkled with bright red ribbons and glittering silver balls dangling from the ceiling on silver cords. The sprays of holly and mistletoe on the tables were a nice touch, and so indicative of Madeline's many talents.

"You're looking well pleased with yourself this evening, my dear."

Her thoughts interrupted by her husband, Cecily smiled at him. "I was just thinking how elegant everyone looks tonight. I do love the welcoming banquet. Most of the work is done and we have all the merrymaking still to come. There's so much to look forward to—the ball, the carol singing on Christmas Eve, the pantomime—"

Her words were cut off by her husband's groan. "Don't remind me. I suppose we have to put up with the daffy Phoebe Fortescue and her even more feebleminded husband."

"Phoebe Carter-Holmes Fortescue would not appreciate being referred to as daffy. You know how protective she is of her image."

"To the point of being ridiculous. Whatever possessed her to marry that addle-brained colonel I'll never know."

Just like Madeline, Phoebe was one of Cecily's best friends. She would not allow such disparagement, especially from her husband. "Colonel Fortescue is a kind and generous man who adores Phoebe. It's not his fault that his mind has been somewhat . . . ah . . . disturbed by his military service in the Boer War."

Baxter uttered a short laugh. "Disturbed? The man is a

20

positive lunatic. How many times have we had to restrain him from attacking the grandfather clock in the foyer with his imaginary sword?"

"I have to admit, he can be tiresome at times. Phoebe, however, seems perfectly happy with him and that's all that matters."

"Happy? Grateful, is more like it. After all, she was thrown out onto the street after her first husband died. She and that timid son of hers. She was lucky to have someone rescue them from abject poverty."

Cecily stirred uneasily on her chair. Madeline had once told her that Phoebe's son, Algie, bore a rather inappropriate liking for men's company, a fact which Cecily had not shared with her husband.

Baxter was intolerant of anything considered improper, and no doubt would avoid all contact with the man. Since Algie was the vicar of Badgers End, and conducted services at St. Bartholomew's, Cecily was not about to risk being barred from attending the church, or being forced to worship alone.

"Perhaps so," she said, with just a hint of reproach, "but since their marriage seems to be working very well, I see no point in berating them." She studied her husband's face. "You're doing it again."

"Doing what?"

"You know full well to what I'm referring."

Baxter's stern features relaxed, and he gave her a rueful smile. "So I am, my dear. I deeply apologize. How may I make it up to you?"

"You can tell me what is troubling you so. It has to be more than a mere picture in a newspaper."

As an answer, he stretched out his hand and patted hers. "Nothing more than that, I assure you. Now finish your pheasant before it grows cold."

She searched his face for a moment or two before picking up her knife and fork. He could deny it all he liked, but she knew her husband. Something was distressing him, and the very fact he wanted to hide it from her told her it was significant. She would not rest comfortably now until she knew exactly what had drawn those furrows on Baxter's brow.

Down in the kitchen, Pansy groaned as she lifted a tray full of dirty dishes from the dumbwaiter. It was the job she disliked the most. The maids piled the trays so high she could hardly lift them, much less carry them across the kitchen to the sink.

She lived in fear that something would fall off the tray and she would have to pay through the nose to replace it. In order to avoid that at all costs, she edged across the tiled floor one step at a time, holding her breath. That usually aroused the ire of Mrs. Chubb, however, who invariably yelled at her, making her jump, putting the dishes in even more peril.

She had almost reached the sink when the dreaded protest bellowed out behind her. "For pity's sake, Pansy! Get a move on with those dishes. You're taking all day!"

Although she'd braced herself for the housekeeper's explosion, Pansy was helpless to prevent the violent jerk of her body. The dishes rattled, and a precious cup wobbled back and forth at an alarming angle.

In a desperate bid to save it, Pansy lunged forward the last two steps and smacked the tray down on the counter.

The cup leapt from the tray and landed on the floor with an almighty crash.

Michel swung around from the stove, his tall chef's cap bobbing up and down. "*Sacre bleu*! What a clumsy oaf you are! You make me spill ze gravy all over the stove. Now you clean it up, *oui?*"

Pansy promptly burst into tears.

Muttering under her breath, Mrs. Chubb hurried over to her and patted her shoulder. "There, there, no need to carry on. Just pick up the pieces." She glared at Michel. "And you can clean up your own stove. You know full well she didn't do it on purpose."

"She never do it on purpose," Michel roared. "She is clumsy, that one. Clumsy like an elephant." He slammed a saucepan lid down hard on the stove, making Pansy cry even louder.

"Now look what you've done." The housekeeper fished a large white handkerchief out of her apron pocket and handed it to Pansy. "Come now, child, blow your nose. It's not the end of the world."

It might just as well be, Pansy thought, as she obligingly trumpeted into the handkerchief. What with Samuel paying her no attention and the new maid flapping her eyelids all the time at him, this was going to be a miserable Christmas.

"Here." Mrs. Chubb took the handkerchief from her and tucked it back in her pocket. "I'll pick up this mess. You can take the tray up to Mr. Mortimer. He's requested his meal in his room tonight." She pointed at the tray on the kitchen table.

Pansy wrinkled her nose at the steaming bowl of soup

and two thick slices of bread. Sitting next to it was a plate of fried roes with beans on toast, and another dish piled high with carrots, peas, and a large slice of steak and kidney pie smothered in gravy.

"I've already sent up a bottle of sherry and a decanter of brandy, so ask the gentleman if he would like a cup of tea and we'll take it up later."

Pansy went on looking at the tray. All that food smelled all right but she didn't have one teeny bit of appetite to enjoy it. The thought of eating just made her feel sick.

"Well go on, girl! Don't stand there gaping at it. Take it up to room nine."

Her thoughts shattered, Pansy leapt for the table, bumping her hip against it as she reached for the tray. "Ow . . . that hurt!"

Michel muttered something and crashed another saucepan lid down on the stove.

Pansy grabbed the tray and fled out the door.

Crossing the lobby, she spotted Ellie hovering in the entrance to the hallway. Pansy frowned. The guests should all be in the dining room, and that's where Ellie was supposed to be, helping Gertie wait on the tables. If it weren't for that blinking girl, she'd be helping Gertie instead of carrying a tray that weighed a ton all the way upstairs to room nine.

She reached the stairs and started up them. As she turned into the curve of the staircase, she glanced down again. Just in time to see Charlie, the footman Gertie had mentioned, dart across the lobby, pull Ellie out under the kissing bough, and smother her face with his.

Mesmerized, Pansy stood and watched. At least it wasn't her Samuel who was acting in such a scandalous manner.

Her lips twitched. She wouldn't mind at all if Samuel acted that way, as long as it was her he was kissing.

"Excuse me, I'd like to pass."

Pansy jumped back from the railing, slopping soup over into the dish beneath it. Her face flamed when she saw one of the guests glaring down at her. Muttering apologies, she slammed her back against the far railing and waited for him to descend the stairs before peeking over the banister again.

Ellie and Charlie had disappeared, which was just as well, considering Sir Walter Hayesbury was now striding across the lobby to the hallway, obviously late for dinner and even more obviously put out by it.

Pansy scrambled up the rest of the stairs and hurried down the hallway to room nine. It would be just her luck for Mr. Mortimer to complain because his dinner was cold. Then she'd be in hot water.

Reaching the door, she tapped lightly on it and waited for a response. Nothing but silence greeted her, and after waiting for several anxious seconds, she curled her fingers and rapped loudly on the door.

"Yes, yes! What is it?"

The voice from the other side of the door sounded grumpy and harsh. A voice Pansy didn't like at all. "It's the maid, sir," she called out. "I brought up your dinner tray for you like you asked."

A couple of grunts answered her, then the sound of the key turning in the lock. The door opened an inch or two and a bony hand appeared. "Give it to me."

"I can't get it through that space without spilling everything, sir."

25

"Oh, very well." The door opened slightly wider. "Bring it in and put it on the bed."

Gritting her teeth, Pansy lifted her knee and nudged the door open. Inside the room a small oil lamp, turned down low, flickered on the bedside table. The stocky figure of Mr. Mortimer stood with his back to her by the window, staring out, though he couldn't possibly see anything since it was pitch dark outside.

Pansy glanced at the back of his head, then let out a small sigh as she placed the tray carefully in the middle of the bed. "Will that be all, sir?"

"Yes, thank you."

Encouraged by the small gesture of appreciation, Pansy went on brightly, "Mrs. Chubb said to ask if you would like a cup of tea brought up later. I'll be happy to bring it up for—"

"No tea! I want nothing else."

Startled by the gruff tone again, Pansy backed away to the door. "Very well, sir. I'll be back to pick up the tray, then—"

"I'll put it outside when I'm finished. Now please, just go away and leave me alone."

Pansy was only too happy to oblige. She slipped outside and closed the door a little firmly to show her displeasure, then marched back down the stairs full of righteous indignation. *How dare he talk to me that way!* Still steaming, she charged across the lobby and ran full tilt into Gertie coming the other way.

"What's the bloody matter with you?" Gertie demanded, jamming her fists into her hips. "You look as if you've got the devil chasing you."

Panting, Pansy flapped a hand in front of her face. "I just came from that Mr. Mortimer's room. He gives me the willies, he does. He wouldn't even look at me. Just stood there looking out the window at nothing but darkness." She shivered. "Did you see him when he arrived? That hat pulled right down over his face, like he didn't want no one seeing him?"

Gertie shrugged. "Maybe he's just shy. He's here on his own, isn't he? Some people just like to be left alone."

"Then why did he come down here if he wants to be alone? Why didn't he just stay home?"

"I don't know. Why don't you ask him?"

Pansy twisted her lips. "Very funny. I tell you, Gertie, there's something creepy about that man. If anyone's the devil, it's him. You mark my words."

CHAPTER
❀ 3 ❀

Having invited Madeline over for breakfast the next morning, Cecily happened to be in the lobby when she arrived earlier than expected. Thrilled to see that her friend held her tiny daughter in her arms, she held out her hands as Madeline approached. "Oh, she is so precious. Do let me hold her."

"With pleasure." Madeline handed over the baby. "She is getting so heavy. She was such a tiny thing when she was born. That's less than six months ago."

"Babies grow fast the first year." Cecily touched the soft cheek. "Hello, little Angelina. I wonder what Father Christmas will bring you for your very first Christmas."

"Too much. Kevin utterly spoils her." Madeline unwound her chiffon scarf from her head and tucked it in the cloth bag hanging from her arm. Her hair gleamed like black gold as it streamed over her shoulders. Glancing up, she murmured, "I'm having second thoughts about that kissing bough. I'm not sure the lobby is the right place to hang it. Perhaps we should hang it in the ballroom, instead."

Cecily frowned. "Baxter said the same thing. I suppose we could move it there. After all there's a lot more room in there."

Madeline chuckled. "You are expecting a good many people to take advantage of it, then?"

"I'm expecting people to admire it, at least. But you're both right. It needs plenty of room to show it off properly. I'll have one of the footmen move it this afternoon. But before I do, I'm going to make use of it right now."

She bent her head and pressed a light kiss to the baby's soft forehead. "Merry Christmas, little one. May this Christmas be the first of very many happy ones to come."

Angelina gurgled in response and stretched up a pudgy hand as if reaching for the huge ball above her head.

Cecily drew her away. "You don't want to play with that, precious," she murmured. "That has holly in it and will prick your fingers."

"You're forgetting whose daughter she is," Madeline said, as Cecily headed for the stairs. "She has a fascination with all kinds of plants."

She'd said it with a note of resignation in her voice, and Cecily felt a thump of apprehension. The one thing Madeline had worried about was that Angelina would inherit her mother's special powers. Dr. Kevin Prestwick would not accept his daughter's abilities lightly. As a man of science, his methods of healing differed vastly from his wife's and had proved a formidable bone of contention in their marriage.

Once inside her suite, Cecily motioned Madeline to take a seat, then sat down herself on the chaise lounge. Still holding the baby, she rocked her for a moment or two, then said lightly, "So how is your husband adjusting to fatherhood? You haven't mentioned much about Kevin recently."

Madeline's expression grew wary. "I haven't seen much of him of late. He spends a great deal of his time in surgery or visiting patients, and it's often quite late before he returns home. That's why we arrived early this morning. Kevin brought us in the carriage before he started his rounds. He sees so little of his daughter. He'll forget what she looks like before long."

"I doubt that." Cecily watched in fascination as Angelina tugged at the strings of her bonnet until they came undone. "She is as beautiful as her mother."

"And just as controversial, I'm afraid."

Cecily looked up. "Are you saying she has your powers? How do you know? What—" She broke off as an urgent rapping on the door interrupted her words. "Oh, that must be our breakfast. I thought it would be better to have it sent up here. You can lay Angelina on the floor and eat your food in peace." Getting up, she handed the baby to Madeline.

"Won't Baxter be joining us?" Madeline asked, as Cecily hurried across the room.

"He's already had his breakfast." Cecily opened the door. "He's gone to the barber's. He likes to get there before it gets too busy." To her surprise, she saw Gertie hovering outside, a breakfast tray in her hands, and by the look on the housemaid's face, something had greatly upset her.

31

"Come in, Gertie." Cecily opened the door wider. "You don't usually deliver trays. Where are the maids?"

"All busy, m'm. Most of them are serving breakfast in the dining room, and Pansy is taking a tray to Mr. Mortimer." Gertie marched into the room, murmured a polite greeting to Madeline, and set the tray down on the table in front of her. "Ellie didn't come in this morning, either, so we're bit short."

"Oh, dear. Is she not well?"

Gertie shrugged. "I dunno, m'm. I haven't heard nothing about it."

"Well, perhaps we should send a footman over to her house later to see if she is all right."

"Yes, m'm."

Gertie seemed in no hurry to move, and Cecily was startled to see her chief housemaid's lower lip trembling. "Is something the matter?"

Gertie glanced at Madeline, then back at Cecily. "I don't like to be the one to tell you this, m'm, but . . . there's been an accident."

Cecily felt as if her stomach had dropped all the way to her shoes. "What kind of accident?"

Gertie swallowed, then blurted out, "It's Charlie, m'm. He got hit in the head. He's . . . I'm afraid he's dead, m'm."

Cecily sat down heavily on the chaise lounge, while Madeline uttered a soft cry of distress.

Gertie looked as if she wanted to run from the room. "I'm sorry, m'm. It were Clive what found him this morning. Said Charlie was lying behind the rose bushes. Good job and all, 'cos no one else could see him. Clive went in to dig up the flower beds and saw him lying there in a pool of blood."

Cecily closed her eyes while Madeline muttered something under her breath.

Gertie struggled on, her words becoming more and more strangled. "Clive says Charlie got hit on the head by a gargoyle from off the roof. It must have been left up there by the workmen last night and got blown off by the wind. It were lying next to Charlie all broken in pieces."

Cecily took a deep breath. "Where is the body now?"

"Still in the rose bushes, m'm. Clive said it was best to leave it there until the doctor could take a look at him." She glanced at Madeline. "Mrs. Chubb has sent for Dr. Prestwick, m'm."

Madeline nodded, and Cecily rose to her feet. "Thank you, Gertie. Please, do let me know the minute Dr. Prestwick arrives."

"Yes, m'm. Oh, and Mrs. Chubb wants to know if we should send for P.C. Northcott."

Madeline groaned. "That's all you need."

Cecily heartily agreed. Police Constable Sam Northcott was more often than not a hindrance rather than a help. Though the sole constable in Badgers End, he usually had little to do, except occasionally arrest one of the customers from the Fox and Hounds for disturbing the peace.

Cecily was forced to summon him whenever a death occurred on the Pennyfoot property. No matter how gruesome the situation, Northcott's main concern was how much food he could consume from the kitchen before he left.

"With any luck at all," Cecily said, "the constable will be leaving for his annual Christmas visit to his wife's family." She frowned. "I suppose, however, that we must inform him of the death, even if it was an accident. Tell Mrs. Chubb to ring the police station, and leave a message for him there."

"Yes, m'm. Sorry, m'm." Bending her knees, Gertie dropped a brief curtsey and left.

Madeline lowered her head to press her cheek against her baby's. "I'm sorry, Cecily. The Christmas curse again. At least this time it appears to be an accident."

Cecily sat down opposite her again. "We have thought so before, only to have it turn out to be murder." She stared hard at her friend. "I don't suppose you . . . ?"

She had left the question unfinished, but Madeline had understood. "I'm sorry, Cecily. My dratted intuition tells me nothing. As you well know, my revelations are far from predictable."

"Poor Charlie. He had only been with us a short time, but he seemed such a nice young lad. I can't imagine what he was doing in the rose garden, though. I do hope Kevin gets here soon. I don't like to think of that poor boy lying out there all morning."

"Kevin will still be on his rounds," Madeline said. "Very few of his patients have telephones. We'll probably have to wait until he gets back to his office."

"Oh, dear. I hope none of the guests see the body. It's hard enough getting visitors to stay here this time of year with rumors abounding about the dratted curse. We do our best to keep it quiet but you know how people love to gossip."

"Well, Clive didn't see him until he went behind the bushes, and in any case, it's chilly out there this morning. I doubt that too many people will be strolling around the rose gardens, especially since all the roses have died."

Cecily reached forward for the teapot. "I suppose you're

right. I know Clive will do his very best to keep the body hidden."

"He certainly seems competent." Madeline gave her a sharp look. "He also appears to be far too intelligent to be a maintenance man."

Cecily concentrated on pouring steaming brown liquid into the delicate china cups. It wasn't her place to repeat Clive's history of the alcohol addiction that had cost him not only a teaching career, but his marriage as well. "He seems happy enough working here. I don't question his motives."

"I sense something in his past. Something that causes him great pain and guilt."

Knowing Madeline's uncanny knack of seeing into people's minds, Cecily concentrated on placing the cup and saucer in front of her friend. "Well, if so, he appears to have laid his ghosts to rest. He's an excellent maintenance man and that's all I ask."

"He's certainly strong enough for any task you may give him." Madeline rolled her eyes. "Those muscles are quite impressive."

Aghast, Cecily stared at her. "Madeline! Let us not forget you are a married woman and a mother."

Madeline's lyrical laugh rang out. "I'm teasing you, Cecily. Forgive me. I was trying to lighten your mood. This is not the time, I know. You're upset about your footman, and rightly so, but try not to worry for now. Wait and see what Kevin has to say." She lowered Angelina to the carpet and laid her on her back. "Let us eat breakfast. It will make you feel better."

She sniffed with an appreciative air. "I'm starving, and this food smells delightful. There's nothing like the smell of bacon and sausage to torment the appetite. It's not my usual fare for breakfast but I'm willing to indulge myself once in a while."

Cecily wasn't at all sure she could eat anything. In spite of Madeline's apparent lack of concern, Cecily couldn't help worrying that the curse was upon them again. The Pennyfoot Christmas curse, which always brought death, and always by someone's hand.

All she could do for now was wait for Kevin Prestwick's verdict and pray that this time would be different.

Pansy's hand trembled when she lifted it to knock on J. Mortimer's door. The shock of hearing about poor Charlie's death had made her feel sick, and she was in no shape to face the sinister Mr. Mortimer. Indeed, she was sorely tempted to place the tray on the floor and knock on the door, then run down the stairs before the spooky old gentleman could open it.

The fear of reprisals should Mr. Mortimer complain, however, kept one hand lifted in the air while she balanced the tray on her knee with the other. She would count to ten, she decided, then rap on the door with her clenched knuckles. One, two, three . . .

The door opened without warning, sending her off balance. Uttering a shrill shriek, Pansy clutched the tray. The poached eggs started to slide off their bed of toast, and she had to jiggle them to get them back in place.

"Good heavens, girl! Do you have to make that unearthly noise?" The tray was snatched from her hands and the door slammed in her face before she even had time to draw breath and apologize.

Grumbling to herself, she fled down the stairs. Next time someone else could take up the tray to room nine. If Ellie had been there like she was supposed to be then she would have taken up the ogre's tray.

Pansy stomped down the last few steps, deciding that the very next time she saw Ellie she'd give her a piece of her mind for making her do twice the work.

She was about to cross the lobby to the kitchen stairs when she heard a soft whistle over by the front entrance. Pausing, she saw the face of a young man peering around the door, smiling at her.

It was a nice face, with twinkly blue eyes and a cheeky grin. A hand appeared next to the face, with a beckoning finger. "Here! Come over here."

Pansy hesitated. She'd seen the young lad on the roof earlier, when she'd gone out to fill the coal bucket. He'd whistled at her, the sort of whistle that made her blush. She'd given him a wave of her hand before going back into the kitchen, and that whistle had warmed her right through, making her forget how cold the kitchen could be before the stove was lit.

"Come here! I want to talk to you!" The words hissed across the empty lobby, inviting and dangerously exciting.

Pansy glanced at the reception desk, where Philip, the desk clerk, sat huddled over a newspaper. He hadn't even looked up. Pansy hesitated a moment longer, then darted across the lobby to the front door.

Slipping outside into the chilly air, she crossed her arms to hug herself against the cold wind. "Whatcha want?"

"I just want to talk to you, that's all. Tell me your name."

"Pansy." She stared boldly into the laughing eyes. "What's yours?"

"Lenny. I'm working up there on your roof."

"Yeah, I saw you." She chewed her bottom lip. "Did you hear about the footman what got killed, then?"

Lenny's eyes clouded with concern. "Yeah, I did. Poor bugger. He was in the wrong place at the wrong time, that's what."

"Yeah, he was." She shivered as a gust of wind whipped her skirt around her ankles. Across the street the empty sands stretched out to the rows of frothy waves racing to shore. The water looked dark and gray, signaling the onset of a storm. Maybe even snow, though it didn't usually last long if it came. Looking back at Lenny, she added, "Mrs. Chubb says as how your boss will be in trouble."

Lenny's eyebrows shot up, giving him a comical expression, though his eyes were anything but amused. "Mick? What's he got to do with it?"

"He left the gargoyle up on the roof where it could fall down, that's what. Mrs. Chubb says that's criminal negil . . . negle . . . neg . . ."

"Negligence," Lenny said, shaking his head. "Nah, it weren't Mick's fault. He's really careful about packing everything down tight. I helped him myself last night and that gargoyle was jammed down in the corner where an earthquake wouldn't have shifted it."

Pansy stared at him. "You sure it wasn't a different gargoyle?"

"We only removed one, didn't we. The others are still on the other three corners of the roof."

"Then how did it fall on Charlie's head?"

Lenny nodded. "That's a good question. I'm beginning to wonder that meself."

Pansy felt a stab of fear, though she wasn't sure exactly what frightened her. "Well, then, your boss must not have done as good a job as you thought. Anyhow, I'd better get along. Mrs. Chubb will be wondering where I am."

Lenny stretched out his hand and laid it on her arm. His fingers felt strong and warm through the thin material of her sleeve. "So when do you get time off?"

"Not until tomorrow afternoon."

"Yeah? Wanna go for a walk somewhere?"

"I might." She pulled away from him, unsettled by the thrills chasing down her spine. "I'll let you know."

He grinned, showing even white teeth. "I'll wait for you by the gate. Tomorrow afternoon. Three o'clock."

Heart pounding, she gave him a quick nod of her head, then shot through the door and slammed it behind her.

Much to Cecily's dismay, P.C. Northcott arrived at the club before Dr. Prestwick later that morning. Madeline had decided to wait there for her husband, thus sparing herself the long walk home with the baby.

Although Madeline was used to walking what seemed to Cecily to be impossibly long distances, carrying her rapidly growing daughter around with her had somewhat limited her stamina. Besides which, flakes of snow had begun to float in on the wind, and Madeline had no desire to trudge through a snowstorm.

Cecily had suggested her friend hire a nanny, or at least purchase a perambulator, neither of which Madeline seemed inclined to do. She preferred to use the methods nature dictated, she'd told Cecily. Even if it impaired her ability to travel as much.

She was therefore in Cecily's suite when Baxter returned from his trip into town. He greeted Madeline with a guarded nod, then turned to his wife. "What the devil is that fool Northcott doing here?"

Cecily rose, dreading having to impart the bad news. "I'm sorry, my love, but I'm afraid one of our footmen has met with an accident."

"Accident?" Baxter's brows drew together in a fierce line. "What happened?"

Cecily explained what she knew. "We're waiting for Kevin to arrive. P.C. Northcott insisted on viewing the body, even though I tried to tempt him with Mrs. Chubb's mince pies. He seemed most determined."

"I thought he was off on his annual Christmas visit to relatives."

"He won't be going this year. Apparently the relatives have decided to stay with him and his wife for a change." Cecily sighed. "He's none too happy with the idea."

"I can imagine." Baxter raised his chin and stared at the ceiling. "I leave for one morning and all hell breaks loose. We seem to have been through all this before."

"I don't think this had anything to do with your absence, dear." Cecily laid a hand on his arm. "Don't worry, Bax. I know it's terribly distressing, but it does seem to have been an accident this time. Poor Charlie was simply in the wrong place at the wrong time. That's all."

"If you ask me, it's a clear case of carelessness on the roofers' part. They should be held accountable."

"Yes, dear. I plan to have a word with them just as soon as Kevin has given us his report."

Baxter stared at her for a moment. "Very well. I have some reports to study. I'll be in your office if you need me." He nodded at Madeline again. "Mrs. Prestwick. Beautiful child you have there."

He was gone before Madeline could respond with more than a surprised, "Thank you!"

"Your husband," she added, after the door had closed behind him, "can be quite charming when he chooses."

Staring after him, Cecily murmured, "Quite. He even surprises me sometimes." Baxter rarely brought work home from the office, and never at Christmastime. Perhaps whatever was worrying him had to do with his business. She would be sure to ask him at the earliest opportunity.

Just then a light tap on the door startled her. "I hope that's Kevin." Cecily hurried to open it, and stepped back as a short, stocky man in a constable's uniform dragged his helmet from his head.

"It's me again, m'm."

"Yes, so I see." She beckoned for the constable to enter, then followed him into the room.

He waited for her to sit down before taking a seat himself. "I 'ave h'examined the body," he said, adopting the pompous tone he used to deliver official business. "It seems clear to me what happened." He paused with an expectant look, waiting for her reaction.

Knowing he would not continue until she had practically begged for information, Cecily took a deep breath. "Do tell me," she said, trying not to sound irritated. "Exactly what do you think happened?"

41

The constable looked immensely pleased with himself. "Well, it went like this, m'm. The gargoyle was either blown off the roof by the wind, or it slipped off of its own accord and fell, where it landed on the head of Charles Baker, who, I believe, was one of your footmen 'ere at the Pennyfoot."

"That's correct," Cecily said solemnly.

"Right. Ah . . ." He paused, fumbled in the breast pocket of his uniform, dragged out a notebook, and flipped it open. "The blow most likely killed him, so I'm putting this down as h'an accident. Should the doctor find anything untoward, which I'm not expecting, I shall investigate further. Otherwise the case is closed."

Relief caused Cecily to rush her words. "Thank you, Sam. I shall make arrangements to have the body collected by Charlie's next of kin just as soon as Dr. Prestwick arrives. Now, if you'd like to have some refreshment in the kitchen, I'm sure Mrs. Chubb will oblige."

The words were hardly out of her mouth before the constable had spluttered his good-byes and disappeared out the door.

"Well," Cecily murmured, "we do know how to get rid of him when needs be." She turned to Madeline, expecting to see an answering smile, and instead, encountered an expression on her friend's face she knew well. Madeline sat staring into space, her features transformed into stone.

Cecily sank down on her chair, knowing there was nothing she could do until Madeline came out of her trance. For long, anxious moments she waited, until Angelina, apparently unnerved by the tense silence, let out a howl of protest.

Madeline blinked, focused for a moment on Cecily's face,

then leaned over to pick up her squalling baby. "Hush, now, little one," she murmured, rocking Angelina back and forth until the crying subsided.

"You saw something," Cecily said, as peace was restored to the quiet room.

Reaching into the bag at her side, Madeline pulled out a soft cloth and dabbed at her daughter's wet cheeks. "Yes," she said quietly. "I did. I'm sorry, Cecily, but I'm afraid P.C. Northcott is wrong. Your footman's death was no accident. He was murdered."

CHAPTER
❀ 4 ❀

Cecily briefly closed her eyes. "I knew it. The moment Gertie walked into the room this morning I felt certain it would turn out to be murder. What did you see? Do you know what happened?"

Madeline straightened the baby's bonnet, which had slid sideways over her face. "Not much that would be of help, I'm afraid. All I could see was the figure of a man standing on the roof, with his hands raised over his head. He was holding a gargoyle."

"That could have been one of the roofers working up there. Perhaps the gargoyle slipped out of his hands and he's afraid to tell anyone."

"It didn't slip, Cecily." Madeline rested her baby's head

on her shoulder. "It was deliberately thrown, and in great anger, I would say."

Cecily collapsed against the back of her chair. "Well, that's it, then. For heaven's sake, don't tell anyone else. Not yet, at least. The last thing I need is Sam Northcott snooping around here again."

"We'll have to see what Kevin says." Madeline settled the baby more comfortably on her lap. "If he so much as smells foul play, you know he'll go straight to the constabulary."

She had barely finished speaking when a knock on the door brought up their heads. Putting a finger to her lips in warning, Cecily walked over to the door and opened it.

The tall, handsome man framed in the doorway smiled at her. "Cecily, my dear. How very nice to see you, though I wish it were under better circumstances."

"Do come in, Kevin. Your wife and daughter are waiting for you."

"Ah, I wondered if they would still be here." Kevin Prestwick strode into the room, dropped a kiss on his wife's forehead, and patted his daughter's cheek. Turning to Cecily, he added, "Jolly bad luck about your footman. He must have been passing under the roof when the gargoyle fell. A second or two earlier or later and he'd still be alive. Must have been his time to go."

Avoiding Madeline's gaze, Cecily concentrated on the doctor. "Dreadful shame. His family will be devastated."

"Well, these things happen, unfortunately. This is an old building, and there's bound to be pieces falling off it now and then. Especially if you have workmen scrambling all over the roof. I'll be happy to take care of the arrangements for the body, if you like. I assume you have the address for the lad's family?"

"Oh, would you?" Cecily clasped her hands together in front of her. "That would be such a help. I'd like to keep this from the guests if possible."

"Of course. I understand." Kevin turned to his wife and plucked the baby from her lap. "Now, I have to get back to my office, so if you're ready, my love?"

Madeline rose and reached for Cecily's hands. "I sincerely hope the rest of your day goes well."

"Thank you, Madeline." Knowing her friend was warning her to be cautious, Cecily managed a smile. "You will both be coming to the pantomime, as well as the carol singing ceremony, I trust?"

Madeline exchanged looks with her husband. "I don't know, Cecily. Now that we have the little one to take care of, we don't do much socializing at all."

"Then bring her along." Cecily stroked Angelina's soft cheek with her finger. "She's such an angel, I'm sure she'll sleep through the whole thing."

Madeline looked doubtful. "Well, I suppose we could, if you're quite sure. . . ."

"I'm certain, so that's settled." Cecily saw them to the door and waved a final farewell before returning to her chair. So the curse had struck again. It would be only a matter of time before the truth came out and Sam Northcott would be back upsetting everyone with his eternal questions.

That was supposing Madeline's vision was accurate, of course. In all the years she'd known her friend, however, Cecily had never known any of Madeline's revelations to be

47

false. She would act on the assumption that Madeline was right and start making enquiries.

At least this time she had a little leeway and a head start on the investigation. She needed to talk to the roofers right away. It seemed the best place to begin, and hopefully Baxter would be closeted in her office for some time, allowing her to conduct her own enquiries without being disturbed.

With luck on her side, she might be able to identify the killer and hand him over to the constable, thus avoiding a lengthy and disruptive investigation that would certainly cast a pall over the festivities.

Without further ado, she reached for her shawl, wrapped it around her shoulders, and headed for the door.

"Well, I think it's nice to have children in the Pennyfoot at Christmastime." Mrs. Chubb wiped her wet hands on her apron and hurried over to the kitchen table, where a large beef roast stood waiting to be carved. Pulling a carving knife from its stand, she waved it at Gertie. "I miss the twins running around here. Those two little ones remind me of your James and Lillian. They must be about the same age—seven or eight, don't you think?"

Gertie sniffed and dashed a hand across her nose. Tears glistened in her eyes due to the stinging smell of the onions she was chopping for the stew. "My twins ain't nothing like those two Millshire brats. Little devils, they are. I caught them swinging on the curtains in the library. It's a wonder they didn't pull them down."

Mrs. Chubb smiled. "They're just excited, that's all. Your

twins get into all sorts of scrapes when they're excited. Especially this time of year."

"My twins don't sauce me back when I tell them off." Gertie wiped her dripping nose again with the back of her hand then went on chopping. "You can tell those two have toffs for parents. They're just as bloody stuck-up as the grown-ups. Talked to me like I was a bleeding worm under their feet, they did."

"Well, they'll settle down after a while." Mrs. Chubb started carving wafer-thin slices of beef from the roast. "Just be careful what you say to them. We don't want them carrying tales to their father, now do we?"

Gertie didn't answer. As far as she was concerned, Lord and Lady Millshire's offspring were spoiled rotten and a sound boxing around the ears would do them a world of good.

"Here." Mrs. Chubb handed a plate of roast beef sandwiches to Gertie. "Mr. Mortimer's tray is on the dresser. Take this up to him, and make up a cheese and fruit plate to go with it. Oh, and pick up a glass of sherry from the bar on the way."

Gertie scowled. "I'm chopping onions, aren't I. Why can't Pansy take it?"

"She's doing Ellie's job, isn't she." Mrs. Chubb shook her head. "I wonder why she didn't come in today. I thought I could rely on that girl. I just hope she isn't ill or something."

"Well, we'll soon find out. Samuel went over her house a while ago to see if she was all right."

Mrs. Chubb raised her eyebrows. "Samuel? What's a stable manager doing running a footman's errands, may I ask?"

Gertie shrugged. "We're short, aren't we. What with Charlie gone and all."

"God rest his soul." The housekeeper walked over to the dresser and put the sandwich down on the tray. "That poor boy's parents. My heart goes out to them. Especially at Christmastime. Makes it twice as hard to bear."

"I still can't believe it." Gertie finished the onion and grabbed another from the bowl. "Fancy taking a morning stroll in the rose gardens and getting bumped off like that. Who'd have thought that could happen." She sniffed and rubbed her nose again. "Wonder what he was doing there so early in the morning. Rotten luck, that's what it was."

"Yes, well, you'll have bad luck, too, if you don't get this tray up to Mr. Mortimer. He's not exactly a patient man, so I've heard."

Gertie put down her knife and the onion with a puff of breath. She wasn't about to admit it to old Chubby, but the truth was, she didn't want anything to do with J. Mortimer after what Pansy had told her about the old geezer. He was a scary old bugger, that's what, and she would just as soon stay out of his way.

Still, she knew how far she could go with the housekeeper, and she wasn't about to let a grumpy old grouch get the better of her. After making up the cheese and fruit plate, she grabbed the tray, muttering, "If I'm not back in ten minutes send Clive up to look for me."

Mrs. Chubb laughed. "You sound like Pansy. What on earth has that poor Mr. Mortimer done to frighten you so?"

"Frightened?" Gertie made a guttural sound of disgust in her throat. "Who said anything about being frightened? We just can't be too careful with strangers, that's all. We never know who they are, do we. Could be that serial killer what's running around London murdering young girls. You just never know these days."

Mrs. Chubb's grin vanished. "Hush, Gertie. Don't say such things. You'll be frightening the maids, and I have enough trouble with them as it is."

"Don't say I didn't warn you." Gertie marched across to the door. Just as she reached it, it flew open, and a skinny young man burst into the kitchen, narrowly missing the loaded tray in Gertie's hands.

Shaken, Gertie glared at him. "Blimey, Samuel! What's your bleeding hurry?"

Ignoring her, Samuel looked at Mrs. Chubb. "I just came from Ellie's house," he said, sounding out of breath.

Mrs. Chubb hurried toward him. "Is she all right? She's not ill, is she?"

Samuel shook his head. "We don't know. She never came home last night. Her mum says she hasn't seen Ellie since yesterday morning. Her brother's out looking for her now."

The housekeeper gasped, her hand flying to her mouth. "Oh, my, I wonder where she went."

Remembering Clive's stricken face when he told her Charlie had died, Gertie felt her stomach start to churn. The tray felt heavy in her hands and she set it down on a chair by the door. "Oh, gawd," she whispered, "you don't think something bad has happened to her as well, do you?"

"Of course not." Mrs. Chubb sounded cross, though her face was creased in worry. "She's probably just gone somewhere and didn't tell her mother. These young girls nowadays can be so thoughtless."

Gertie felt sick. "Where would she go without telling someone?"

"I don't know. But it's not for us to say, anyway." Mrs. Chubb turned to Samuel. "Have you told madam yet?"

"No, I couldn't find her. She's nowhere in the club, and Mr. Baxter is in her office. He doesn't know where she is, either." Samuel pulled his cap from his pocket. "She must be outside. I'll go and look for her."

"Just try not to alarm her," Mrs. Chubb said, as he crossed to the door. "She's upset enough about Charlie. We don't want her thinking the worst."

Samuel nodded, but he didn't look too convinced when he left.

Gertie didn't feel all that reassured either as she picked up the tray again. "I'd better get this up to Mr. Mortimer," she said, and followed Samuel out the door.

The stable manager had already disappeared up the stairs when she stepped out into the hallway. Too bad, Gertie thought, as she followed him up to the lobby. She would have liked to ask him how things were with Pansy. He might have said something she could pass on to her friend to cheer her up a bit.

Not that Pansy was the only one who needed cheering up. Gertie had her own problems with Dan, and now there was this awful business with Charlie dying and Ellie missing. What a blinking Christmas this was turning out to be.

Reaching the top of the stairs, she glanced up to look at the kissing bough. To her dismay, it had disappeared. Someone must have taken it down. Maybe because of Charlie.

More depressed than ever, she crossed the lobby to the stairs. The kissing bough had looked so cheery hanging up there.

It was the first thing people saw when they walked in the door. Not that anyone would feel like celebrating once word got around about Charlie. It was bound to get around, like it always did, no matter how hard they tried to keep such bad news under their hats.

She reached the first landing and stomped around the railing to the second flight of stairs. Two small bodies barred her way and she came to an abrupt halt. Just her luck to bump into the Millshire brats.

"Excuse me," she muttered. "I have to go upstairs."

Wilfred, a freckle-faced lad with orange hair, stood on his toes to look at the tray. "What's that?"

Gertie resisted the temptation to tell him to mind his own business. "It's somebody's meal, that's what. Now please move aside so I can take it upstairs."

Adelaide was a smaller version of her brother, except that her hair, a much darker shade of red, hung almost to her waist. "Who's it for?"

"A gentleman."

"Can Harriet have some?" She held up a china doll, beautifully dressed in pink satin and white lace. A pink hat sat on the yellow woolen curls, decorated with flowers, ribbons, and a tiny white dove.

The doll reminded Gertie of Phoebe Fortescue, and she hid a smile. Mrs. Fortescue would not be flattered by the comparison.

"I don't think your dolly would like roast beef sandwiches."

"Harriet likes anything to eat. I give her some of my food all the time."

"She doesn't eat it," Wilfred said, his tone thick with disgust. He looked up at Gertie. "She thinks her doll is really alive. She gives it stuff to eat and drink and sings it to sleep every night."

Adelaide snatched the doll to her chest and stamped her foot. "She *is* real, so there." She rocked the doll, murmuring, "There, there. Don't let the nasty boy upset you, then."

Wilfred laughed. "I can't hear it crying. Where are its tears?"

"You just can't tell, because you're a stupid boy and boys don't know anything."

Sensing a squabble coming on, Gertie raised the tray above the children's heads. "I have to take this upstairs now, so kindly get out of my way."

Adelaide shifted sideways, but Wilfred held his ground. "Why doesn't the gentleman eat his meals in the dining room, then?"

Gertie gritted her teeth. "Because he doesn't want to be bothered with naughty little children who won't do what they're told." Shoving her hip forward, she nudged Wilfred aside and charged up the stairs.

The last thing she heard as she reached the landing was Adelaide declaring, "Harriet is alive, I tell you. She wets her drawers and everything."

Gertie didn't hear Wilfred's answer, but she was pretty sure it wasn't polite.

Reaching room nine, she balanced the tray on her hip and rapped on the door with her knuckles. After waiting for longer than her patience would allow, she rapped again. Louder this time.

The door swung open, but all she could see was hairy fingers clutching the edge. "What is it?"

The harsh tone seemed to grate right inside her head. "Your tray, sir." Her own voice had sounded higher than usual and she cleared her throat.

"Leave it there. I'm indisposed at the moment. I'll pick it up in a while."

Concerned, she edged closer to the door. "Are you ill, sir? I can bring some powders up for you, if you like?"

"I am not ailing, woman! Just leave the tray and go away." The door snapped shut again.

Offended, Gertie bent her knees and dropped the tray none too lightly on the floor. Serve him bloody well right if the ants got to it before he did. Straightening, she thumbed her nose at the door and turned her back on it. That was the last time she was taking up a tray to that old bugger. He could starve inside that bloody room for all she cared. Having settled that in her mind, she tramped back down the stairs to the kitchen.

Cecily shivered as she rounded the corner of the building.

Stray snowflakes still floated down on the wind, but turned to water the moment they hit the ground. With any luck, they would have no snowfall to spoil the Boxing Day hunt.

Her skirts whipped around her ankles as she entered the rose garden, and she drew her shawl closer around her throat. She was thankful to see Clive raking the flower beds as she passed under the trellis arches that supported the roses in the summer.

Although Charlie's body had been removed from the premises, viewing a crime scene was never one of her favorite things to do, and it was comforting to have someone else present.

The big man paused when he saw her coming, and propped his rake up against the wall. "I'm sorry about what happened to Charlie," he said, as she approached. "I would have come and told you myself, but I thought it best to stay here until the body had been taken away."

"Of course, Clive. Thank you." Cecily glanced at the rose bushes. "Whereabouts did you find him?"

"Right here, m'm." Clive stepped into the row of bushes and pointed at the ground. "I picked up the gargoyle pieces and raked it all over. I hope that was all right."

Cecily would rather have seen the murder weapon still in place, but she was reluctant to tell Clive what she suspected. He would find out soon enough if Madeline's vision proved to be correct. "Where did you put those pieces?" she asked him instead.

"In the dustbin, m'm." He gave her a sharp look. "I can retrieve them if you like?"

She shook her head. "No, that won't be necessary. Both Dr. Prestwick and P.C. Northcott are satisfied with their investigations." She glanced up at the roof, unable to suppress a shudder at the thought of that heavy masonry hurtling down on Charlie's defenseless head. "I suppose the men are still doing the repairs on the roof?"

"No, m'm. They finished up this morning. They left a short while ago."

"Oh, dear. I really needed to talk to the foreman."

"Mick Docker?" Clive looked even more curious. "Well, he did say he'd be back this afternoon to pick up his money."

"Oh, good. I can talk to him then." Of course, how silly of her. The man had to be paid, and she would take care of that herself, as usual.

"The constable talked to Mick this morning about the accident," Clive said, reaching for his rake. "I heard Mick tell him he packed everything down tight last night and he can't understand how the gargoyle got loose."

Avoiding Clive's probing gaze, Cecily said hurriedly, "Well, these things happen. It could have been the wind, or maybe a cat brushing up against it."

"Yes, m'm. If you say so."

She was about to answer him when she heard someone call out behind her. Turning, she saw Samuel hurrying toward her. One look at his face told her he was bringing bad news. Clutching her throat, she prayed it wasn't another so-called accident.

"It's Ellie, m'm," Samuel said, panting a little. "She's gone missing and her mum doesn't know where she is."

Cecily felt as if someone had punched her right in the ribs. "Missing? For how long?"

"Since last night, m'm. According to Mrs. Tidwell, Ellie never went home from here."

"I see." Aware of her maintenance man's steady gaze on her face, Cecily made an effort to recover her composure. "Well, perhaps we should pay Mrs. Tidwell a visit, Samuel. Please have a carriage ready at the front door in half an hour."

"Yes, m'm." Samuel touched his cap with his fingers and hurried off in the direction of the stables.

"Thank you, Clive." Cecily gave him an uncertain smile. "I appreciate you taking care of things here."

"Not at all, m'm. My pleasure." Clive's dark eyes raked her face. "I hope you find Miss Ellie, m'm."

A chill that had nothing to do with the cold wind chased down her spine. "So do I, Clive," she muttered as she turned away. "So do I."

CHAPTER

🏵 5 🏵

Baxter was still in her office when Cecily returned a few minutes later. As she pushed open the door and entered, he snapped shut the ledger he had in front of him, and replaced his pen in its stand. "Excellent timing," he said, as she reached the desk. "I was about to come looking for you."

"Oh?" She glanced at the ledger and then back at his face. "You have something to tell me?"

A flicker of discomfort tightened his mouth for a moment, then he smiled. "Only that I've missed your pleasant chatter. What have you been up to this morning? I assume Mrs. Prestwick has left?"

"She has indeed." Cecily hesitated, wondering if she should tell him that Ellie was missing. In the next instant she dismissed the thought. It would only worry him, and if he had the slightest inkling that she suspected foul play and intended to look into it, he would immediately launch into a hundred reasons why she shouldn't.

She had been through that particular argument with him more than enough times already. If she had to resort to a little subterfuge now and again to avoid unpleasantness then that's exactly what she would do.

"Well, then." He rose, tucking the ledger under his arm. "What say you to a pleasant lunch in our suite?"

She would have liked nothing more, but the fate of Ellie lay heavily on her mind. She couldn't rest until she had at least spoken to the maid's mother in the hopes of uncovering a clue as to where the young girl may have gone.

"I'm sorry, Bax, really I am, but I have to prepare the envelope for the roofers, and then I have an errand to run in town. I'm afraid it will have to be a very late lunch, unless you would prefer to dine alone?"

For an anxious moment she thought he might protest, but then he sighed, and headed for the door. "One of these fine days we really do have to reexamine our lives. When you have free time in the spring, that's when I'm at the peak of my business. Then, when I have time to spare, you are always busy here. We never seem to have any time when we can enjoy some relaxation together."

"Perhaps tomorrow my time will be a little less in demand." She smiled at him, hoping to soften his scowl. "You know I would much rather spend it with you."

He opened the door, his words almost lost as he stepped outside. "Would you? I'm beginning to wonder." The door closed behind him, leaving her staring after him.

She didn't have much time to ponder his words. She had

barely finished stuffing pound notes into an envelope when Pansy arrived to announce that Mick Docker was waiting for an audience with her.

Inviting him in, she waited for him to seat himself. He was a stout man, almost as tall and broad shouldered as Clive, but carried a great deal more flesh on his belly. His cheeks glowed, more from a penchant for ale than from the biting wind, and his graying dark hair had thinned considerably above his brow.

He sat with an expectant look on his face, and she indulged him by passing the envelope across the desk. "I think, Mr. Docker, that you will find this pays for all the repairs in full."

"Thank you, m'm." He reached for it, and without opening it, stuffed it into the breast pocket of his coat. "I trust you found everything satisfactory?"

The roofer's thick Irish accent confused her, and it took her a moment to realize what he'd said. "Well, I haven't observed the repairs myself, but I'm sure everything is in order. We shall soon find out with the next fall of rain, no doubt."

He uttered an irked laugh. "I can assure you, m'm, there will be no more leaks from that part of the roof, at least."

She felt a pang of dismay. "Oh? Are you saying the rest of the roof is in need of repair?"

"Not at this very moment, no." He leaned back with a smug expression that did not sit well with her. "But if I were you, I'd look into replacing a few more tiles before too long, or you're likely to have some damp patches in your ceilings."

Cecily made a mental note to send Samuel up to examine the roof before she ordered any more repairs from this man. There was something about his attitude that she didn't quite trust. Maybe it was the fact that he hadn't mentioned the death of her footman. She found that callous in the extreme.

He was about to rise when she stopped him with a quick raise of her hand. "Just a moment, Mr. Docker. I'd like to ask you about the gargoyle that struck and killed one of my trusted employees this morning."

The roofer's face was instantly devoid of expression. He sat down again as if lowering himself on a prickly bed of nettles. "Yes, m'm. Please accept my sincere regrets. A very unfortunate accident, indeed."

"Indeed." She folded her hands in front of her and leaned forward. "I don't suppose you have any idea how that gargoyle happened to slip off the roof just as my footman was passing below?"

A muscle started twitching at the roofer's cheekbone, and his blue eyes grew wary. "I haven't the slightest idea, m'm. I secured it myself, I did. I just can't understand how it got loose."

"How did you secure it?"

"I tied it down with rope around the chimney stack, and wedged bricks on either side of it. Then we covered it with a tarpaulin." He shook his head, as if in bewilderment. "Can't understand that, at all."

She stared at him for a moment. "Tell me, did you happen to see the spot where the young man was killed?"

"No, m'm, I didn't. First I heard about it was when the constable asked me about the gargoyle this morning. I never did see the body."

"Well, thank you, Mr. Docker. I'm sure we'll be seeing each other again."

He looked worried about that for a moment, then his brow cleared. "Oh, right. For the rest of the repairs. Just let me know when you need me, Mrs. Baxter. I'll do a good job for you. That's a promise."

She simply nodded, and didn't bother to get up as he let himself out the door. Her mind was focused on what he'd told her. The roofer said he'd tied down the gargoyle to the chimney stack, which was several feet farther along the roof than the spot where Charlie had died.

Had the gargoyle simply slipped down from its moorings, it would have easily missed him. There seemed no doubt now that either Mick Docker had lied or someone had untied the masonry, carried it over to the edge of the roof, and waited for Charlie to pass by below.

If so, all she had to do was find out who had wanted her footman dead, and why.

Pansy hummed to herself as she carried the vase of fresh flowers along the hallway to the ballroom. Madeline Prestwick had ordered them especially, to stand on the grand piano at the ball that evening. Beautiful they were, all different colors and shapes and sizes.

Pansy didn't know the names of half of them, but it didn't stop her enjoying the fragrance right under her nose. She took another sniff as she reached the doors, then paused, one hand frozen in the act of pushing them open.

The doors were already ajar and she could see inside the ballroom. The kissing bough hung just a few feet away.

Someone must have moved it from the foyer. She squinted at it. Unless it was another one.

It wasn't the bough of greenery that held her attention, however. It was the couple standing beneath it. The young man had his arms around the lady, and he was kissing her as if he was never going to let go again.

Pansy felt a warm feeling trickling all over her. She recognized the honeymoon couple, and it made her feel all squishy inside to watch them.

The new Mrs. Danville must have caught sight of her, since she drew back with a gasp.

Pansy quickly pushed the doors open. "I'm so sorry to disturb you, m'm," she said, her voice breathless with embarrassment. "I have to put these flowers on the piano. I won't be but a moment or two."

The bride blushed, but her husband swung around with a laugh. "You must catch quite a few couples taking advantage of this." He pointed at the kissing bough above his head. "After all, that's what it's for, right?"

Aware that he was trying to alleviate his wife's discomfort, Pansy lied. "Oh, yes, sir, all the time. People do like to kiss each other under it. It's tradition, sir, isn't it." She hurried over to the stage and ran lightly up the steps. Some of the water in the vase slopped over her arm, but she pretended not to notice.

"There you are, my dear." The young man's voice carried across the room. "Didn't I tell you no one would think anything of it?"

Pansy put the vase down on the polished surface of the piano. It looked really nice with its colorful sprays of blossoms. She turned back to the Danvilles.

The gentleman stood smiling at her, while his bride hid her face behind his shoulder. Pansy thought the young girl was really silly. If she, Pansy, was being kissed by her husband she wouldn't care who saw her.

She skipped down the steps and past the couple, her heart giving a little jump when Mr. Danville gave her a knowing wink. She grinned in answer, and darted from the room, practicing how she would tell Gertie about her encounter.

She found her friend in the dining room, setting new candles in the candlesticks. "Where have you been?" Gertie demanded, the moment she set eyes on her. "I've been waiting for you to help me in here."

"Mrs. Chubb asked me to take the flowers into the ballroom." She let out a giggle. "You'll never guess what I saw."

"Madam was dancing with Clive."

Pansy stared at her. "What?"

Gertie shook her head. "I was teasing, that's all. What did you see, then?"

Still confused, Pansy told her about the honeymoon couple. "Mr. Danville winked at me when I came out of there," she said, smiling at the memory. "I do wish Samuel had been there to see it."

Gertie laughed. "You don't really think that would make him jealous?"

Pansy tossed her head. "Maybe not, but I know what would. Lenny asked me out and I'm going, too."

Now it was Gertie's turn to stare. "Who the hell is Lenny, then?"

"He's the lad that works on the roof with that big Irishman."

"Mick Docker? Saucy blighter he is and all. Mrs. Chubb said he was whistling at the maids all day."

Pansy thought it better not to mention that Lenny had whistled at her. "Well, anyway, Lenny asked when my afternoon off was and I told him it was tomorrow so I'm meeting him by the gate and we're going for a walk."

Gertie pursed her lips. "So what if he gets fresh with you?"

"Fresh?"

"You know, what if he tries to take advantage of you. What're you going to do then?"

Pansy laughed. "I'm only going for a walk with him, that's all."

"Yeah, well, don't let him lure you into the woods. There's all sorts of horrible things he could do if he got you in the woods."

Pansy didn't like the sound of that but she wasn't about to let Gertie know she was upsetting her. "You're teasing again," she said, without too much confidence. "It's too cold to walk in the woods, anyhow."

"You'd go walking in the woods with Samuel, though, wouldn't you?"

"Samuel wouldn't ask me."

"Well, if he did."

"I dunno."

"You'd be daft not to go with him." Gertie turned back to the table and set another candle in its stick. "If you want a man you have to grab every opportunity he gives you."

Pansy shivered. She'd be only too happy to do anything Samuel asked, but she wasn't so sure about Lenny. Maybe she'd made a mistake promising to meet him after all. Then again, she didn't exactly promise. All she'd done was nod her head. That could have meant anything.

She had no time to dwell on the problem, however. Gertie thrust a bundle of candles into her hands. "Here, finish these for me. I have to get ready to meet Dan. We're going for a walk on the pier this afternoon and I have to put more pins in my hair or it'll blow all over the blinking place."

"Isn't it a bit cold to go walking on the pier?"

"Nah." Gertie headed for the door, throwing words over her shoulder. "I'll have Dan to keep me warm, won't I." Laughing, she disappeared into the hallway outside.

Sighing, Pansy stuck a candle into the silver candlestick. It would be so nice to have someone to keep her warm. Especially if it was Samuel. At least that giddy Ellie wasn't there to get in the way.

Pansy felt a stab of guilt. Ellie was missing, possibly hurt or worse. She felt sorry for that, but part of her hoped that Ellie never came back. She had enough trouble keeping Samuel's interest without some frivolous little twerp grabbing his attention. No, it would be a lot better for all of them if Ellie Tidwell never came back to the Pennyfoot ever again.

Samuel was waiting in the carriage right in front of the main entrance when Cecily hurried down the steps a while later.

Shivering as the wind nipped her nose, she waited for him to open the door, then clambered up onto the seat and sank back against the creaking leather.

The cold seeped through her thick woolen coat and every layer of clothing underneath. Wishing she'd brought her shawl for extra warmth, she glanced out of the window as the carriage jerked forward.

The gray ocean churned up white foam on the waves racing to shore. That meant an east wind, which could bring a cold snap to the southeast coast. Cecily tugged her collar closer to her throat. They would have to stoke up the fires in the bedrooms, as well as the library, dining room, and the bar. The ballroom had no fireplace, but usually there were enough people dancing to keep everyone warm enough.

Thank goodness they'd just had the coal shed filled up. They would need lots of it to keep all those fires going. Thinking about the coal shed reminded Cecily of her meeting with Stan Whittle, the coal man. He'd been in a dreadful hurry, and had become quite impatient with her while she was preparing his payment envelope. She never had liked the man, but his rudeness yesterday had been inexcusable.

The attitude of workmen lately was quite deplorable. It upset her no end to have to accommodate them. In the old days, when she owned the Pennyfoot, Baxter served as the manager and dealt with all the tradespeople that came to the hotel. Now she was forced into that unenviable position and it didn't sit well with her at all.

The carriage jerked, sending her forward and jolting her out of her thoughts. She heard Samuel shout out something as the carriage lurched to a halt, then the horse's hooves clicked on the pavement again and once more they sailed smoothly on their way.

Another of those dratted motorcars, Cecily thought, as she caught sight of the gleaming white machine trundling past her window. All that banging and smoking, and they were constantly breaking down. They caused more problems on the road than any skittish horse might. That was the price they paid for progress.

Ellie's house lay just on the edge of town, for which Cecily was most thankful. Badgers End was little more than a village, but at this time of year the High Street resembled one of the busy shopping streets in nearby Wellercombe. It would take forever to get the carriage through a crowd of determined pedestrians, intent on getting their Christmas shopping done before the shops closed.

Cecily peered out the window as the carriage jerked to a stop. They had pulled up outside a small white gate and fenced front garden with neatly trimmed hedges and well-pruned fruit trees. The carriage door opened and Samuel offered her a hand as she prepared to climb down.

Catching sight of a black smear on his coat, she frowned. "You must ask Mrs. Chubb to remove that stain, Samuel. It looks most unsightly."

Samuel rubbed a hand across his chest, smearing the smudge even more. "Sorry, m'm. I didn't notice it until I was sitting waiting for you in the carriage. Didn't have time to change it, did I. I'd been cleaning out one of the motorcars. It was covered in dirt and I must have rubbed my hand across me like this."

He dragged his fingers across his chest again and Cecily uttered a cry of protest. "You're just making things worse, Samuel. Do try not to touch it again until you can give it to Mrs. Chubb to clean."

"Yes, m'm. Sorry, m'm." Looking contrite, Samuel helped her to the ground. "If you've got a minute, m'm, I'd like to ask you something."

Impatient to talk to Ellie's mother, Cecily gave him

a quick nod. "Very well, but do hurry. I'm catching cold standing out here."

"Yes, m'm." Samuel pulled off his cap and started rolling it up in his hands. "Well, it's like this. I found this stray dog. It's been lurking around the stables, looking for food, I reckon."

"Oh, Samuel." Cecily shook her head. "I do hope you didn't feed it. We'll never be rid of it if you did."

Samuel looked down at his feet. "Well, yes, m'm, I did." He looked up again, his eyes wide and pleading. "She's a really good dog, m'm. Doesn't cause no trouble, comes when I call, and she's caught three rats since she's been around. I thought, since we've had trouble with rats in the past, that I might keep her around, m'm, just to help out, like. If that's all right with you?"

Cecily puffed out her breath. In her opinion, horses and motorcars didn't mix well with dogs, and she would never allow one inside the Pennyfoot. Samuel, however, was not only a trusted employee, he was just as much a part of her family as the rest of her staff. Those beseeching eyes were simply too hard to ignore.

"Very well." She held up her hand as Samuel gushed his thanks. "Just remember, you are responsible for the animal. One hint of trouble with her and out she goes."

"Yes, m'm. There won't be no trouble, I swear. I'll take really good care of her. Just wait until you meet her, m'm. She's really lovable and cuddly. You'll love her to death, I know."

Cecily hid a smile. It was unusual for Samuel to be so forthcoming. He was a somewhat serious young man, always sticking strictly to protocol. Whenever she wanted to know what he was thinking it took considerable effort on her part to drag it out of him.

To see him so enthused and excited gladdened her heart, and she looked forward to meeting the creature that had inspired her stable manager to such eager anticipation. "Well now," she said briskly, "I must talk to Mrs. Tidwell. You are welcome to come inside with me, if you like."

He donned his cap and touched his forehead. "Thank you, m'm, but I'd prefer to wait out here if it's all the same to you."

"Of course. Whatever you wish." She left him then, and walked up the narrow gravel path to the porch. Empty plant pots sat on either side, waiting for the spring so they could be filled again with gorgeous blossoms. Cecily looked forward to that time. How she disliked the winter, with its dreary skies and chilly winds.

She disliked even more having to face the mother of a missing child. She could only hope that Mrs. Tidwell would be able to tell her something that would help find Ellie. Lifting her hand, she rapped on the door.

CHAPTER
❀ 6 ❀

The door opened moments later, emitting the heavenly fragrance of freshly baked bread. Having eaten hours earlier, Cecily hungered for a thick slice of buttered toast.

The woman who stood framed in the doorway wore an anxious frown. A white cap was perched on her graying curls, and wrapped around her waist was a threadbare apron covered in flour. Her fingers were covered in the white stuff as she lifted a hand to her face, leaving a powdery streak across her cheek.

"Mrs. Baxter! How good of you to call! Is it Ellie? Have you found my daughter?"

Cecily thrust out her hand to lay it on the woman's slender arm. "I'm so sorry, Mrs. Tidwell. Actually, I was hoping you'd have word of her for me."

The woman's face crumpled. "I wish I did, m'm. I can't think where she'd be." As if remembering her manners, she drew back. "Please, do come in."

"Well, just for a moment." Cecily stepped inside the cozy cottage, where the aroma of the baking bread was even more enticing.

Mrs. Tidwell motioned her to a seat on the chintz-covered sofa. "Would you like a cup of tea?"

Cecily was about to politely refuse when the other woman added, "Perhaps a slice of bread and jam? I've just baked a loaf of bread. I always bake when I'm worried. Gives me something else to think about, it does."

Cecily almost smacked her lips. "Well, if you insist. That sounds wonderful." She took a moment to look around as Ellie's mother hurried off to the kitchen.

It was a pleasant room, small but comfortable, with bright flowered curtains at the windows and a soft green carpet under her feet. An oil lamp had been lit to ward off the early winter dusk, and hot coals glowed a dark red in the fireplace.

In one corner shelves had been crammed with books, and unable to resist, Cecily got up to scan the titles. She was still studying them when Mrs. Tidwell returned with a loaded tray.

"I see you enjoy reading," Cecily commented, as she returned to her seat. "I notice you have the latest book by Sir Arthur Conan Doyle."

"Yes, *The Return of Sherlock Holmes*. I do so love his books." She put the tray down on a table beside Cecily and began pouring the tea. "My favorite, of course, is *The Hound of the Baskervilles*. I read every episode in the *Strand*."

"As did I." Cecily took the cup and saucer from her. "I've read everything that man has written. He is my favorite author. Such a talent."

"Indeed." Mrs. Tidwell offered her a plate with two slices of buttered bread smothered in thick strawberry jam.

Cecily hastily put down her tea and took the plate. "This looks delicious. Thank you."

Nodding, Ellie's mother sank on a chair across the room. "Mrs. Baxter, do you have any idea at all as to what might have happened to my daughter?"

Cecily paused, the delectable treat halfway to her mouth. "I wish I did. I'm afraid no one has seen Ellie since she left the Pennyfoot last night." She took a dainty bite, feeling guilty for enjoying the morsel. "Does she perhaps have friends she might be visiting?"

"None that I know of." Mrs. Tidwell rubbed her forehead with her fingers. "Ellie has changed, though, since she went to work in London. I never thought she'd go. She wasn't the sort of girl who would act on impulse, but after the problem she had with Mr. Docker, she seemed almost desperate to leave Badgers End."

Cecily swallowed her mouthful of bread a little too fast. Coughing, she sought her handkerchief tucked in her sleeve and drew it out to blow her nose. "Please excuse me," she muttered, a little hoarsely, "but you did say Mr. Docker, didn't you? Is that, by any chance, Mick Docker, the roofer?"

Mrs. Tidwell nodded. "The big Irishman. He was sweet on my Ellie. She met him two years ago, and he kept pestering her to go out with him, but she kept putting him off. He'd been married before, you see. Lost his wife when she caught a cold and it went into pneumonia. Ellie said as how she didn't wanted secondhand goods. Besides, he was much too old for her."

Still trying to clear her throat, Cecily nodded.

"Anyway," Mrs. Tidwell continued, "she finally got up the courage to tell him how she felt. Well, he must have flown into a rage or something. She wouldn't talk about it but I could tell she was worried about it. Right after that she told me she'd got a job as scullery maid at Rosewood Manor in London."

"I see." Cecily put down her plate. "Has she had any dealings with Mr. Docker since she's been back?"

"I really couldn't say. Our Ellie doesn't tell me much these days. I do know she wasn't happy in the city. She was only there a few months before she came back. I think that serial killer really frightened her. It was in the same district where she lived that they found the bodies of those poor young girls." Mrs. Tidwell shook her head. "I know she was troubled about something, but she won't talk to me about it. Got really secretive, she has."

"I understand your son is searching for her."

"Yes, he is. He's got some of his friends helping him and all, so I'm hoping they find her soon. It's not like her to stay out all night without telling me where she is."

She paused, as if remembering something. "Though, I have to say, she did it once before. Last summer, it was. Worried me sick. I thought something terrible had happened to her, but she turned up the next morning right as rain. She said she spent the night on the beach. Told me she didn't feel like coming home. I could tell something had upset her then, but she wouldn't say what it was."

Cecily finished the last piece of her bread and jam, then reached for her tea. "It's a little cold to be staying out on the beach this time of year."

"Yes, I know. I'm hoping she found somewhere warm to stay, though why she feels she can't come home and tell me about things, I really don't know."

Having drained her cup, Cecily rose. "Well, these young girls are hard to understand sometimes. I do hope you find Ellie soon. Please tell her that we miss her at the Pennyfoot, and look forward to her return."

"I will do that, Mrs. Baxter. Thank you." Mrs. Tidwell got to her feet, her face lined with worry.

Having said her good-byes, Cecily headed down the path to where Samuel waited in the carriage. She still felt guilty for enjoying the woman's hospitality when she was so obviously worried about her daughter.

Riding back along the Esplanade, however, Cecily managed to convince herself that the visit had relieved her mind to a degree. According to her mother, it wasn't the first time Ellie had stayed out all night, though the news had surprised Cecily. She hadn't thought the timid maid would have that much gumption. Apparently she had misjudged her newest employee.

Nevertheless, the news had raised her hopes that Ellie had merely been vexed over something and had sought refuge elsewhere to soothe her injured feelings. If so, she could stop worrying about the maid and concentrate on finding out who had caused Charlie's death.

She frowned, reminded of her conversation with Mick Docker earlier. She'd had no idea he was that well acquainted with Ellie. As far as she could remember, he had said nothing to indicate he knew of her disappearance. Nor if, indeed, he'd had any contact with her. Nevertheless, perhaps she should talk to him again.

The carriage jerked to a halt in front of the Pennyfoot's front steps, and she did her best to dismiss the problem from her mind. Ellie would be found sooner or later, no doubt unrepentant for causing so much upheaval. In fact, if the young girl did return to work, Cecily intended to make it her business to have a word with the maid, and try to impress upon her the error of her ways.

Having arrived at that conclusion, she alighted from the carriage, thanked Samuel, and hurried up the steps to the front doors.

The moment she stepped into the foyer, she remembered her last words with Baxter. She glanced at the grandfather clock. Almost half past two. Perhaps it wasn't too late to have a small meal with him, though she had little appetite after eating that delicious bread and jam at Ellie's house.

In her haste to reach her suite, she failed to see Sir Walter Hayesbury until, just as she reached the foot of the stairs, he called out her name.

Reluctantly she paused, and turned to face him. "Sir Walter! I trust you are having a good day?"

"As well as can be expected, madam." The gentleman before her looked grave, his classic features drawn into harsh lines. His mouth was pinched, as if he was in pain.

He must have been remarkably handsome in his youth, Cecily thought, as he peered down at her over his white silk cravat. Too much indulgence in food and spirits had now begun to rob him of his looks and possibly his health.

If he continued on that path, it would be only a matter of time before he would acquire a heavy paunch and sagging jowls. That would, indeed, be a shame. There was something distinctly charismatic about the man.

"I understand you have suffered a tragedy this morning," he said, his voice low and apprehensive. "One of your staff has passed away?"

Inwardly cursing the loose tongue that had betrayed her rules, Cecily did her best to look composed. "We had an unfortunate accident, yes, involving one of our footmen. I can assure you, Sir Walter, that there will be no inconvenience to our guests, and I would greatly appreciate it if you would not discuss the matter in public."

He nodded emphatically, then winced, passing a hand across his forehead. "Of course, madam. You can rely on me not to betray your confidence."

"Thank you, Sir Walter. We would rather not depress our guests with such tragic news. Rest assured that we shall endeavor to carry on with the festivities as usual."

"Oh, quite, quite, madam. I quite understand." He appeared to make an effort to dismiss his concern. Tilting his head to one side, he smoothed his mustache with the tips of his fingers. "My wife tells me there is to be a ball tonight in the ballroom. Is that so?"

Relieved at the change of subject, Cecily brightened. "Yes, indeed. I do hope you and your wife will join us?"

"Oh, most certainly, madam." He moved closer to her, bringing with him a faint minty fragrance of snuff. "May I be permitted to take this opportunity and extract a promise for a dance or two?"

Taken aback, Cecily momentarily lost her tongue. Before

she could find it again, a familiar voice spoke from behind her, with some considerable force. "Do pardon my intrusion, sir, but my wife will be fully engaged this evening, taking care of her guests."

Cecily swung around to face the cold gaze of her husband. She was not in the least interested in dancing with Sir Walter, but neither was she about to allow her husband to dictate her actions in such an arbitrary manner. "Why Baxter, darling, I can't possibly refuse such a charming request from one of our esteemed guests." She turned back to Sir Walter. "Thank you for your kind invitation. I shall be delighted to join you for a dance this evening."

Sir Walter lowered his head in a stiff bow, then sent Baxter a look that clearly stated his victory before heading away toward the main doors.

Baxter's gray eyes were pure ice. "I had no idea you were so enamored of that pompous ass."

Cecily smiled. "Actually I find him rather charming. His manners are impeccable." Her tone suggested that she found her husband's manners, on the other hand, somewhat wanting. "Besides," she added, as he made way for her to mount the stairs, "his wife is rather pretty. Since you will be forced to reciprocate and invite her to dance, no doubt you will enjoy the exchange."

Baxter's snort assured her otherwise, and still smiling, she climbed the stairs.

Gertie's afternoon walk with Dan was not turning out as she'd envisioned. For one thing, he flatly refused to walk on the pier. "Why the hell would you want to walk out over the ocean in a wind that could cut you in half?" he complained, when she suggested it.

"It will do you good." She took his arm and began to pull him toward the jetty. "Blow the cobwebs out of your head."

"That wind would blow my ears off." He shook her off. "Why don't we go back to my cottage where it's warm."

She felt her heart thump. So far she'd resisted his efforts to take her back to his home. She knew where that might very well lead. That's how she'd ended up with the twins, thank you very much. Wild horses wouldn't drag her into that situation again.

Still, she couldn't help remembering what she'd told Pansy just that morning. *If you want a man you have to grab every opportunity he gives you.* After all, she was big enough and old enough to take care of herself, wasn't she? Besides, she trusted Dan. He wouldn't do anything she didn't want him to do.

She ignored the little voice that warned her she might want more than was good for her. She was a big girl. She knew what she was doing. "All right," she heard herself saying, before she had time to really think about it. "If that's what you want, we'll go to your cottage."

Dan looked at her as if she had invited him to fly to the moon. "Really? You sure?"

No, she wasn't sure. She studied his face. He was the best-looking man she'd ever set eyes on, and she'd spent many sleepless nights wondering what it was he saw in her. She loved him as she'd never loved anyone before, and all she wanted was to be his wife and make him happy for the rest of their lives.

The trouble was, Dan didn't seem to want to settle down.

He was happy the way things were, he'd told her, though she knew by the way he kissed her good night that he wanted more than she could give him.

"It's not as if it's your first time," he'd told her once. That had made her angry. He just didn't understand. She'd made that mistake once before, and she wasn't about to make it again. This time she wanted a ring on her finger before she did anything like that again. And much as she adored him, nothing Dan could say or do would ever change her mind about that.

Still, she'd told him she'd go to the cottage and she could hardly take it back now. "Of course I'm sure," she said, and inwardly prayed that she wasn't making a big mistake.

In spite of her depleted appetite, Cecily managed to enjoy a light lunch of cheeses, fruit, and pickles, and even succeeded in reviving her husband's good humor. In fact, he seemed so much more cheerful than previously, she felt compelled to question him about it.

"I assume that whatever was worrying you earlier has been resolved?"

To her dismay, he avoided her gaze as he reached for another slice of Gorgonzola cheese. "What gave you that assumption?"

She hesitated, before replying, "You just seem a little more lighthearted. You've been walking around with a ferocious scowl for the last two days."

"Ah." He broke off a piece of cheese and popped it in his mouth. "As a matter of fact, I would like to talk to you about that."

She felt an uneasy thump of her heart. "I hope it's not bad news?"

"That depends on how you look at it."

"Look at what?"

"Well, my dear, I think you should know that—" He broke off as a loud rapping on the door interrupted him. "Blast it! Are we ever going to have any peace in this place?"

"I'm sorry, dear. I won't be a moment." Feeling flustered, Cecily crossed the room and opened the door. Pansy stood outside, her forehead scrunched up in a worried frown. "I'm sorry to disturb you, m'm, but I'm worried about the gentleman in room nine."

Cecily thought hard for a moment, then nodded. "Oh, yes, Mr. Mortimer. Is something wrong?"

"I don't know, m'm. He's not answering his door. I went to fetch his tray that I took up two hours ago and it's not outside in the hallway like he usually puts it, and I knocked and knocked on his door but he's not answering." She swallowed. "Not even to tell me to go away."

"He's probably gone out for a walk."

"Then why didn't he leave his tray outside like he always does?"

"Perhaps he forgot."

Pansy looked unconvinced. "I don't know, m'm. He's mentioned before that he wasn't feeling well. I just got a feeling that something's wrong. I would ask Mrs. Chubb, but she's resting in her room and gets really cross if I disturb her. Perhaps if you could come and knock on his door . . . ?"

Cecily sighed, and glanced back at her husband. "I won't be a moment, dear. I have to go downstairs to enquire after Mr. Mortimer."

"Quite all right, my love. I have to take care of some business myself. We'll talk later." He got up from his chair, crossed the room, and followed her out the door.

Reluctant to see him go, Cecily led Pansy down the hallway to the stairs. She would not rest now until she'd heard what Baxter had to say about what had been troubling him so. He had aroused her curiosity, and not without a certain amount of alarm. She knew him well enough to know that this was no frivolous matter he wished to discuss.

She couldn't imagine what it was, but she had a nasty feeling that it concerned her, and could possibly affect her life in some way. But there was one thing she would not do, no matter what it was he had to tell her. She would not give up her position at the Pennyfoot Country Club. Somehow he would have to understand and accept that. Deeply troubled, she walked down the stairs and along the landing to room nine.

After smacking the door with her knuckles several times and receiving no answer, Cecily told her maid to fetch the master keys. Fitting one into the lock, she turned it and carefully opened the door.

Pansy stood shivering outside while Cecily edged into the room. It was in total darkness, the curtains drawn against the fading daylight. She could see nothing except the faint outline of the window.

Wishing she'd bought a lamp with her, Cecily coughed. "Mr. Mortimer? Are you there?"

She jumped violently when a harsh voice answered her from the direction of the bed. "What the blazes . . . ? Who are you? What the hell do you want?"

Cecily backed away, bumping into the door and sending it closed shut. Frantically seeking the door handle in the dark, she muttered, "I'm terribly sorry, Mr. Mortimer. My maid could get no answer and we thought you might be indisposed."

"For heaven's sake, woman, I'm taking a blasted nap! Why on earth do you give me a room with a lock if you're just going to barge in here whenever you feel like it? Surely I'm entitled to a little privacy?"

Cecily went on fumbling for the door handle. "Of course, sir. Please accept my sincere apologies. It's just that you didn't answer your door and your tray is not outside in the hallway and—"

The irate voice interrupted her. "I didn't hear anyone at the door. I was asleep. My tray is still here because there's still food on it. Now, is there anything else you'd like to know?"

At long last her fingers closed around the handle. Pulling open the door, she backed outside, still muttering apologies, then closed the door with a loud snap.

Pansy stood with her head down, her hands clasped in front of her. "I'm sorry, m'm. Really I am. I was worried about him, that's all."

Cecily let out her breath on a puff of exasperation. "It's quite all right, Pansy. You were showing concern for a guest and that's commendable. Mr. Mortimer is a rather unpleasant man who could use a lesson in manners. Just do your best with him and try not to let him upset you."

She had raised her voice deliberately in the hopes that the man inside would hear her. There was no doubt in her mind that Mr. Mortimer had deliberately refused to answer their frantic assault on his door. Drat the man. As if she didn't have enough problems.

Pansy dropped a curtsey, and sent an apprehensive glance at the door of room nine. "Yes, m'm. Thank you, m'm. I'll be getting back to the kitchen now."

"Please do. Oh, and tell Mrs. Chubb we need all those coal scuttles filled to the brim. It looks as if we'll have a cold night."

"Yes, m'm." Pansy turned and ran for the stairs, disappearing down them at a speed that Cecily envied. Once she'd been able to run that fast. It seemed a century ago. Things had seemed so much simpler then.

Now she had so much more to contend with—rude, disgruntled guests, a husband with a troubling secret, not to mention a missing maid and a murder to solve. To echo Baxter's sentiments, were they ever going to have any real peace again?

CHAPTER

❀ 7 ❀

"Gertie!" Mrs. Chubb's voice rang out across the kitchen. "What are you doing?"

"I'm bloody putting the dishes away," Gertie yelled back. "What do you think I'm doing?" She smacked the last dish down on the shelf and slammed the cupboard door.

"What's got your hackles up?" The housekeeper sounded cross as she marched out of the pantry, closing the door behind her.

"Nothing." Gertie seized the tray of silverware and started sorting out knives, forks, and spoons, slotting them into their compartments in the dresser.

"Well, something's up. You're not usually this disagreeable to me."

"Sorry." Gertie scowled as a knife slipped from her hand

and fell to the floor. "Bloody hell. Now I'll have to wash the flipping thing all over again."

Mrs. Chubb walked over to her and took the knife from her fingers. "I'll wash it. The coal buckets need filling. Why don't you go and fill them. The fresh air will do you good."

Gertie thought about arguing, then shut her mouth. Anything she said right now was going to come out wrong anyway.

Grumbling to herself, she picked up the coal scuttles and slammed out of the kitchen into the dark, chilly yard. This was the crowning insult on a horrible day.

She'd had a terrible row with Dan, bad enough that she didn't know if she'd ever see him again. He'd accused her of tormenting him, when all she'd done was go with him to his cottage and let him kiss her.

It wasn't enough for him, though, was it? Oh, no. He had to go and spoil everything by trying to get more and got really nasty when she'd shoved him away.

Tromping across the yard, she swung both coal scuttles so hard they almost came off their handles. She'd promised herself she wouldn't get all upset again remembering all the nasty things he'd said. He was upset, and didn't mean them. She knew that.

He'd come around tomorrow and tell her how sorry he was and promise it wouldn't happen again. He'd done it before.

Only he'd broken his promise, and how did she know he wouldn't break it again? How could she trust him when he couldn't keep his hands to himself?

A slight sound from across the yard brought her to a halt. The maids had been talking in the kitchen about the serial killer, making her sick with all the gory details of what he'd done to them poor girls.

Not that she thought a killer like that would bother to come all the way down to Badgers End, when he had so many girls to pick from in London. Still, you never know.

The sound came again. Shuffling feet, and some sort of swishing sound, as if someone was dragging something across the cold ground. *A dead body?*

Gertie's teeth started chattering, and she bit down hard to make them stop. If only she could see. Heavy clouds obscured the moon, however, and obliterated everything except the faint outline of buildings.

Gertie could barely see the coal shed. She never bothered to bring a lamp with her, because there was one hanging on a nail in the shed. With her hands holding two heavy coal scuttles, it was impossible to carry a lamp anyway.

The skin on the back of her neck tingled as the shuffling sound came closer. It was just around the side of the building now, and any second whoever it was would turn the corner and be right in front of her. Very slowly and quietly, Gertie began to back up.

She had gone no more than a few steps when her heel came down hard on a stone. Her shoe twisted sideways, wrenching her ankle. In an effort to prevent the sharp cry of pain, she slapped a hand over her mouth. Unfortunately, she had to let go of a scuttle to do so. It rolled away from her with a clattering and banging that would have awoken the dead.

At the same time, a male voice uttered a startled oath. "What the hell was that?"

Sheer relief gave Gertie the giggles as the coal scuttle finally came to rest against the wall with a resounding whack. "Sorry, Clive," she said, between hiccups of laughter. "I thought you was the serial killer."

Clive muttered something, but her giggles smothered his words. She didn't know why she was laughing, considering what a miserable day she'd had. She just couldn't seem to stop. Then she wasn't laughing at all, but crying real tears that ran down her cheeks and onto her shawl.

Embarrassed, she turned away. She never cried. Not even when her mother died, or when she found out the father of her twins had somehow forgotten to mention he was married. She didn't know why she was crying now. Angrily she dashed the unfamiliar tears away with the back of her hand.

"Here."

Clive's voice had softened. She squinted at him in the dark, seeing only his outline and unable to see his expression. She felt like a fool, furious with herself for acting like a baby in front of him.

Something cold touched her hand and she realized he was handing her the coal scuttle she'd dropped. She hadn't even seen him pick it up. "Thank you, Clive." She took it from him, holding it awkwardly by the edge instead of the handle.

"Are you all right?"

She nodded, then realizing he couldn't see her, she said quickly, "I think I'm coming down with a cold."

He didn't answer right away. She was about to speak again when someone put a lamp in the kitchen window. The flickering light spread across the yard, and now she could see his face. He was smiling.

"Here," he said again, and held up a white handkerchief. "You'll need this."

She managed a shaky grin. "Thanks. I generally use my sleeve."

He took one of the scuttles from her and pushed the handkerchief into her hand. "This is better."

He turned away and started walking toward the coal shed, and while his back was turned she quickly dabbed at her eyes and blew her nose. She thought about giving him back the handkerchief, then decided it would be better if she washed it first. Tucking it into her sleeve, she followed him over to the coal shed.

"I'll light the lamp for you," he said, as she unlocked the door.

She waited while he struck a match, the flame flaring up in his face. Funny, she never really noticed before, but he had a really nice face. Not good looking, like Dan, but a kind face, sort of square and dependable. The kind of man who would take care of his family.

She wondered why he didn't have a wife. Or perhaps he did somewhere. A wife and children, waiting for him to come home to them. No, Clive wasn't the kind of man who would just go off and leave them. Either he wasn't married, or something must have happened to them.

She realized then how little she knew about the big man. He'd been a good friend to her, protecting her when she'd needed it, always looking out for her and the twins, yet she knew nothing about him. Nothing at all. She made up her mind there and then that when she had more time, she'd make it her business to talk to him and find out more about his life.

The light from the oil lamp swung across her face and

she jumped. A shovel leaned against the wall nearby and she snatched it up. "Thanks. I can manage now."

"Give me that." He took the shovel from her and started piling the gleaming black lumps of coal into the scuttle.

She appreciated his help, yet felt awkward just standing there. Moving deeper into the shed, she looked around for another shovel.

That's when she saw it. A black shoe, lying in the middle of the coal pile.

Her strangled gasp brought Clive's head up. "What's the matter? Spider? Rat?"

"No, a shoe." Her finger trembled when she pointed at it. "Look. Over there."

Clive straightened his back. "What the heck is it doing there?"

He started to move forward, but Gertie thrust out a hand to grab his arm. "Don't! Don't touch it!" Her stomach heaved, and she slapped the other hand over her mouth.

Clive frowned. "It's just a shoe, Gertie."

Her throat felt so tight she had to force the words out. "The last time I saw a shoe like that," she said, her voice so hoarse she hardly recognized it herself, "there was a bloody foot in it."

Clive's eyebrows shot up. "What?"

Gertie swallowed. "It's true. One of our maids had been murdered and the killer flung her body into the shed out by the tennis courts. I was the one what found her, and that's how I saw her first. Just one shoe."

Clive reached for the lamp and swung it high above his head. The patent leather gleamed in the light. "Looks like one of your shoes."

Gertie looked down at her feet. The toes of both her shoes poked out from under her skirt. "It's not mine."

"Then it must belong to one of the other maids."

"If it does, we'll soon find out. Mrs. Chubb makes us write our names in our shoes so we won't get them mixed up."

"Well, then, let's find out who it belongs to."

He started forward again, but Gertie grimly hung on to his arm. "It could be Ellie."

For a moment she saw a flash of alarm in his eyes, then he quickly masked it. "It's not Ellie, Gertie. It's just a shoe. Not a dead body."

She watched him hang the lamp on a hook on the wall. "What are you going to do?"

"I'm going to get the shoe so you can see for yourself there's no foot inside it. Or anything else, unless a rat or a spider has decided to make it its home."

Gertie shuddered. "I can't look." She closed her eyes, wincing as she heard Clive scrabbling up the coal pile, sending chunks of it sliding down to the floor.

He grunted, then more scrabbling, and his voice speaking almost in her ear. "Well, it's not Ellie, that's for sure. It is, however, her shoe."

Feeling only slightly reassured, Gertie took the shoe from him and held it up to the lamp. "Oh, gawd. This is Ellie's shoe all right." She lowered it and stared at Clive. "So then, why would she leave it in here and walk out without it? Where the bloody hell is she?"

"Look at that. Disgusting behavior, I call it." Baxter nudged his head at a spot across the ballroom by the doors.

Seated at the table opposite him, Cecily followed his gaze, and caught sight of Geoffrey and Caroline Danville sharing a chaste kiss under the kissing bough. "I'd hardly call it disgusting, dear. After all, they are newly married, and it was quite an inoffensive embrace."

Baxter rolled his eyes. "Public displays of affection in an exclusive hotel ballroom? Where will all this lead, I'd like to know?"

Cecily felt her neck tightening. She was in no mood for Baxter's intolerance this evening. All afternoon she had been trying to decide how to proceed with the investigation of Charlie's death without even a glimmer of an idea.

She had so little upon which to base her suspicions. The position of Charlie's body, that was all. In fact, if it wasn't for Madeline's vision, she'd be inclined to think that the whole thing was a tragic accident, after all. It was just that Madeline's visions invariably transpired, and she had learned never to dismiss her friend's unusual powers.

"You are not paying attention, Cecily."

She gave a guilty start and covered it by smiling at him. "I'm sorry, my dear. You were saying?"

"I was saying that the world is going to rack and ruin, with all these corrupt standards abounding everywhere. We are leaving decency and ethics behind in our frenzied pursuit of modernization. I blame the French. They always were a loose lot."

Cecily sighed. "Why Bax, darling, you are always impressing upon me the importance of progress, and how change is good for the country and the soul."

Baxter grunted. "When it applies to mechanical conveniences like motorcars and telephones, yes. I shudder to think, however, of the detrimental effects all this will have on the morals of young people."

"Piffle." Cecily leaned forward and lowered her voice. "I seem to remember, my dear husband, you and I sharing such a kiss in this very room. And without the benefit of a kissing bough to make it acceptable."

Baxter's eyebrows lifted. "We were quite alone at the time."

Keeping a solemn face, Cecily nodded. "You are quite certain of that?"

She watched a shade of pink creep over her husband's cheeks. "Were we not? I don't—"

He broke off abruptly as Sir Walter Hayesbury paused in front of their table. The gentleman bowed, and offered his hand. "I do believe this is my dance?"

Cecily glanced at her husband and encountered a face of thunder. For a moment she was tempted to make some excuse, but having penciled Sir Walter's name into her dance card earlier, she was under an obligation to accommodate him.

She rose, murmuring, "I shan't be long," and received a curt nod in answer.

Much as she tried to suppress her emotions, she had to confess to a certain thrill of pleasure as the aristocrat took her hand for the two-step.

He was a strong dancer, guiding her around the floor with such ease she felt as if she were floating. Feeling somewhat guilty about the pleasure she was experiencing, she murmured, "Your wife looks particularly elegant tonight, Sir Walter."

He glanced over to where Lady Esmeralda sat in deep

Kate Kingsbury

conversation with Lady Millshire. "She does, indeed." He returned his dark gaze to Cecily's face. "If I may say so, madam, you look every bit as elegant, if not more so."

Normally Cecily would ignore such blatant flattery, but she couldn't suppress the rush of warmth his words gave her. "Why, thank you kindly, sir."

Together they swept toward the stage, gracefully weaving in and out of the other couples. Sir Walter turned her to face the door, where Geoffrey and Caroline Danville still lingered. "It seems that some of your guests are making good use of the kissing bough," he murmured.

Cecily couldn't remember when she had felt such heat in her cheeks. "A charming Christmas tradition, don't you think?"

"Indeed. Such a shame it is only utilized during the Christmas season. Think what pleasure such an enjoyable practice could bring year-round."

Catching sight of Baxter's disapproving scowl, Cecily laughed. "I'm afraid there are some people who would not agree with you."

"Perhaps, but then some people have difficulty appreciating such a pleasurable experience."

Having no answer to that, she decided it was high time she changed the subject. "I do hope you and your wife are enjoying your stay at the Pennyfoot?"

"Most assuredly, madam. This is a charming place to enjoy the celebrations." His gaze swept the room. "It would seem all of your guests are having a good time. Your efforts are well appreciated, I'm sure."

"We do our best to please."

"I trust the unfortunate incident with your footman has not impeded your plans?"

Startled, she glanced up at him. "What? Oh, no, of course not. It was a nasty accident and we are all shocked and dismayed, of course, but our first and foremost duty is to entertain our guests in the manner to which they are accustomed, and nothing is allowed to interfere with that."

Sir Walter nodded. "I'm glad to hear it. A dreadful thing to happen any time of the year, but losing a loved one at Christmastime must be quite unbearable."

Uncomfortable with the way the conversation was going, Cecily was thankful when the music ceased and she could return to her table.

She thanked Sir Walter, who kissed her gloved hand, then gave Baxter a slight bow of his head before returning across the room to his wife.

"I trust you enjoyed that," Baxter said, with just a hint of resentment in his voice.

She couldn't resist teasing him. "I did, indeed. Such a gentleman, Sir Walter. He looks quite dashing on the dance floor."

Baxter snorted. "He wouldn't look quite so immaculate had he not borrowed a bow tie from me this morning. He was lucky I had a spare. Apparently his valet had forgotten to pack one for him. Seems to me he needs to get his household in order."

Cecily smiled at her husband's feeble attempt to discredit the charming aristocrat. "Well, the dance was very nice, dear, but I'd much rather dance with you. So much more relaxing. Besides, he doesn't have your light foot on the turns."

Baxter's scowl disappeared, and his mouth twitched in a smile. "Then what are we waiting for? Will you do me the honor of having the next dance with me?"

"Of course."

"In that case—" He broke off as Gertie appeared at the table, her pale face taut with anxiety.

"Sorry, m'm, but I thought you ought to know at once."

Her good mood shattered, Cecily felt a pang of misgiving. "What is it, Gertie?"

The housemaid cast a furtive glance over her shoulder at the couples dancing behind her. The orchestra on the stage played a lilting waltz, loud enough to cover her words, and apparently reassured, she leaned forward. "I just found one of Ellie's shoes, m'm."

For a moment Cecily stared at her, wondering why that was such momentous news she had to be disturbed. "Ellie's shoe?"

"Yes, m'm." Again Gertie looked over her shoulder. "I found it in the coal shed, m'm."

"In the coal shed?" Cecily exchanged a puzzled look with Baxter. "What on earth was it doing in there?"

"That's why I came to tell you, m'm. We thought it queer that she'd leave her shoe in the coal shed. I mean, where would she go with only one shoe? What with her gone missing and everything."

Baxter leaned an elbow on the table and covered his eyes with his hand. "Oh, good Lord."

Cecily let out her breath. "Thank you, Gertie. I'll look into it."

A look of relief crossed her housemaid's face. "Yes, m'm.

Thank you, m'm." She backed away, narrowly missing being struck in the face by the energetic elbow of Lord Millshire.

Muttering an apology, Gertie rushed across the floor and out the door.

Cecily smiled at the Millshires as they swept past her, then encountered Baxter's gaze.

His brows practically met over the bridge of his nose. "Just when were you going to tell me that one of our maids is missing?"

Aware that the musicians had ceased playing, she sent him a warning look with a finger pressed to her lips. "I'm sorry, dear. I didn't want to worry you. You seemed so preoccupied with something I didn't want to add to your troubles. Besides, Ellie has only been gone one day and her mother said she often stays with a friend when she's upset. . . ." She let her words trail off as his frown deepened.

"You spoke to her mother?"

"Yes, dear. This afternoon. I was doing a spot of shopping and thought I'd drop in to see her."

He narrowed his gaze. "Why?"

"Why what, dear?"

"Why would you take time out of one of the busiest days of the year to visit the mother of a maid who has been in our employ exactly a week?"

Cecily felt a stirring of resentment. "I thought Ellie might be ill. Besides, it's not as if her mother is a stranger. Mrs. Tidwell supplies the hotel with apples and cherries from her garden. I have met her on more than one occasion."

"What does all this have to do with you chasing after a

missing maid? Why didn't you send one of the footmen to enquire after her health?"

Cecily raised her chin. "I do not question the management of your business, Baxter. I would thank you for not questioning mine."

He at least had the grace to look somewhat contrite. "I didn't mean to criticize, my dear. I was merely concerned that you were getting yourself involved in another nasty mess that seems so prevalent around this time of the year. I—"

Once more they were interrupted, this time by a petite woman in a purple velvet gown and a pink wide-brimmed hat weighed down by an assortment of flowers, feathers, and bright red cloth cherries.

"Cecily, my dear! It has seemed simply ages since we last saw you, hasn't it Frederick, dear?" She looked over her shoulder. "Frederick? Drat the man. He was right behind me. Where has he gone now?"

"The bar, most likely," Baxter said dryly. He rose to his feet and gave the newcomer a light bow of his head. "Mrs. Carter-Holmes Fortescue. What a pleasure."

"Oh, the pleasure is mine, dear Mr. Baxter." Phoebe Fortescue giggled behind her fan. "As always."

Cecily smiled at her friend. "Hello, Phoebe. I'm so happy you could join us."

"Yes, well, I'm afraid we are a little late. Frederick takes such an inordinate amount of time to get ready. I swear that man falls asleep while he's dressing." Phoebe sank onto a chair and fanned her face, blowing little tendrils of hair about as she did so.

Cecily was never quite sure whether or not to believe the rumor that Phoebe was quite bald and wore a wig under her massive hats. The fact that she had rarely seen her friend without a hat seemed to add credence to the supposition. Not that it mattered to her, of course. Phoebe was a dear friend, bald or not.

"Yes, well," Baxter said, making no effort to sit down again, "perhaps I should seek good old Frederick out, in case he has nodded off somewhere."

Phoebe looked up with a little gasp of gratitude. "Oh, would you, Mr. Baxter? So very good of you, I'm sure."

"Not at all." Ignoring his wife's cynical shake of her head, Baxter bowed again and hurried off.

Cecily watched him leave, feeling an acute disappointment at having been robbed of her chance to dance with him. There was such little opportunity these days, and she missed the pleasure of whirling around the floor with him.

Much as she had enjoyed her two-step with Sir Walter, it could not compare with a lively waltz in the arms of her beloved husband.

"Such a gentleman, your husband." Phoebe closed her fan and laid it on the table. "Tell me, Cecily, will Madeline and the good doctor be attending the ball tonight?"

"I'm afraid not, Phoebe." Cecily picked up a plate of hors d'oeuvres and offered it to her friend. "Madeline didn't think it was a very good environment to bring a baby."

"Oh, of course." Phoebe sniffed. "I forgot. She doesn't have a mother with whom she can leave the poor child. Such a detriment to her social life. I wonder how Dr. Prestwick feels about being trapped in his house for the entire Christmas season. He always so enjoyed going out and about."

Cecily resisted the urge to say something biting. Phoebe

and Madeline had been at each other's throats for as long as she could remember, and she had never understood why. She doubted very much if either of her friends knew why. It was a silly feud that went on and on without any signs of being resolved, and there were times when Cecily grew quite tired of having to resolve their arguments and keep the peace.

Phoebe took a miniature sausage roll from the plate, studied it for a moment, then popped it in her mouth. "I suppose she will have a good excuse not to attend my pantomime. She will be missing an excellent performance this year."

Cecily rather doubted that. Phoebe's presentations were known more for their mishaps than for any glowing tributes. Her cast of dancers had much to do with that. Not only were they miserably inept, their contempt for their director was made obvious both on and off the stage.

Phoebe usually lost control of the proceedings, and much to the delighted expectations of the audience, the result was, at times, utter chaos.

"As a matter of fact," Cecily murmured, "Madeline will be at the pantomime. She and Dr. Prestwick will be bringing little Angelina with them. I think they would both be quite disappointed to miss your performance."

"Oh!" Phoebe lifted her hands to straighten her hat. Having recovered from her surprise, she added, "Well, it is the highlight of the season, after all. I shall look forward to seeing the baby."

She went on prattling, but Cecily wasn't listening. She was envisioning a single shoe lying in the coal shed. Mrs. Tidwell's words ran through her mind, shutting out all else. *The big Irishman. He was sweet on my Ellie. Must have flown into a rage or something.* First thing in the morning, she promised herself, she would pay Mr. Docker a visit. All she could hope was that the maid's disappearance was not connected in some way to Charlie's death. For if so, things did not bode well for Ellie Tidwell.

CHAPTER
❀ 8 ❀

The following morning brought a heavy shower, and Pansy lifted her skirts as she stepped across the puddles in the courtyard. She'd been sent with a message for Samuel, and she intended to make every moment count. It wasn't often she had an excuse to see him alone in the stables. She wasn't about to squander the opportunity.

She'd taken a moment or two to pull strands of hair out from under her cap. Mrs. Chubb would have a fit if she saw that, but it was worth the risk to look modern and daring like the models in Mrs. Chubb's magazines that her daughter sent her all the time.

Humming to herself, Pansy skipped across the last big puddle and smoothed down her skirt and apron. She pinched her cheeks to give them color, then spit on her finger and smoothed it across her eyebrows.

Secure in the knowledge that she looked the best she could, she marched into the stables. The smell took her breath away for a moment, and she tried not to breathe in too deeply as she scanned the stalls for a sight of Samuel.

She heard his voice before she saw him. By the soft tones he used she could tell he was talking to one of the horses. Creeping forward, she noticed three motorcars in the stalls opposite the horses.

Samuel had told her about them the first night they'd arrived. The first one, a sleek silver machine, belonged to Lord and Lady Millshire. Then the dark blue one in the next stall, that was Sir Walter Hayesbury's. The third one, a small dark green motorcar, belonged to the crackpot in room nine, Mr. Mortimer.

"You have to learn to drive it first," Samuel said from a few yards away.

She jumped, and swung around. "What?"

"The motorcar. If you're thinking of stealing it, you have to know how to drive it."

She tossed her head, wafting strands of hair across her face. Snatching them out of her eyes, she muttered, "I wasn't thinking of stealing one. I never stole nothing in my entire life."

Samuel laughed. "I know that. I was just teasing." He walked a few steps toward her, then stopped. "I want you to meet a very good friend of mine. She's sweet and pretty and I think you'll like her."

Pansy's heart sunk. If it was that twerp Ellie, well, she'd already met her thank you very much. She didn't want to meet any girl that Samuel thought was pretty and sweet. "I can't stop," she said, already turning away. "I just came to give you a message, that's all."

"It won't take a minute." To her surprise, Samuel looked over his shoulder and whistled. "Come here, Tess! There's a good girl!"

A large brown head poked around the corner of a stall, then a furry body followed, ending with a long wagging tail.

With a cry of delight, Pansy rushed forward. "Oh! She's beautiful! Where did she come from?"

"I found her a few days ago, wandering around in the rain. She looked so sorry for herself, I brought her in here and got her dry."

"She's so thin." Pansy ran a hand over the bony ribs sticking out above the dog's taut belly. "Poor thing must be starving."

"Well, not anymore." Samuel grinned. "She's been eating everything I bring in for her for the past two days."

Pansy gasped. "You've been feeding her? What will Mrs. Chubb say?"

"Madam said I could keep her, seeing as how she's a good ratter. Caught three of them, she did."

"Eeew. I hope she didn't eat them."

"Nah, I buried them."

Pansy shuddered. "When did madam see her, then?"

"She didn't. I just told her about Tess and she said it was all right to keep her."

Pansy stroked the soft fur. "She looks really clean for a stray."

"Yeah, well, I had to give her a bath. She smelled horrible."

Pansy smiled up at him. "As bad as your horses?"

"Worse."

Obviously put out about losing her attention, the dog nudged her arm.

Pansy laughed. "Well, I hope I can come and see you sometime, Tess."

"You can come anytime you want."

Catching her breath, Pansy looked up at him. "I'd really like that. I love dogs."

For a moment she saw something in Samuel's eyes that made her heart beat faster. She snatched her gaze away, before he could see her confusion. He knew how she felt about him. She'd told him she loved him. More than once. He always answered with a joke, telling her she was too young to know her own mind.

In the end she'd grown tired of him treating her like a child. True, he was a few years older than her. Well, almost twelve years older, but that didn't make no difference to her and it shouldn't to him. So now she was careful what she said. She could afford to wait. One day he'd see her as a woman, and she'd be there waiting for him.

"Tell you what," Samuel said, his voice sounding a little strained, "I'm taking Tess to the woods this afternoon. Since it's your afternoon off and all, perhaps you'd like to come for a walk with us?"

Pansy leapt to her feet so suddenly Tess backed away in alarm. "I'd love to come with you! I'll meet you back here at half past two."

Keeping his gaze firmly on the dog, Samuel stooped to pet her. "We'll be waiting for you."

Bursting with excitement, Pansy fled for the door, only

to pause as she remembered why she'd come. "Oh, I forgot. Madam said to tell you she wants a carriage at the front door at ten o'clock this morning."

She barely waited for Samuel's "Right ho!" before flying across the courtyard on winged feet. She couldn't wait to tell Gertie. Samuel had actually asked her to go for a walk with him! He'd never asked her before. She'd always been the one to engineer their meetings.

Now she ached for the afternoon to come. Any time she could spend with Samuel was precious time, and she was going to enjoy every single second of it.

It wasn't until she had burst into the kitchen, busting to tell her friend the great news, that she remembered. It was her afternoon off, and she had already told Lenny she'd meet him at the gate at three o'clock. Now what was she going to do?

Mick Docker had been hard to track down. After calling on his home, Samuel had been redirected to a farmhouse on the outskirts of town, where Mick was working on the roof.

Cecily was quite frustrated when they arrived to find the roofer had already moved on to the next job—at the Fox and Hounds, on the other side of town.

By the time they arrived at the pub, she was seriously thinking about her midday meal. Without Baxter by her side, however, it would be improper for her to take lunch at the pub.

Samuel helped her down from the carriage with a worried frown. "You're here to talk to Mick about Charlie, aren't you, m'm."

Cecily gave him a warning look. "Perhaps. If you're thinking of telling me, however, that Mr. Baxter would not ap-
prove, and that you are not comfortable helping me without
his knowledge, then may I remind you that this is certainly
not the first time, nor is it likely to be the last."

Samuel looked even more unhappy. "That doesn't make
me feel any better, m'm."

"I'm not here to make you happy, Samuel. I'm here to
find out if Mr. Docker can tell us anything useful."

"Yes, m'm."

Cecily glanced up at the roof. Although she could see no
one, the clamor of banging and thudding told her the men
were working up there. "Now that we have that settled, perhaps you would be so good as to attract Mr. Docker's attention, and let him know I wish to speak with him."

Samuel opened his mouth, looking as if he were about
to protest, when the sudden silence took them both by surprise. "Must be time to knock off," he muttered.

"They are probably going into the public bar for lunch."
Cecily gave him a gentle prod with her elbow. "Hurry, Samuel. I want to speak to Mr. Docker before he goes in there."

Samuel hurried off, and she took a seat at one of the out-
doors tables in the garden to wait for him. By the time he returned, with a frowning Mick Docker in tow, the cold wind
had chilled her to the bone.

Anxious to be on her way home, she wasted no time in
her quest for answers. "Mr. Docker, do you have any idea
where we might find Ellie Tidwell?"

The roofer seemed taken aback by the blunt question.
He sat down heavily on the bench opposite her, shaking his

head, his eyes dark and wary. "Why would I know where she is? She's probably run off, that's what."

Cecily raised her eyebrows. "Run off?"

"Yes, m'm. Scarpered." He leaned forward, lowering his voice. "She was sweet on that footman what got killed. I reckon she saw it happen, got scared, and ran." He straightened up again. "She'll be back as soon as she gets hungry enough, you mark my words."

Cecily narrowed her eyes. "How exactly did you learn that Ellie was missing?"

Mick swiped at his nose with the back of his hand. "I heard the maids talking about it, didn't I."

"Did you also know that one of Ellie's shoes was found in the coal shed last night?"

Mick's eyes widened. "The coal shed? What the devil was it doing there?"

"That's what I'd like to know."

"Look, I don't know what you're getting at, Mrs. Baxter, but I don't know nothing about Ellie or where she might have gone. She and me were done a long time ago. I haven't even spoken to her since she came back to Badgers End." He pulled a watch from his vest pocket and studied it briefly before stuffing it back. "If that's all, m'm, I have to get back to me mates. I only give 'em half an hour to eat, then it's back on the job."

Frustrated, Cecily nodded. "Of course. I would appreciate it, however, if you would let me know if you should hear from Ellie."

Mick laughed as he got up, and it wasn't a pleasant sound. "You can rule that one out, m'm. I'd be the last person on earth Ellie would talk to, no matter how much trouble she's in." He touched the peak of his cap with his fingers. "Good day to you, m'm."

"Thank you, Mr. Docker." Cecily watched him stride off across the courtyard; then, turning to Samuel, she murmured, "Well, that was a wasted journey."

Samuel looked at her, an odd expression on his face.

Sensing something amiss, Cecily leaned forward. "What is it, Samuel?"

Her stable manager shook his head, then said slowly, "He said he hadn't talked to Ellie at all since she got back from London."

"Yes, he did." Nerves tightening, Cecily waited.

"Well, m'm. I could be wrong, but I could swear it was him I heard Ellie arguing with the night before we found Charlie's body. I heard her yelling at someone, and I'm sure it was Mick I heard. I recognized his accent."

"Are you quite sure, Samuel?"

Samuel shrugged. "As sure as I could be, I reckon."

"What time was this?"

"Around nine o'clock. I'd just finished putting away the last motorcar and locked everything up. I was on my way to my room when I heard Ellie yelling in the kitchen yard. Then I heard Mick yelling back at her."

Cecily tapped her fingers on the table. "I shall have another chat with Mr. Docker later. Right now, however, we have to return to the Pennyfoot. Mr. Baxter will be wondering where I am."

At the mention of Baxter's name, Samuel leapt to his feet. "We'd better go, then, m'm."

Rising more slowly, Cecily drew her scarf closer around

her neck. She was thinking about Mick Docker. Had he lied when he said he hadn't talked to Ellie? He'd mentioned that the maid was fond of Charlie. Had he seen them together and argued with Ellie that night? Perhaps, driven by jealousy, he'd dropped the gargoyle on Charlie's head the next morning. It was certainly a possibility, but how in the world would she find out for certain, much less prove it? That was the question.

"You'll have to tell Lenny," Gertie said, waving a spoon at Pansy for emphasis. "You can't just leave him waiting for you at the gate."

Leaning back against the kitchen sink, Pansy twisted her apron between her fingers, her stomach tied up in knots. "He'll be cross with me. I daren't tell him."

"Just tell him you have to do something else this afternoon. You don't have to tell him what it is." Gertie turned her back on her and went on folding serviettes into the shape of swans. "Tell him you'll go out with him another time."

"But I don't want to go out with him. Ever." Pansy felt a tear forming and blinked it back. "I only said I'd go out with him to make Samuel jealous, and now Samuel's asked me out so I don't have to make him jealous anymore."

"Well, Lenny will be a lot more cross if you don't tell him and he has to wait in the cold for you and you don't turn up." Gertie turned back to face her. "If I were you I'd be there at the gate to meet him."

"I can't." Pansy glanced at the clock. "I'm supposed to meet Samuel at half past two. Lenny won't be at the gate until three o'clock."

Gertie pursed her lips. "Looks like you've got a bleeding problem then, doesn't it. Perhaps you should tell Samuel about Lenny and meet him later."

Pansy swallowed. "I can't. He'll be upset with me and I'd rather make Lenny angry than Samuel."

"Well, then, I suppose it's up to you what you do. Just don't come crying to me if Lenny has a row with you later." She turned back to the table, putting an end to the conversation.

Pansy went back to washing the glassware, wishing she'd never agreed to meet Lenny. She must have been out of her mind. Now she'd got herself in a mess, and Gertie wasn't any help.

She thought about asking Gertie to meet Lenny and tell him she wasn't coming, except she knew Gertie wouldn't like that at all, and she was upsetting enough people as it was. No, she'd just have to meet Samuel and leave Lenny waiting at the gate.

After all, she hadn't actually said in words that she'd meet him. She'd just nodded her head. In any case, he'd probably be so cross with her he'd stay out of her way and never talk to her again.

The roof job was finished, and unless they got another leak, it could be months before he worked on the Pennyfoot again. By then, he would have forgotten all about her leaving him at the gate.

Feeling a little better, she carefully stacked glasses on the draining board. All she wanted to do was look forward to her walk with Samuel and Tess, and she couldn't wait to get out of there.

As it was, the guests lingered longer than usual over their

midday meal, and it was already half past two by the time all the dishes were cleared from the table and stacked by the sink ready to wash.

Fighting a sense of panic, Pansy thrust a pile of dishes into the hot soapy water. "If I don't get out to the stables, Samuel will go without me," she cried, as Gertie picked up a tea towel ready to dry the dishes. "He'll never ask me again and I'll just die."

Gertie grinned. "No, you won't." She took a wet dish out of Pansy's hands. "Here, go on with you. I'll finish these."

Pansy rose up on tiptoe and flung her arms around Gertie's shoulders. "Thank you, thank you!"

"You can do the same for me someday," Gertie said, shaking her off. "Now get out to those bloody stables before Samuel leaves."

Pansy needed no more nudging. Dragging off her apron, she flew to the door, pausing only long enough to hook the apron on the wall before racing out into the hallway.

Reminding herself that the staff were not allowed to run inside the building, she slowed her steps as she crossed the lobby, but once outside in the cold fresh air, she flew as fast as she could across the backyard and into the courtyard.

Samuel was just emerging from the stables, the lanky dog skipping around his feet, as she turned the corner. He waved as she hurried toward him, one hand smoothing the stray hairs that had escaped the tight knot at the back of her head.

Flushed and panting, she stopped to pat Tess's head before smiling up at Samuel. "Sorry I'm late. They was late getting out of the dining room."

"That's all right." Samuel grinned back at her, warming her through and through. "Tess is anxious to get to the woods, though, aren't you, girl?"

Tess wagged her tail and bounded over to the gate. For a moment Pansy worried that Lenny might arrive there early, but there was no sign of the lad as they stepped out onto the Esplanade.

"We'll take the back way," Samuel said, leading her down the alleyway that bordered the country club. "Tess doesn't like carriages, for some reason. I think she might have been hit by one at some time."

"Oh, poor thing!" Pansy reached out a hand to pat the dog's head again but Tess bounded away, out of reach. Not that Pansy minded. She was too relieved that they were taking the back way, thus avoiding any chance of bumping into Lenny.

The next half hour or so went by in a flash as she and Samuel walked side by side, talking and laughing at Tess, who stopped every two minutes to sniff at the roadside.

Pansy did her best to forget about Lenny waiting for her at the gate, though every now and then she'd be struck with a pang of guilt.

Samuel must have sensed her uneasiness. As they climbed the path across the Downs, he paused, one hand on her arm. "Is there something wrong?" he asked, his eyes full of concern. "You're awfully quiet all of a sudden."

She was tempted to tell him the truth, but perhaps he wouldn't think much of a girl who left another man waiting while she went off with someone else. So she made up a lie. "I was thinking about that Mr. Mortimer in room nine." She gave him a quick smile. "He's really strange. Gives me the willies, he does. I think he's evil."

Samuel frowned. "What did he do? Did he say something to you?"

Pansy shook her head. "Not really. It's just the way he looks and acts." She shuddered. "I wouldn't be at all surprised if he's that serial killer from London."

Samuel laughed. "What would the Mayfair Murderer be doing down here in Badgers End?"

Offended, Pansy turned away. "I dunno. Maybe he's hiding from the police. Anyway, I'm not the only one that thinks so, neither."

Samuel's grin faded. "Who else thinks so, then?"

"The other maids. After all, we're the only ones that see him. He stays in his room all day. Even eats his meals in there."

"He's probably just shy, or doesn't like being with people he doesn't know. After all, he's down here on his own, isn't he?"

"So, if he's shy and doesn't like people he doesn't know, what's he doing staying at the Pennyfoot Country Club at Christmastime?"

Samuel shook his head, and whistled to the dog, who had gone bounding ahead. "I don't know, but if I were you, I'd be careful what you say about him. If he is the Mayfair Murderer, he won't like you going around telling everyone he is, will he."

He was grinning, but Pansy couldn't be sure if he was teasing or not. In any case, she felt shivers running down her back every time she thought about it after that.

In no time at all, it seemed, they had reached the path to the woods. Tess plunged ahead of them into the trees, making Samuel call out anxiously after her when she disappeared from sight.

"I don't want to lose her," he said, as they quickened their steps to catch up with the dog. "She's used to being on her own, though. She might decide she likes it better being free."

There was such anxiety in his voice, Pansy felt like hugging him to make him feel better. "She won't run off," she said, hoping she was right. "Why would she? She has someone to feed her and brush her coat and take care of her. More than anything, she has someone to love her now. What more could she want? What more could anyone want?"

He must have picked up something in her voice, as he paused and looked back at her. For a moment they stared at each other, looking deep into each other's eyes, while her heart drummed in her chest.

Samuel's voice sounded strange when he spoke. "Pansy, I—"

To her intense disappointment, the sound of barking cut off whatever he was going to say. He turned, looking in the direction of the urgent summons. "That's Tess. Something's upset her."

Sensing the precious moment fading away, Pansy grabbed his arm. "It's probably only a rabbit, that's all. What were you going to say?"

He shook his head. "No, that's an alarm bark. We'd better go and find out what's bothering her."

He took off at a run, leaving her to follow, seething with frustration. She was sure he was going to say something important. Maybe something that would change her life forever. Drat the dog. Tess had taken away her chance of finally hearing Samuel say the words she longed to hear.

Sulking, she trudged after him, the dog's barking echoing in her ears. Samuel disappeared among the trees, and shortly after that Tess's barks dwindled to soft whines.

Thinking the dog might be hurt, Pansy quickened her steps. The forest smelled of wet wood and damp earth, blending with the tangy fragrance of pine. Needles and dried leaves crunched under her feet as she hurried up the trail toward the spot where Samuel had disappeared.

She couldn't see any movement ahead, and above her the thick branches of the evergreens shut out the light, so everything around her was clothed in murky shadows. Even Tess had stopped her whining, and only the rustling of the wind in the trees competed with the thump of her heart.

Pansy halted, clutching her thin scarf to her throat. "Samuel?" Her voice sounded thin and high. She cleared her throat and tried again. "Samuel? Tess? Where are you? I can't see you."

No one answered. Frightened now, she took a few steps deeper into the woods. "Samuel? *Samuel!*"

"I'm here."

The harsh voice had drifted out to her from the dense thicket of trees. She took a nervous step in that direction, then all at once Samuel appeared from behind the thick trunk of a gnarled old oak tree.

Relief swamped her, until she saw his face. His skin had turned as pale as a bleached sheet. His eyes looked huge and stared back at her as if she were some wild animal getting ready to attack him.

"Samuel?"

She took a step toward him and his hand shot up, freezing her to the spot. When he spoke his voice sounded so different she hardly recognized it.

"Don't come any closer."

Her own voice barely above a whisper, she answered him. "What? Why not?"

Samuel clutched his stomach and leaned the other hand against the oak's trunk. His next words chilled her to the bone. "Because I just found Ellie, and it's not a pretty sight."

CHAPTER
❀ 9 ❀

Gertie stacked the last dish on the draining board and reached for the soggy tea towel. It had taken her twice as long without Pansy, but she knew, only too well, what it was like to be late on a day off. When you only got one afternoon a week, every minute was precious. Especially if you were spending it with someone you really liked.

Gertie sighed. She used to long for her afternoon off so she could spend it with Dan. That was when they were first getting to know each other and every moment with him was exciting.

Nowadays, all they seemed to do was argue with each other. She knew that Dan missed living in the city, and was getting bored with the sleepy little village of Badgers End. He kept telling her there was nothing to do down there, and the winters were too long.

Twice he'd asked her if she'd move to London with him, and both times she'd refused to consider it. She didn't want her twins growing up in London. She'd seen what the city could do to people, and she wanted none of that for her children.

Besides, everyone she knew and loved lived in Badgers End. She'd miss them all, and her job. She loved working at the Pennyfoot, meeting new people every week or so.

She loved living across the street from the ocean and all that fresh air. Not like the black fog from the coal fires that choked the streets of London. They didn't call it The Smoke for nothing.

No, she wouldn't give up her life again for a man. She'd done it once, moving to Scotland to be with Ross. How she'd hated it up there. The bitterly cold winters, the strange customs and accents that were impossible to understand. Much as she loved Dan, and she loved him far more than she'd loved Ross, she wouldn't do it again. She and her twins belonged in Badgers End and that's where they'd stay.

"I want to give Harriet a bath."

The high-pitched voice piping behind her startled her out of her wits. She spun around, the bone china plate slipping through her fingers. It landed with a splintering crash on the floor, making the little girl in front of her jump back in horror.

"You dropped the plate!"

Gertie scowled. "Now how on earth did you find out about that?"

Adelaide drew her brows together. "I didn't find out. I saw it."

Obviously sarcasm was wasted on the child. Gertie

stooped to pick up the pieces. "What are you doing in the kitchen anyway? You're not supposed to be in here. Does your mummy know where you are?"

Adelaide shrugged. "She's sleeping."

"What about your nanny?"

"She's reading in the library. I crept out when she wasn't looking."

"And your brother?"

"He crept out, too. I don't know where he went."

Some other lucky blighter being bothered by him, no doubt, Gertie thought darkly. "Well, you'd better go back to the library before your nanny sees you missing and decides to raise the alarm."

Adelaide ran her finger down the edge of the table then licked it. She pulled a face, and stuck the offending finger into the pocket of her apron. "What's an alarm?"

"It's a loud bell that tells people something is wrong so they come running."

"The bell can talk?"

Gertie muttered a word under her breath so the child wouldn't hear it. "No, it can't talk."

"Harriet can talk." The little girl held the doll's face up to her ear, frowned in concentration, then announced, "Harriet wants a bath."

"Then you'll have to take her to the lavatory. There's no bath in here."

"She wants a bath in there." Adelaide pointed to the sink and held the doll over it as if about to drop it in.

Abandoning the scattered pieces of china, Gertie surged to her feet and grabbed the doll. "No! You'll spoil all its clothes. They'll get all wet and stained." She fingered the delicate silk and lace in awe. "She has such beautiful clothes. Better than I've ever seen. I wish I had clothes like this to wear."

"Mommy will buy me more clothes for her. She buys me anything I want." Adelaide stretched out her hand for the doll but Gertie held it up out of reach.

"You're not getting her back until you promise not to give her a bath. Or at least, take her clothes off before you get her wet."

Adelaide pouted, and just then the door opened and Mrs. Chubb bustled in. She took one look at Adelaide and her eyes widened in dismay. "What on earth is that child doing in the kitchen?"

"Causing a lot more trouble than she's worth," Gertie muttered.

Mrs. Chubb gasped. "Don't tell me that's one of our best china plates all over the floor. Who did that? Did she do that?"

Adelaide promptly opened her mouth and let out a blood-curdling scream. "No, I didn't! She broke it, and she's hurting Harriet! She's going to drown her in the sink!"

"Don't be daft." Gertie thrust the doll at her. "You was the one that wanted to drop her in there. Besides, you can't drown a doll. She's not alive like a real baby."

"She is, she is!" Adelaide hugged the doll to her chest, her cries drowning out Mrs. Chubb's next words.

The housekeeper sent Gertie a murderous look, then ushered the sobbing child out of the kitchen, muttering, "There, there, precious."

Gertie rolled her eyes as the door closed behind them. As if she didn't have enough to put up with, what with all the extra work that Christmas brought.

She stooped again to pick up the pieces of the shattered plate. Fine bloody Christmas this was. She missed the twins. It wasn't Christmas without them. Sighing, she dropped the broken china into the lap of her apron. Soon they'd be home, and then maybe she'd feel better about things.

She climbed to her feet, then holding the corners of her apron up, walked over to the back door. Stepping outside, she looked up at the sky. Dark clouds scurried overhead, driven by the brisk winds from the sea.

Shivering, she trudged over to the dustbin and opened the lid. The broken pieces of china clattered as she dropped them in, and she closed the lid with a bang. As she turned around to hurry back inside, a man appeared, seemingly from nowhere, and stepped in front of her.

Startled, she drew back with a gasp. "Lenny! You made me jump. Where did you come from?"

"The gate." His eyes glittered with anger. "I've been waiting there half an hour. Where's Pansy? She was supposed to meet me there."

Gertie looked around as if expecting to see her turn up any minute. "I don't know where she is. I haven't seen her in a while."

Lenny looked about ready to explode. "Well, you tell her from me, I don't like being made to look like a fool. No one does that to me and gets away with it. You tell that little bitch I'll be seeing her."

With an angry punch in the air with his fist, he spun around and marched off, banging the gate so hard behind him Gertie was sure it had come right off its hinges.

She was shaking as she hurried back to the kitchen. She didn't like the look in Lenny's eyes one little bit. She'd have to warn Pansy to stay out of his way. Nasty temper that young man had, and she for one wouldn't want to be on the wrong end of it. She pitied Pansy if he ever caught up with her.

She shut the door, feeling a little safer now that she was back inside the kitchen. Even so, the uneasy feeling hovered in her stomach for the rest of the afternoon. She couldn't help worrying that Pansy was in for trouble, and there didn't seem to be any way to avoid it.

Cecily was relieved to find her suite empty when she returned. Baxter, it seemed, had found something to occupy his time. Thankful she didn't have to answer any awkward questions, she took off her coat and hung it in the wardrobe.

Having missed lunch, she decided to ask Mrs. Chubb to send up a sandwich and a pot of tea. She was about to pull the bell rope when a sharp tap on the door stayed her hand.

Opening it, she saw at once that her messenger had brought bad news. Samuel's face was pale and drawn, his mouth a tight line. "Come in," she said sharply, and closed the door behind him. "Tell me. What's happened now?"

Samuel opened his mouth, swallowed, and then cleared his throat.

Cecily moved over to her chair and sat down. "It's Ellie, isn't it?"

Samuel nodded. He sounded as if he had a bad cold when he finally spoke. "I'm sorry, m'm."

"Where is she?"

"Buried in the woods. Tess found her."

"Tess?"

"My dog. We heard her barking and I went to see what was upsetting her. I . . ." Samuel's voice wavered and he cleared his throat again.

"Take a moment, Samuel." She needed a moment as much as he did. "Sit down and take your time."

He glanced at the chair she'd pointed to but made no move to sit down. "I saw her hand, sticking out from a pile of leaves. I brushed them all away and she was lying there with her eyes open, staring right up at me." He gulped, and grabbed his throat. "Sorry, m'm."

"Quite all right, Samuel."

"I knew she was dead. Covered in what looked like coal dust she was. All over her. She must have been buried in the coal shed or something." He shook his head. "Who would have wanted to kill her? She was such a sweet girl. Wouldn't hurt a fly. I can't . . . I don't . . ."

He turned away, and Cecily rose swiftly and went to him. Laying her hand on his shoulder she said gently, "You must pull yourself together, Samuel. I know this has been a terrible shock and I don't blame you for being upset. But now we must find out who did this and bring them to justice."

Samuel nodded. "Yes, m'm. Do you think whoever killed her killed Charlie, too?"

"I don't know." Sighing, Cecily sat down again. "That's something we will have to find out. I will have to ring the constabulary, of course. Dr. Prestwick will have to examine her."

"They will go right away, won't they?" Samuel dashed the back of his hand across his eyes. "I didn't want to leave her out there all alone. I covered her up again, in case someone else came along. It seemed the right thing to do."

"Very good, Samuel. Now please try to put it out of your mind as best you can. We have our jobs to do and we can't let something like this get in the way of our duties, no matter how much pain we are suffering."

"Yes, m'm. I'll be off, then." He moved to the door, pausing to look back at her. "You will let me help you find Ellie's killer, won't you, m'm? I'd like to see whoever did this get his just desserts."

"Of course, Samuel. You know I'd appreciate the help." She smiled, more out of habit than because she felt like it. "Thank you."

"Yes, m'm."

The door closed quietly behind him, only to open a moment later. Cecily rose to greet her husband as he stepped into the room. "Baxter, darling! I wondered where you were."

"I was wondering the same thing about you." He waited for her to sit before sinking onto his favorite chair. "I had to eat alone. You know how I hate that."

"I'm sorry, dear. I had some errands to run. You know how it is this time of the year. Always something else one must buy."

"Ah, yes." He laced his fingers across his chest and regarded her with a raised eyebrow. "Are you telling me you went Christmas shopping?"

"Among other things."

"And would these other things involve an investigation into Charlie's death and that little maid's disappearance, by any chance?"

She sighed. "I'm afraid Ellie didn't simply disappear. Samuel's dog found her body this afternoon."

His entire face seemed to crumple. "Oh, God, no. Not another one."

"I'm afraid so, dear."

"This is utterly intolerable." He sat for a moment, contemplating the news, then said heavily, "I suppose you've summoned that idiot, Northcott?"

"Not yet." She plucked a piece of lint from her navy skirt. "I was rather hoping you would do that for me. As well as Dr. Prestwick. They both will have to be notified."

"Of course." He sent her a curious look. "Is there a reason you don't want to do it? You are usually so determined to handle such things yourself."

She laid a hand on her stomach. "I haven't eaten since early this morning. I'm afraid I'm feeling a little light in the head."

"Good Lord, why on earth didn't you say so." He got to his feet, and was halfway to the door before he spoke again. "I'll have the kitchen send up a tray, and then ring the constabulary. You stay there and rest, and when I come back, we'll discuss your part in all this."

She pulled a face at the closing door. She adored her husband, and wouldn't change him for anyone else in the word, but there were times when he could be an insufferable nuisance with his concerns over her safety.

He should know by now that no matter how much he worried, she was honor bound to hunt down a person who had taken the life of someone close to her. Her heart ached for the two young people taken so early in their lives.

No matter how brief their acquaintance, Ellie and Charlie had been members of her staff, the next best thing to family, and she would not rest until their killer, or killers, had been brought to justice.

The thing that really frightened her was that two of her staff had been struck down in close succession. It was imperative she find out the motive behind the deaths, since the possibility existed of an insane murderer intent on wiping out the entire Pennyfoot staff. As far as she could see, that was the only link between the two victims.

Such a disaster seemed impossible, yet she had seen enough in her years at the Pennyfoot to know that anything and everything was possible, no matter how bizarre.

She must summon Madeline again, she decided. If anyone could help her gain insight into the reason behind the murders, it was her friend and her remarkable powers.

She started to rise, just as a loud rap on her door announced a visitor. Hurrying to the door, she threw it open, to reveal Pansy standing there, eyes red rimmed and face paper white, holding a tray in hands that shook so violently, tea slopped out of the teapot's spout.

Taking the tray from the frightened girl, Cecily said gently, "Come inside for a moment, Pansy, and sit down."

"Yes, m'm."

Her voice had been hardly more than a faint whisper, and she scurried past as if the devil himself was after her. She waited for Cecily to lay the tray down and take a seat before perching on the very edge of her chair.

"You were friendly with Ellie, weren't you?" Cecily gave the girl an encouraging smile. "Did she ever talk about someone she was seeing?"

Pansy's bottom lip quivered. "She didn't talk much to me, m'm. We didn't get along that well."

Surprised, Cecily nodded. "I see. When was the last time you saw her?"

Pansy blinked, her brows drawn together. "It must have been two days ago. I went out to fill the coal scuttles and I saw her out in the yard talking to Stan, the coal man." Her frown deepened. "Or I should say more like arguing."

Cecily leaned back in her chair. Ellie hadn't worked for her that long, and apart from the first interview, she hadn't had much occasion to talk to the girl. Her impression, however, was that the new maid was a shy little thing, hard-working and unassuming, polite and eager to please.

Yet what she had heard about her lately had been quite different. Ellie, it seemed, had been involved in arguments with more than one person, and was at odds with Pansy, who got along with everyone. It would seem she had indeed misjudged the girl. The point was, what had all the arguments been about?

It seemed unlikely she'd ever find out. Neither Mr. Docker nor Mr. Whittle were likely to tell her. Especially if one of them was guilty of murder.

Cecily sighed. "Thank you, Pansy. You may go. I'll bring the tray down to the kitchen myself later. You will be busy getting the dining room ready for the evening meal."

Pansy curtsied, then fled through the door.

Cecily contemplated her roast pork sandwich, torn with indecision. How she hated to simply give up at such an early stage, yet there was so little evidence to help her. One thing seemed clear. According to Madeline's vision, Charlie's death was not an accident. Ellie's certainly wasn't. Someone had wanted them both dead, and until the reason for that became clear, there didn't seem to be any path to follow.

Ellie seemed to have had some kind of disagreement with both Mick Docker and Stan Whittle. Mr. Docker had apparently lied about his argument with her, if Samuel was right about what he'd heard.

As for Mr. Whittle, he'd also been heard arguing with her. Not only that, he was a coal man and Ellie's shoe had been found in the coal shed. Also, Samuel was saying he thought Ellie's body was covered in coal dust.

On the other hand, just because Ellie had possibly been killed in the coal shed, that didn't necessarily condemn Stan Whittle. Anyone could have killed her and left her in there.

Nevertheless, Mr. Whittle could be considered a suspect, and she should start there. Christmas, however, was just a few short days away. She had little time to go chasing after everyone asking them questions, not to mention the obvious peril in doing so.

Then there was Baxter's disapproval to take into account. Perhaps she should simply hand this one over to Sam Northcott, and hope that he would make a real effort to find whoever had done these dreadful deeds.

It was all extremely upsetting, to say the least. She would feel better, she decided, once she had talked to Madeline. Until then, she would just have to take one step at a time.

CHAPTER
❧ 10 ❧

That first step came an hour later, when P.C. Northcott arrived on the scene. "The doctor h'examined the body," he told Cecily, when she took him into her office to discuss the matter. "The girl was strangled. No doubt about that. Her neck was black and blue. I could actually see the thumb prints on her throat."

Cecily shuddered. "Has her mother been informed?"

"The doctor is with her now. I thought it best he be the one to break the bad news. Just in case she went into shock or something." The constable rocked back on his heels, hands behind his back.

He always did that when he was embarrassed, and Cecily guessed he had asked Kevin Prestwick to tell Mrs. Tidwell her daughter had been murdered because he was too spineless to do it himself.

"Do you have any idea who might have done this?" She was still reluctant to share her suspicions just yet. Perhaps, with Madeline's help, she wouldn't have to leave it up to him to solve the murders, after all.

Northcott puffed out his chest and stuck his thumbs in the breast pockets of his uniform. "Yes, m'm, I do. I have all that worked out."

She stared at him, unable to believe what she had just heard. "You do? Who——?" She broke off as someone rapped on the door.

A second later Baxter stuck his head in the gap and glared at P.C. Northcott. "I thought I told you to alert me when you arrived."

"Didn't see you around, did I." The constable turned his back on him, infuriating Baxter even more.

Cecily winced. There had always been bad blood between her husband and the constable, due to Northcott having stolen away Baxter's sweetheart when they were quite young. The feud had simmered for years, and although neither man ever spoke of it, the air bristled with hostility anytime the two of them were together.

"The constable was just about to tell me who killed our maid," Cecily said, as Baxter charged across the room like a wounded elephant.

"How terribly decent of him," Baxter muttered.

Northcott sniffed. "I wasn't going to tell you anything, Mrs. B. After all, this is police business. Seeing as how you asked, however, I s'pose it wouldn't hurt to inform you of the events of two nights ago, h'as I see it."

"Spit it out, then." Baxter folded his arms and looked menacing. "We're both waiting with bated breath."

He got a dark glare from Northcott, who then turned to Cecily. "It were like this. It came to my notice that the deceased were fond of each other. Or, at least, the young footman was sweet on the maid, but she had eyes for another. Namely, your stable manager, Samuel."

Cecily exchanged a startled look with Baxter. "Samuel? Are you certain?" She was remembering Samuel's distress when he told her about finding the body. At the time she'd thought he was simply in shock at seeing such a grisly scene, but now she wondered if he had a deeper reason to be so upset.

"Oh, yes, m'm. One of your other maids saw them together. She told me all about it. It was quite plain, she says, that the deceased female—"

"Her name, sir, was Ellie Tidwell," Baxter said, rudely butting in. "Please have the decency to use her proper name. She may be dead, but she still deserves some respect."

The constable didn't even glance in his direction as he continued, "—was sweet on the young man. Any'ow, this is what I think happened. Your footman saw them together, and in a fit of jealous rage, strangled the maid. You'd be surprised how many young men decide that if they can't have the object of their affection, then no one else will have 'em, either."

"Really. How terribly selfish of them." Cecily sent Baxter a shake of her head as he opened his mouth to interrupt again. "Do go on, Sam."

"Yes, well, then once he realized what he'd done, he was full of remorse, weren't he. So he rushed up to the roof and threw himself orf."

"Threw himself off," Cecily repeated solemnly.

"Yes, m'm. That's what I said. He threw himself orf. Head first. Like he was diving into the sea." He stroked his chin. "Of course, if he had dived into the sea, instead of the cement path of the rose garden, he might well have survived. Not that he wanted to survive, of course, otherwise he wouldn't have thrown himself orf the—"

"For God's sake, man, get to the blasted point!"

Northcott drew himself up as tall as he could manage and glared at Baxter. "I thought I had."

"In that case, there's just one thing I'd like to know."

Baxter's expression made Cecily nervous. She tried to catch his eye but he avoided looking at her. "Did he happen to throw the gargoyle down first and then deliberately fall on top of it, by any chance?"

Northcott lifted a finger in the air. "Ah, I was coming to that."

"Oh, jolly good. I was afraid we'd be left to puzzle that one out for ourselves."

Cecily loudly cleared her throat. "Please, Sam, go on."

"Yes, well, it's quite obvious to someone what is an expert at deductions, isn't it. He changed his mind at the last minute, didn't he. That's what happened." He nodded at Cecily, his bottom lip jutting out. "Not the first time I've seen that happen, neither."

"He changed his mind," Baxter said. "How utterly inconvenient."

"Yes, well, he must have grabbed ahold of the gargoyle to stop himself from falling. Of course, it wasn't tied down enough to hold his weight, was it, so down it came with him. Poof! He's dead, isn't he. Cracked his head open, poor blighter. Though I suppose some would say

136

it's poetic justice. Having taken the life of that young girl and all."

Cecily sent a wary glance at her husband. His face had turned scarlet and she could see he was gathering breath to explode. "That's extremely astute of you, Sam," she said hurriedly. "I suppose this means you will be closing the case in your report?"

"Quite, Mrs. B. After all, we don't want to have any unpleasantness over the Christmas season, now do we? I shall give a full report to the inspector right after the New Year, and I'm quite sure he will agree with my deductions."

Baxter rolled his eyes but mercifully kept quiet. Cecily let out her breath. She was certain now that she did not want Sam Northcott bothering her guests with his endless questions and ridiculous assumptions. Far better that he believe the scenario he had given them and leave them in peace.

Meanwhile she had a week or so to find the killer before the inspector became involved. That was something she would try to avoid at all costs.

Inspector Cranshaw had long ago formed the opinion that the Pennyfoot was a den of iniquity and should be shut down forever. Anytime he had reason to investigate a crime on or near the premises, it raised the possibility of him getting his wish.

So far Cecily had managed to stay one step ahead of him at all times. She would be the first to admit, however, that sooner or later, he would find the excuse he was looking for to be rid of the Pennyfoot and everyone connected with it. She was equally determined to prevent that happening anytime soon.

"Well, if that be all, I'll be orf." P.C. Northcott reached

for his helmet and shoved it on his head. "I'm sorry this here unfortunate incident has put a dampener on your festivities, Mrs. B., but in spite of everything, I do wish you a very happy Christmas."

"Thank you, Sam. And I wish the same to you and your family."

Northcott touched his helmet with his fingers and inclined his head. "I . . . ah . . . don't suppose Mrs. Chubb has a mince pie or two to spare?"

"I'm sure she will be able to find something for you." Cecily ignored her husband's grunt of disgust. "Just stop by the kitchen and tell her I sent you."

"Much obliged, Mrs. B., I'm sure." Without looking at Baxter he passed him by, muttering, "Good day, sir."

"It will be," Baxter said, as the door closed behind the constable, "now that he's gone."

"Hush," Cecily warned, raising her finger to her lips. "We can't afford to annoy him. We don't want him bringing Cranshaw down on our heads."

Baxter frowned. "I should say that Inspector Cranshaw is exactly what we need. That confounded fool, Northcott, would say anything to avoid having to do his duty and investigate a murder during his Christmas holidays. He must be really irked that he had to stay in Badgers End this year. Usually when something like this happens, he's away visiting relatives. Dashed convenient for him if you ask me."

"Yes, dear. We don't, however, need the inspector breathing down our necks, either. Not while we are attempting to entertain our guests."

Baxter tilted his chin down and frowned at her. "May I

remind you that two of our servants have died by someone's hand in quick succession. Obviously some madman. There could be more deaths. We must notify the inspector as soon as possible. If he can't come himself he can at least send someone more capable than that clown, Northcott."

Cecily drew a deep breath. "Can we at least wait until the New Year? By then Sam will have given his report to Cranshaw and he can make his own decisions."

"Don't you mean that by then you might just have solved the murders and apprehended the killer?"

She gave him a small smile. "There's always that possibility, I suppose."

Baxter drew himself up and shook his head. "Absolutely not!"

Cecily tightened her mouth. "You are not, by any chance, forbidding me to look into this, are you?"

Some of the fire went out of his eyes. "I know how futile that is, my dear. I would, however, ask you to reconsider, knowing my feelings on the subject."

"As you do mine. I am every bit as aware as you are that we could have a killer in our midst who just might strike again. All the more important for me to get busy and find out who is behind these murders."

"Isn't that why we have policemen?"

"You know very well that our only constable in Badgers End is Northcott. If we go to the constabulary in Weller-combe, Inspector Cranshaw will be only too happy to make our lives miserable. You also know how devastating that could be for our guests, not to mention the very real possibility that the inspector will finally lose patience and use the opportunity to shut us down."

Baxter sighed. "I wonder why I inevitably end up losing this argument."

Cecily smiled to soften her words. "I often wonder why you even give me an argument, knowing the outcome."

"One always lives in hope that good sense will prevail." He moved to the door. "I trust that we have the same arrangement as always? That you do not put yourself in harm's way without telling me where you are going and with whom? Preferably me."

"Of course." She held up her hand to prevent him leaving. "Wait! You were about to confide in me earlier, about what has been keeping you in such a morose mood. This business of poor Ellie put it completely out of my mind until now. What was it you wished to tell me?"

He opened his mouth to answer her, then closed it again with a shake of his head.

Dismayed, she moved toward him. "Are you in some kind of trouble?"

"No." Again he sighed. "Well, I suppose so. Not me, personally, but the business. It hasn't been doing well. I'm thinking of closing it down."

"Oh, Bax, I'm so sorry. I know how much you enjoyed working for yourself."

"Not really." His smile barely made it past his lips. "It has become quite a bore traveling to and from the city on the train. I have so little time to spend with you. When I do close the office and have time to spare, in the summer and at Christmastime, that is when you are most busy. It's all getting a little tiresome."

Worried now, she reached for his hand. "Bax, I know how important your work is for you. Can't you continue your

140

business from here? You could have my office, while I could move my things—"

"No!" He shook his head and clasped her hand to his chest. "Cecily, my precious, this isn't the time to discuss it. I do have some suggestions, but they can wait until we have this appalling business of murder cleared up and our guests are safely on their way back home. Then we can sit down and talk about our future."

She felt a cold pang of fear and clutched his hand more tightly. "*Our* future?"

"Well, of course." He kissed her fingers and let her go. "My future is inevitably fused with yours, is it not? Now, I have some work to do. I trust we shall be able to enjoy a quiet meal this evening in our suite?"

Full of misgivings, she nodded. "Yes, but perhaps we should—"

"No buts." He opened the door and walked out into the hallway. "Until this evening, my love."

Before she could answer him, he was gone.

She closed the door and returned to her chair. Sighing, she rested her chin in her hands. Something told her that she was not going to like Baxter's suggestions for their future. Right now, however, she could not allow herself to stew over it.

Knowing him as well as she did, he would tell her in his own good time and not before, so she would be simply wasting her breath trying to dig it out of him. She would simply have to wait until he was ready.

Meanwhile, she had enough on her mind to deal with, and the sooner she got to work on her investigation the better. Reaching for the telephone, she lifted the receiver to her ear. The operator answered her a few seconds later and she asked to be put through to Dr. Prestwick's office.

Moments later his efficient voice answered her. "Cecily! How nice to hear from you. I'd be flattered that you rang me were I not certain that you are calling to ask about the murder of your maid."

She smiled. "How did you guess?"

"As soon as I realized that she was one of your employees, I expected to hear from you."

"Well, my reason for ringing you is twofold. It's true, I would like to know your thoughts on Ellie's murder."

"Not much to tell you, I'm afraid. She was strangled. Her body was covered in coal dust, suggesting she had either been killed in your coal shed, or thrown there afterward. Probably until the killer had an opportunity to move the body."

"Oh, my." Cecily briefly closed her eyes. "Can you tell me when she died?"

Prestwick hesitated, as she'd expected.

"Kevin, I know you're not supposed to tell me anything, but Ellie and Charlie were members of my staff, and you know what that means to me. I'd like to help, if I could, and knowing when Ellie and Charlie died would help a great deal."

She heard the doctor's sigh. "Very well, Cecily. If it were anyone but you . . ."

"Yes, I know, and I'm deeply grateful, Kevin. I promise I won't mention to anyone what you tell me."

"All right, then. The best I can estimate, Ellie's death occurred somewhere between seven and ten o'clock two nights ago. Charlie died maybe an hour or so later." He paused, then added, "I assume you know what is in Northcott's report?"

"Yes, he believes Charlie killed Ellie then threw himself from the roof. Is that what you think?"

"I try not to second-guess the constable," he said, with just a hint of rebuke. "All I can tell you is how and roughly when they died."

"I understand, Kevin. Thank you."

"I can tell you this," he went on, surprising her. "It would seem that she had been wearing a necklace of some sort, which is now missing."

Cecily caught her breath. "A necklace? Could it have broken while she was being strangled?"

"I don't think so. There's a deep slit in her neck above the bruises. I'd be more inclined to think the necklace was deliberately torn off her."

It wasn't much, Cecily thought. Still, it was something. A necklace, deliberately torn from Ellie's neck. Why? And if so, where was it now?

"I have just one small favor to ask of you," she said, as Kevin Prestwick prepared to hang up. "I'm having some crumpets delivered from Dolly's tea shop tomorrow morning, and I was wondering if Madeline would like to join me for a spot of tea around eleven. With Angelina, of course. Would you pass on my invitation?"

"I'd be happy to do so. Madeline mentioned that she wanted to do a spot of shopping. I'm sure she'd be delighted to stop by. I know how much she loves Dolly's crumpets."

He bid her good day and hung up. Cecily was about to replace the receiver on its hook when she heard a cough on the line. "Is that you, operator?" she demanded, incensed by the intrusion. "May I remind you that eavesdropping is breaking the rules and could very well cost you your employment."

The line clicked, and then hummed. Frowning, Cecily replaced the receiver. It had never occurred to her before that someone could be listening in to her conversations. As far as she knew, this was the first time this had happened. Perhaps the telephone exchange had hired a new operator.

Now the news could be all over town that two of her employees had been murdered and that she was investigating the crimes. Not only would that alert the killer, it could put her life in danger, as well as cause a great deal of trouble for Kevin.

From now on, she decided, she would have to conduct her private conversations in person. Apparently there were a good many disadvantages to this modern technology. Thoroughly disgruntled, she went in search of Samuel.

She found him in the courtyard, throwing a stick for a large, lanky dog who looked as if a good bath would do wonders for her appearance.

"I need you to do something for me," she said, as Samuel greeted her. "I need you to search the coal shed and the backyard to see if you can find a necklace."

Samuel looked at her in surprise. "You lost a necklace in the coal shed, m'm? What does it look like?"

"I don't know what it looks like, Samuel. It isn't mine." She paused, then added quietly, "It belonged to Ellie. It was missing when the doctor examined her and I just wondered if perhaps it got lost in the scuffle."

Samuel's expression changed, and he looked down at the

ground. "Oh, I see. I'll take a look, m'm. I'll let you know if I find anything."

"Samuel?"

He looked up, but now she could see nothing in his face to tell her what he was feeling.

"Were you and Ellie . . . involved romantically?"

Samuel's cheeks glowed red and he shuffled his feet as once more he dropped his gaze. "Course not, m'm. We were just friends, that's all. I liked her, but not in that way, if you get my meaning."

Feeling relieved, though she wasn't quite sure why, Cecily said cheerfully, "Of course I understand, Samuel. Forget I asked. I would appreciate it if you would tell me if you find the necklace."

"Yes, m'm. Right away." He turned and whistled to the dog, who came loping over to him with her furry tail wagging.

"This is your new pet, I assume." Cecily offered the back of her hand to the dog and received a wet lick across her fingers.

"Yes, m'm. This is Tess. She's a good dog. If it hadn't been for her we might never have found Ellie." He patted the dog's head, and a pair of adoring eyes stared back at him. "I hope Pansy is feeling better. She just about fainted when I told her. I wouldn't let her see the body." He looked at Cecily then and once more his eyes were moist. "I'd like to get my hands on whoever did that to Ellie."

Cecily patted his shoulder. "We'll find him, Samuel, never you fear. And when we do, we will see that justice is served."

145

"Yes, m'm."

"Meanwhile, Samuel, keep a sharp lookout, will you? Not only for yourself, but for everyone downstairs."

Alarm slashed across his face. "You don't think he's after someone else, do you?"

"I don't know what to think. I certainly hope not, but I don't think we can rule out the possibility." She tried to sound confident when she added, "Just be on your guard, though, all right?"

"You bet I will, m'm." Samuel patted the dog again. "So will Tess, won't you, girl."

Cecily rather doubted that the friendly dog would be much defense against a ruthless killer, but if it made Samuel feel better to think so, then she certainly wouldn't argue.

On her way back to the building she spotted Clive digging up potatoes in the vegetable plot and hurried over there to have a word with him.

He straightened when he saw her, and wiped a sleeve across his forehead. "Nasty business, this, m'm."

"It is, indeed." Cecily peered up at him. "I suppose Samuel told you he found Ellie?"

"Yes, m'm. He was shaken up, all right. It must have been a shock for him."

"I'm sure it was." She hesitated, then added, "Clive, I'm sure you're aware that we could have a dangerous criminal still lurking around the Pennyfoot. With two of our staff dead, I'm worried there could be more. I've asked Samuel to be on guard, and I'd appreciate it if you would keep an eye open for anything unusual or suspicious."

"I already made up my mind on that, m'm."

"Good. That makes me feel a little easier. Thank you, Clive."

She left him, somewhat reassured. Clive was big enough and strong enough to wrestle a bear, and she had no doubt he would take care of anyone who threatened to harm one of her staff. She had done all she could do to protect everyone. Now it was time to start looking for answers. All she could hope was to find them before someone else got hurt.

CHAPTER
❧ 11 ❧

"It's the Mayfair Murderer, I just know it." Gertie stood in the middle of the kitchen, hands on hips, feet spread apart. "I told you it was him that killed Charlie and now Ellie. Who's blinking next, I wonder?"

"You, I hope," Michel snapped, dropping a saucepan lid on the floor with a loud crash. "How can I make my souf-flés rise with all this racket going on? All that screeching is making them flat. I do not cook soufflés until you shut up, *comprenez-vous?*"

"Oh, put a bloody sock in it, Michel." Gertie turned back to Mrs. Chubb, who was beating eggs in a basin so rapidly, froth was flying over the edge of the bowl. "We're not safe in our beds, that's what. I was worrying about my twins being in London with that maniac on the loose and now I have to worry about them coming home to him."

"It is not the serial killer!" Michel shouted. "You are a stupid woman to frighten everyone. He kills only the young girls, *oui*? Why would a serial killer come here to kill a footman and a maid? It makes no sense." He glared at the housekeeper. "Stop beating my eggs to their death, *s'il vous plaît*! There will be nothing left of them to put in my soufflés."

Mrs. Chubb put down the bowl. "Some of the maids think the man in room nine is the Mayfair Murderer."

Michel snorted, and wiped his nose on his sleeve. "Pansy is ze idiot as well."

Gertie glared at him. "She's not an idiot. She could very well be right about that man. He's really strange."

"There are many strange people who come to the Pennyfoot. They are not serial killers."

"People don't usually come here alone, stay in their rooms all day, and cover their faces with a hat."

"He *is* rather unsociable," Mrs. Chubb put in. "I passed him in the corridor and wished him good morning. He just grunted at me."

"Was he wearing that big hat?" Gertie demanded.

"Yes, as a matter of fact, he was."

Gertie swung around to give Michel a triumphant wave of her hand. "See? I told you!"

"Wearing a big hat does not make him a serial killer." Michel bent over to pick up the saucepan lid. "Now give me the eggs and be quiet, both of you. I need complete silence for my soufflés."

"You'd better go and help Pansy with the tables," Mrs. Chubb said, glancing at the clock. "It's almost time to ring the dinner bell."

Gertie needed no second bidding. There were times

when she'd like to sock Michel in the jaw. Him and his fake French accent. Give him a bottle of brandy and that accent disappeared fast enough. Telling her to keep quiet, the saucy blighter. He made more noise than anyone when he was in a bad mood. Which was pretty much all the time.

She stomped up the stairs and across the lobby, her mind churning over the news that Ellie's dead body had been found. Pansy had cried when she'd told her. Poor Pansy. She'd been so excited about going for that walk with Samuel. What a horrible way for it to end.

She turned the corner of the hallway and halted with a gasp as she collided with someone tall and stout. To her dismay Sir Walter Hayesbury stood looking down at her, his eyes gleaming in the flickering light of the oil lamps. She could smell a faint aroma of whiskey, and guessed he was on his way back from the bar.

"I'm terribly sorry, sir," she stammered, as she leapt backward. "I was thinking so hard I wasn't looking where I was going."

"That's quite all right." He smiled at her, and a dimple flashed in his cheek.

Fascinated, she stared up at him. He might be getting on in years, but he was still a good-looking chap. She and Pansy had both said what a handsome couple he and his wife were. In fact, they'd fought over who should serve them in the dining room. So far Gertie had won, and although she would never admit it, she'd been flustered more than once by a smile and a wink from the charming aristocrat.

"So," Sir Walter murmured, "what was it that occupied your mind so intensely? A young suitor, no doubt."

Gertie shook her head, her face growing warm. "Oh, no,

sir. I was thinking about the Mayfair Murderer." Horrified, she slapped a hand over her mouth. She'd committed the cardinal sin. Her mind had been boggled by the handsome gentleman's seductive voice, and she'd forgotten she wasn't supposed to mention the murders to anyone outside the staff.

She saw the aristocrat's face change, and her heart sank. Now the word would be all over the Pennyfoot and she was to blame. Madam would be really cross with her when she found out. Trust her to go and blabber it all out. She looked up at Sir Walter. "You won't tell no one, will you? It's supposed to be kept a secret."

He stared back at her. "What is supposed to be kept a secret?"

Inwardly cursing her stupidity, Gertie shook her head. "Nothing, sir. It's nothing. Forget I said anything."

He glanced over his shoulder, down the empty hallway. "Are you talking about the footman who was killed?"

She felt a small ray of hope and clutched at it. "You already knew about that?"

"Mrs. Baxter mentioned it, yes. I understood it was an accident."

"Oh, yes, sir, it was." Relieved now, she started to back away. "I must be getting down to the dining room, sir. It's almost dinnertime."

"So what was all this about the Mayfair Murderer?"

Gertie's nerves jumped. "Oh, nothing sir. Er . . . my twins are in London and I worry about them with that serial killer running around, that's all."

"Ah, I see." He nodded, his expression amused. "Well, run along then. I don't want to keep you from your work."

"Yes, sir. Thank you, sir." She dropped a curtsey and rushed down the hallway without looking back. What a fool he must think her, blabbering like an idiot out there. Pansy would have a good laugh when she told her. Nearly spilt the milk, she did. You'd think she'd learn to keep her bloody mouth shut. Thank goodness he didn't know what she was talking about. She'd have been in hot water, all right, if madam had found out she'd let it slip about the murders.

Still, she couldn't help being nervous about Ellie being dead as well. She never really liked the girl, but it was sad to think she was dead. Gertie shivered as she entered the dining room. She only hoped it wasn't the Mayfair Murderer, or none of them would be safe in their beds.

By the time all the guests had left the dining room and the tables had been cleared, Pansy was ready to crawl into bed and forget the horrible day. She kept picturing Samuel's face when he told her he'd found Ellie lying dead among the leaves in the woods.

She didn't think she would ever go into those woods again. Certainly not by herself. She kept imagining a sinister figure dragging poor Ellie by her feet, her head bumping along the ground. It made her sick to think about it.

Stacking the last of the dishes on the cupboard shelf in the kitchen, she breathed a sigh of relief. The day was over at last. Not that she was looking forward to falling asleep. She was sure she'd have terrible nightmares about Ellie.

"Pansy!"

She jumped and spun around to find Mrs. Chubb glaring at her.

"Did you, by any chance, forget to bring down Mr. Mortimer's tray again?"

Pansy grabbed her stomach, feeling it start to churn. The last thing she wanted to do was climb those stairs to that room.

"I could get it first thing in the morning," she offered, without much hope.

"Oh, no, you won't." Mrs. Chubb folded her arms across her ample bosom. "This is the third time you've forgotten. I'm beginning to think you forget on purpose."

Pansy pinched her lips. "I've been busy. Why can't someone else get it?"

"Because I told you to take care of it." The housekeeper pointed at the door. "Now you get upstairs this minute and fetch that tray. We don't want any of the guests falling over it, now do we?"

"No, Mrs. Chubb." Dragging her feet, Pansy headed toward the door.

Gertie stood by the kitchen cabinet and gave her an encouraging smile as she went by, which did nothing to make her feel better.

She hated going up to that room. That old man frightened her, and she was sure he was the killer everyone kept talking about, come down from London to do his horrible deeds.

What if he came out when she was picking up the tray and pulled her into his room? She'd end up like poor Ellie, dragged by the feet into the woods.

She felt reasonably sure Ellie had been dragged by her feet because of the missing shoe. It must have come off when the killer grabbed her feet. Pansy shivered. She wished she'd brought a knife with her. Then again, there'd be a knife on

Mr. Mortimer's tray. Feeling only slightly reassured, she climbed the stairs.

No one passed her on the way up. Most of the men would be in the gambling rooms or the bar, while the women were either in the library or in their rooms. As she turned the corner of the landing, she shivered again. The gas lamps were turned down low this time of night, and shadows leapt along the walls as she crept down the hallway.

She was almost at the door of room nine when she noticed the tray wasn't sitting on the floor outside. Mr. Mortimer must still have it in his room. That old man'd had plenty of time to finish his meal. He must have fallen asleep in there and forgotten about the tray.

Now she really did feel sick. Mrs. Chubb wouldn't like it if she went back down without it, and she'd just have to come all the way back up again for it.

It took several long moments of indecision before she gathered the courage to tap on the door. She wasn't terribly surprised when she received no response. Holding her breath, she rapped louder. Still no answer.

Pansy turned away and started walking slowly back down the hallway. She'd just tell Mrs. Chubb that the old man had the tray in his room and wouldn't answer her knocking.

She reached the stairs and paused, her inner voice telling her that if she went back to the kitchen empty-handed, the housekeeper would simply shout at her and send her right back upstairs again.

Sighing, she retraced her steps back to number nine and pounded on the door. Taking her by surprise, it swung open, banged against something, and swung back to rap her raised knuckles.

"Ouch!" She jammed her knuckles in her mouth and glared at the offending door. Expecting any minute to see the disagreeable old man scowling at her in the doorway, she braced herself for the confrontation.

Seconds ticked by while she nursed her bruised knuckles, her stomach tying itself up in knots. When she heard no movement from inside the room, she took a tentative step forward. "Mr. Mortimer?"

No answer. Taking a deep breath, she spoke louder. "Are you in there, Mr. Mortimer?"

Still no answer.

She waited a moment or two longer, wondering if she should go and fetch Mrs. Chubb. What if he'd died in his sleep? What if he wasn't the Mayfair Murderer after all, but had been killed by him? Thinking about Samuel's face that afternoon, she knew, without a shadow of a doubt, she did not want to go in there and find a dead body.

Once more she plodded back down the hallway, only to halt again at the top of the stairs. She didn't have to look at him. All she had to do was creep in there and pick up the tray. Someone else could go and see if he was all right, but at least she wouldn't be yelled at for not bringing down the tray. Maybe if she took the tray down, she'd be forgiven for not making sure the old man was all right.

Turning back, she clenched her fingers into tight balls and crept back to the open door. If only someone else would come along right about now. She looked hopefully down the corridor, but all she could see were the dancing shadows of light from the gas lamps.

There was nothing for it but to go in there and get the

flipping tray. Steeling herself, she pushed the door open wider and stepped into the darkened room.

Blinking, she peered at the bed. She couldn't see much in the dark, but it didn't look as if anyone was lying down. She caught her breath. What if he was on the floor? She couldn't see properly. She could step on him and fall over him.

The thought of being tangled up on the floor with a dead man was just too horrible to contemplate. She backed away, then paused. The tray had to be somewhere. Could it possibly be on the floor?

She stretched out a foot and tapped the toe of her shoe in front of her. Seconds later she was rewarded with the chink of china. Relief made her giddy, and she stooped to reach for the tray, blindly feeling around in the dark.

Her fingers touched a cup and sent it crashing onto its side. She froze, expecting to hear a grunt of annoyance from somewhere. The silence stretched on, and she let out her breath. Praying the cup wasn't cracked or broken, she felt for the edges of the tray, picked it up, and backed to the door, the cup rolling noisily around in its saucer.

Backing out into the hallway, she was never so thankful to see gaslight in all her life. Stooping again, she laid the tray on the floor, closed the door, then reached for the tray again. That's when she saw the crumpled ball of paper.

It sat in the middle of the dinner plate, nestled against a lump of mashed potatoes. The old man had cleared everything else off his plate. He must have thrown the paper on the floor, forgetting the tray was there.

Pansy tried to ignore the paper, but she could see writing on it, and being the curious type, she was finding it terribly difficult to pretend it wasn't there.

If she took the tray to the kitchen, she would be expected to scrape the food off the plate and into the stove, paper and all. Then she'd never know what was written on it.

Down the stairs she went, holding the tray in front of her, eyes firmly on the steps so she wouldn't trip up. She reached the bottom and crossed the lobby. All was quiet, and no one was around. Maybe if she took a quick peep.

Pausing by the hall stand, she rested the tray on the shelf and held it there with her stomach while she picked up the rumpled ball of paper. Unfolding it, she smoothed it out against the hall stand mirror.

At first she couldn't make out the scrawled words, but then gradually one by one, they became clear. Stunned, she read them a second time, then shrieked and dropped the note. It fluttered to the floor, and she stooped to pick it up, forgetting the tray. Bone china plates, cup, and saucer slid off and fell to the floor with a crash and a thud.

She didn't even stop to pick up the pieces. She left it all there, lying on the floor of the lobby, and fled down the stairs to the kitchen.

Mrs. Chubb swung around, her mouth dropping open as Pansy burst through the door, while Michel smacked a saucepan down with a muttered, "Sacre bleu!"

"It's him," Pansy said, panting. "Here, look!" She held out the note in shaking fingers. "Look at this. I told you that horrible man in room nine is the Mayfair Murderer! Look! I was right!"

*　　*　　*

"I think I should have Mr. Docker and his men come back to inspect the rest of the roof," Cecily announced.

Baxter, seated on his favorite chair in their suite, looked up from his newspaper. "I thought they had finished the repairs."

"On that section, yes." Cecily took a dainty sip from her glass of sherry and put down the glass. "But I thought I saw a stain on the ceiling above the attic stairs, and I would like the roofers to look at it before it gets to be a bigger problem. Then it would cost twice as much for repairs."

"Whatever you say, dear."

"I'll ring for them first thing in the morning." She picked up the book lying next to her and opened it at her bookmark.

"Wouldn't it be better to wait until after Christmas?"

She looked up again to find Baxter staring at her over the top of his newspaper. "I beg your pardon, dear?"

"I said, it might be better to wait until after the guests go home. We have so much going on, what with the pantomime tomorrow, and the carol singing in the library Christmas Eve, not to mention Christmas Day and the hunt on Boxing Day."

"Yes, we do." She smiled at him. "But a leaky roof can cause all sorts of problems, and I'd like to be sure that we won't have to worry about rain-soaked beds while our guests are sleeping in them."

"And this wouldn't have anything to do with the unfortunate deaths of our servants, I suppose?"

Cecily opened her eyes wide. "Goodness! Whatever gave you that idea?"

Baxter grunted, but just then a light tap on the door turned his head. "Good Lord, what now?"

"Probably someone come to collect our trays." She raised her voice to call out, "Come in!"

The door opened, and much to Cecily's surprise, Mrs. Chubb poked her head around the door.

"Sorry to disturb you, m'm. May I have a quick word with you?"

"Oh, do come in," Baxter said, rattling his newspaper. "There's a dreadful draft coming through the door."

The housekeeper hastily stepped inside and closed the door behind her. Moving forward, she fished a stained and creased sheet of paper out of her apron pocket. "I thought you might want to see this, m'm."

Cecily took it from her and peered at it. Holding it farther away from her eyes, she read the words out loud. "Hide dagger in drawer by bed and wait until victim is asleep. Stab in neck, then leave by window."

"Good Lord!" Baxter put down his newspaper and stared at the housekeeper. Leaning forward, he took the note from his wife's fingers. "Where did you get this?"

"Pansy found it, sir. In the mashed potatoes. That's why it's a bit messy."

Cecily raised her eyebrows, while Baxter frowned. "In the mashed potatoes? What the devil does that mean?"

"It was on Mr. Mortimer's dinner plate, sir."

Cecily caught her breath. "In room nine?"

"Yes, m'm." Mrs. Chubb wiped her brow with the back of her sleeve. "Pansy went up to fetch his tray and this was on it. I thought you should see it right away."

"Yes, thank you, Mrs. Chubb. We will take care of this. Try not to worry and please don't alarm the staff. It could mean nothing at all."

"Yes, m'm." The housekeeper moved to the door, then paused. "Pansy thinks he's the Mayfair Murderer, m'm."

Cecily tried to ignore the little thump of fear under her ribs. "I doubt that very much, Mrs. Chubb. Please tell Pansy not to mention this to another soul."

"I will, m'm, though Gertie overheard her, as did two of the maids. And Michel."

"Oh, dear. Well, do try to keep it among yourselves." Cecily waited until the door closed behind her housekeeper before turning to Baxter. "What do you think?"

Baxter stared at the note, turning it this way and that as if hoping to see something different in the menacing words. "I don't know what to think. Mortimer is a strange old chap, but he doesn't strike me as particularly dangerous."

"Me, neither." Cecily gazed uneasily at the note in her husband's hands. "Then again, I have been acquainted with enough murderers to know that appearances can be deceiving."

"Indubitably." Baxter shook his head. "I suppose we should pass this along to the inspector."

"Not yet." Cecily pulled the note from his hands and folded it up. "It could all be quite innocent, and if so, Mr. Mortimer could be embarrassed by some unwarranted attention from the constabulary. I should hate to put one of our esteemed guests through that, only to find out he is perfectly innocent. It would not look well for our reputation."

Baxter sighed. "How did I know you were going to say that? Now, I suppose, you are going to place yourself in dire peril in order to find out if Mortimer is indeed a serial killer. After all, who goes around scribbling reminders of how to do away with someone without being caught?"

"I admit, it does look rather troubling." Cecily leaned forward and patted her husband's hand. "I shall take great care not to confront Mr. Mortimer unless I'm certain he can do me no harm."

"I don't know how you can be certain of that," Baxter muttered, as he picked up his newspaper again. "I can only hope that you know what you are doing and that Mortimer is harmless."

Cecily couldn't agree more.

CHAPTER
12

Cecily awoke early the next morning from a restless sleep, and climbed out of bed leaving Baxter snoring under the covers.

The coals in the fireplace were down to their last embers, and she used the tongs to transfer several small lumps from the coal scuttle to the fire, then gently stoked them until flames began to lick around them.

Drawing her dressing gown closer around her, she walked over to the window. Tiny flakes of snow were blowing about in the wind, but the ground was wet and the lawns still green, relieving her mind. The last thing she needed right now was a snowfall to hamper her efforts.

She dressed quickly, and Baxter had just begun to stir by the time she was ready to go down to her office. "I'll meet you for breakfast in the dining room," she told him, and hurried from the room before he could enquire about her haste.

Reaching her office she rang the operator and asked to be put through to Mick Docker. He seemed surprised to be hearing from her so early in the morning. When she told him she needed his services again, however, he seemed only too happy to oblige her.

She had barely finished entering invoices in her ledger when she heard the breakfast bell. Baxter was waiting for her when she entered the dining room. Seated at their customary corner table, he hid behind the daily newspaper as usual.

He lowered it when she greeted him, and rose to pull out her chair for her. Having seated her, he sat down again, his face a mask of apprehension.

Cecily removed her serviette from its silver ring and spread it on her lap. "Bad news?"

He didn't answer her right away, and she felt a shiver of uneasiness. "Bax? What's wrong?"

He tried to smile, but she could see his features were tight with tension. "I was just reading about that dratted Mayfair Murderer."

"Oh? Have they caught him?" She felt a wave of reassurance. Until that moment she hadn't realized she had actually considered the idea that Mr. Mortimer might be the villain for whom all of Scotland Yard was hunting.

Her relief was short-lived, however, when Baxter shook his head. "As a matter of fact, there have been no more murders committed by him in some time. They think it's entirely possible that he has left the city."

Cecily's craving for the bacon, sausage, and fried tomatoes she'd been looking forward to suddenly disappeared. "Oh?" she said again, only far more faintly this time. "Have they had no murders at all in London, then?"

"None, apparently, with the trademark of the infamous serial killer."

"Perhaps he has changed his trademark," Cecily said, clinging to a faint ray of hope.

"Unlikely. He has used the same method and left the same memento with over a dozen other murders. According to the chief inspector, serial killers almost always stick to the same routine."

"Then it can't possibly be our killer. He has left no memento of any kind."

Baxter looked worried. "I hadn't even considered that possibility. I suppose there's always the exception to the rule."

"Oh, my." Cecily grasped her throat, the macabre words on the stained sheet of paper racing through her mind.

"I know what you're thinking." Baxter leaned toward her and lowered his voice. "I think we must talk to Inspector Cranshaw and tell him what we have found."

"Not yet. Not until I've talked to Mr. Mortimer." Seeing his stubborn frown, she laid her hand on his. "We can hardly accuse one of our guests of being a mass murderer without evidence of the fact."

"I should think mere suspicion would be enough to warrant a report to the constabulary. You are playing a dangerous game, my dear, and I fear not only for your safety but for that of everyone here in the Pennyfoot as well."

"I promise you, Bax, I will be careful. I shall not rest,

however, until I have discovered who is responsible for the deaths of Charlie and Ellie. I owe it to them to bring their killer to justice."

Baxter was prevented from answering as Pansy arrived at the table with a tray. She looked pale and sleepy as she unloaded bowls of steaming porridge and a covered platter, which she laid in the center of the table.

Guessing her maid hadn't slept well, Cecily gave her a sympathetic smile. "I hope you are feeling a little better this morning, Pansy?"

"Yes, m'm, thank you." Pansy hesitated, then added, "I had bad dreams last night. I kept imagining Ellie lying in the leaves, her eyes all wide and staring."

"Shsh!" Baxter glanced over at the next table, where Sir Walter sat in earnest conversation with his wife. "We are trying to keep all that quiet."

"Sorry, sir. It slipped out." She bent her knees in a swift curtsey and hurried off, holding the empty tray at her side.

"Poor Pansy." Cecily gazed after her. "It must have been such a dreadful shock."

"Well, I just hope she keeps her mouth closed about it all. The last thing we need is for the guests to find out."

Cecily nodded in agreement, though she didn't have much hope of keeping the news a secret. People let things slip, just as Pansy had done, and sooner or later the word would spread. Her only hope was to find out who was responsible as quickly as possible, before the killer could strike again.

Pansy shivered as she crossed the yard to the coal shed. The dark gray skies overhead threatened rain, or even snow.

Clutching her shawl to her neck she leaned into the wind, the coal bucket swinging in her hand.

She had almost reached the door of the shed when a heavy hand descended on her shoulder, squeezing so hard she cried out in pain.

Lenny's face loomed in front of her, his mouth twisted in an ugly smile. "So there you are. I wondered when you'd turn up again."

Pansy drew back, trying to break the cruel grip on her shoulder. "What are you doing here? What do you want?"

"I'm working here, aren't I." His chuckle sent shivers of fear down her back. "You can't get rid of me that easy. I'll be here for the whole day, maybe two."

Again she tried to shrug him off, but he only gripped her tighter. She looked about, hoping to catch sight of Clive, or better yet, Samuel, but the yard and the lawns beyond were deserted. Glaring up into Lenny's grinning face, she said loudly, "Let me go, or I'll scream and someone will come running."

"I don't think so." He brought his nose down to hers. "You owe me, you little bitch. You were supposed to meet me yesterday afternoon. I waited nearly an hour for you."

"I was busy, wasn't I." She met his gaze squarely. "It wasn't my fault. It's Christmastime and all of us have extra work."

"Yeah, extra work running off into the woods with your boyfriend?"

Startled, she tried to back away. "I don't know what you mean."

"Oh, yes, you do." He pulled her closer to him and wrapped an arm around her waist. "I saw you, in the woods

167

with your boyfriend when you were supposed to be with me."

She stared up at him. "How could you have seen me in the woods if you waited an hour for me?"

"I saw you on me way home, didn't I. Though I have to say, you didn't look too happy. If you ask me, you were crying. See? That's what you get for going off with some country lout instead of coming out with me."

Once more she struggled to be free, her fear gradually turning to anger. "It's none of your business what I do, so there. Now let me go before I scream for help."

"You won't scream, ducky. I know what you want, and I'm the one to give it to you."

He bent his face closer, and desperate now, Pansy swung the bucket as hard as she could against his head. It made a dreadful clanging noise as it hit, and Lenny pulled back with a look of surprise and let her go.

Every instinct shouted at her to run, but fear held her rooted to the spot.

Lenny staggered backward, shaking his head.

Horrified at what she'd done, Pansy began stammering. "I'm sorry, I shouldn't have done that but you wouldn't let me go when I told you to and—"

She shut her mouth abruptly as Lenny slowly turned toward her. Too late she realized her mistake. She should have run when she had the chance. She dropped the bucket and backed away. "Don't you touch me—"

Her words ended in a scream as Lenny raised his hand and smacked her hard across the face. Stunned, she dropped to her knees, little spots dancing in front of her eyes.

The next thing she knew, Lenny's hand was on the collar of her frock, dragging her to her feet. "This is what you get for daring to hit me," he snarled, and raised his hand to strike her again.

She lifted her hands to shield her face and closed her eyes, bracing for the blow.

It never came. There was a shout, a thump, and someone grabbed her from behind.

Opening her eyes, she saw Samuel, fists raised, standing over Lenny who was lying on the ground. "Get up you bloody coward," Samuel yelled. "See if you can pick on someone your own size."

Lenny just lay there, eyes closed.

Aware of the big hands on her shoulders, Pansy twisted her neck and saw Clive peering down at her. He looked worried, and let her go, then gently touched her cheek.

It stung, and she drew back.

"Are you all right?" Clive sent a murderous look at Lenny, who now was struggling to his feet. "I'd have hit him myself if Samuel hadn't reached him first."

Pansy tried to speak and felt something warm trickling down her chin. She dabbed at it with her fingers then looked at them. They were smeared with blood.

She heard another thud and a grunt of pain. "You dare to touch my girl again and I'll bloody well kill you!" Samuel yelled.

Lenny staggered back, holding his jaw. "All right," he snarled. "You asked for this."

Pansy screamed when she saw the knife in his hand. Samuel jumped back, but Clive stepped forward and with one mighty blow sent the weapon clattering across the yard. Samuel scrambled after it, but by the time he'd picked it up Lenny was racing to the gate. He had it open before Samuel could catch up with him and disappeared into the street.

Sobbing, Pansy ran up to Samuel and grabbed his arm. "Let him go, please! Don't get into a fight with him. He'll kill you!"

"Not if I kill him first," Samuel muttered.

"She's right, lad." Clive joined them at the gate. He gently pried open Samuel's fist, then took the knife and slipped it in his pocket. "He's not worth that kind of trouble. You sent him on his way and that's what matters."

Pansy choked, tears running down her cheeks. All she could think about now was Samuel's words, yelled in fury. *You dare to touch my girl again and I'll bloody well kill you!*

Did he mean it? Was she really his girl? The thought made her forget all about the pain in her lip, which now felt twice its size when she ran her tongue over it. All she could feel was a fuzzy warmth way down deep in her tummy. She would hear those words in her head, she told herself, over and over again for as long as she lived.

"Are you all right, little lady?" Clive looked down at her, then pulled a big white handkerchief from his pocket. Very gently he dabbed at her chin and her swollen lip. "You'll have a bruise for a couple of days, but you'll live."

Pansy tried to smile, but it hurt too much, so she nodded instead.

Clive stepped back and then Samuel stood in front of her, a look in his eyes she'd never seen before. "You need someone to take care of you," he said gruffly, "and I think that should be me."

Even the pain couldn't keep Pansy from smiling. She

wasn't sure exactly what that meant, but right at that moment she didn't care. Samuel was looking at her the way
she'd always dreamed he would, and now it was real. That
was all she asked for right now. "I can't think of anyone I'd
rather have take care of me," she said unsteadily.

Now Samuel grinned. "I'd kiss you, but I'm afraid it
would hurt you too much."

Pansy lifted her face. "Try it."

Samuel didn't need any more prompting.

"I am quite sure I paid you the right amount!" Seated
in her office, Cecily flipped the pages of her ledger back
to where she had entered the amount of the check she'd
given Stan Whittle. "Look, here it is. Three shillings and
ninepence."

"It should have been four and six." The craggy face of the
coal man glared down at her.

"I ordered five hundredweight. At fifteen shillings a ton
that's three shillings and ninepence."

"I had two extra bags so I added them in."

Cecily puffed out her breath. "I didn't ask for two extra
bags. When I order five hundredweight that's exactly what I
expect and what I'm prepared to pay. No more, no less."

The coal man jutted out his chin. "You got the coal, so
you pay for it."

"Why didn't you mention all this when I paid you two
days ago?"

"I didn't look at the check until after I left." He leaned
over her desk. "I thought I could trust you to pay the right
amount."

Cecily met his angry gaze squarely. "Is this what you were arguing about with Ellie?"

Stan Whittle straightened, his face turning to stone. "I don't know what you're talking about."

"I heard that you and my new maid, Ellie, were in the kitchen yard, arguing about something."

"I talk to a lot of people. I don't remember which one Ellie is, do I." He strode to the door, tossing words over his shoulder. "Keep your money. I'll just leave two bags less next time."

"As you wish." She was talking to empty air. The door had closed behind him. Furious, she snapped the ledger shut. Infuriating man. She had never cared for his attitude, and now she thoroughly disliked the man. Perhaps her first thoughts were right, after all, and Stan Whittle had killed Ellie. But then why would he have killed Charlie as well?

No, it was far more likely that Mick Docker was the culprit, and all she had to do was prove it. She wasn't quite sure yet how she would do that, but she had asked Samuel to send the roofer to her office as soon as he arrived, which should be just about any minute now.

Even as the thoughts passed through her mind, a loud rap on the door announced the arrival of her next visitor. Crossing her hands on the desk, she called out, "Come in!"

Mick Docker's round face appeared in the gap. "You wanted to see me, m'm?"

"Yes, Mr. Docker. Please, come in." She waved him to a chair, and waited for him to sit down.

"I've sent the men up to take a look at the roof," he said, tucking his cap into a back pocket. "As soon as I know what needs doing, I'll give you a report and then you can decide what you want us to do."

"Very well. Thank you." She fixed her gaze on his face as she added, "I'm afraid I have some very bad news. It's about Ellie."

She saw a flicker of alarm in his eyes. "Ellie? She's all right, isn't she?"

"I'm afraid not." She paused, then added quietly, "My stable manager found her body yesterday afternoon. She'd been strangled."

He made an odd sound in his throat, as if he were choking. "Dead? Ellie's dead?"

If he was, indeed, the murderer, Cecily thought, he was a remarkably good actor. He certainly looked as if he'd received a tremendous shock.

He swallowed a couple of times, and when he spoke, his voice was hoarse with emotion. "Who did this?"

"I was rather hoping you could tell me."

Mick's eyes widened. "Me? How the hell should I know who did it?"

"According to a witness, you were probably the last person to see her alive."

He stared at her for a moment as if he didn't understand the words, then he violently shook his head. "That's impossible. The last time I saw Ellie was three days ago. I'd come down from the roof to have a bite and she was walking across the kitchen yard. I knew there was no point in talking to her. She'd made it very clear how she felt about me. So I went around to the rose garden and ate my lunch there. That was the last time I saw her."

Cecily frowned. "You didn't see her that evening? You didn't have an argument with her in the yard?"

Again he shook his head. "It wasn't me, Mrs. Baxter. I

swear it. Ask Lenny. We knocked off around four o'clock that afternoon, when it was getting dark, and we went straight down the pub. We had dinner down there and stayed until closing time. Left there just after eleven and then went home." He buried his head in his hands. "I can't believe she's dead. Who would do this to her?"

"That's what we'd all like to know." Cecily sighed. "I'm sorry, Mr. Docker. I know this has been a shock for you."

"Yes, it has." He got up from his chair, slowly, as if he were lifting something heavy with his shoulders. "I'll be getting along now, m'm. I'll let you know what we find on the roof."

Cecily watched him leave, letting out her breath as the door closed behind him. She didn't know whether to believe him or not. Samuel had seemed fairly certain that he'd heard the roofer arguing with Ellie that night, but he could have been mistaken. There was one way to find out. She would talk to the new publican of the Fox and Hounds, Barry Collins.

Since she couldn't trust the operator not to listen in, she would have to go down there in person. Meanwhile, she must go at once to the foyer. Madeline would be arriving any minute. Baxter was probably still in the suite, going over his records, which, he told her, would take most of the morning. She would have to have her conversation with her friend in the library and hope that they wouldn't be interrupted.

For what she had to ask Madeline was definitely not for anyone else's ears.

CHAPTER
❁13❁

"Samuel kissed you!" Gertie stopped curling coils from the slab of butter and stared at Pansy. "Go on! What happened next?"

Pansy shrugged. "Nothing. He had to go back to the stables and I came back in here."

"Well, you was lucky he was around, that's what I say." Gertie picked up the lump of butter again and swiped the curler across it, letting a soft spiral of butter join its companions on the silver dish. "Wait until Chubby sees that lip. She'll faint from shock."

The voice from the doorway froze Gertie's hand. "How many times do I have to tell you not to call me Chubby!"

Gertie winced. She hadn't heard the kitchen door swing

open, with all the racket Michel was making over by the stove.

"Sorry, it just sort of slipped out."

The housekeeper switched her gaze to Pansy and let out a gasp of horror. "What happened to you?"

"She had a fight with her boyfriend," Michel said, slapping a metal pot on the stove. "With all this fighting and upset going on, it is impossible to concentrate. How am I supposed to produce my magnificent meals in this chaos?"

"Same bloody way you always do," Gertie muttered. "Throw it all together and pray."

She cringed as Michel crashed a lid on the pot. "I do not have to put up with such impudence! I go somewhere else, where I am more appreciated."

"Oh, be quiet, Michel. Can't you see this child is hurt?" Mrs. Chubb rushed over to Pansy and tilted her chin up with her fingers. "Great heavens. Your lip is swollen twice its size. You can't go into the dining room like that. What on earth happened to you?"

Gertie groaned. More work for her.

Pansy's words were muffled as she recounted the argument with Lenny. "It wasn't just Samuel that helped me," she said, as the housekeeper soaked a face flannel in cold water over the sink. "It was Clive." She looked at Gertie. "He was so gentle and kind. Brave, too. He knocked the knife right out of Lenny's hand."

Gertie smiled. "That sounds like Clive. He's always coming to someone's rescue."

"Well, that Lenny sounds like a really nasty person." Mrs. Chubb dabbed at Pansy's lip, ignoring her muffled cry of pain. "If I were you, Pansy, I'd stay out of his way."

"He frightens me," Pansy said, as the housekeeper let her go. "I thought he was going to kill me. Samuel, too."

"Well, I'll talk to Mrs. Baxter about it. She'll see he never works around here again." She hurried to the door. "Meanwhile, Gertie, you had better get a move on. The tables haven't been laid yet and it will soon be time for the bell. Get one of the other maids to help you. Pansy can give us a hand in here."

"That blinking bell drives me crazy." Gertie scraped the last curl off the butter and carried the knife over to the sink. "We live our life by that bell. We're always rushing around to get things done and we always have to ring it before we're ready."

"Then you will all have to rush faster, *non?*" Michel smacked a saucepan down on the stove. "Instead of standing around talking all the time."

For once Gertie didn't have a smart answer for him. She was thinking about Clive, and what Pansy had said. Kind and gentle, and brave, too. That was Clive. Didn't have much to say, but when he did say something, it was always warm and thoughtful. So different from Dan.

Dan was clever and funny, exciting to be with, always wanting to go places and do something. He was the restless type, never standing still. For a long time she'd thought that was what she wanted in a man, but the longer she was with Dan, the more she realized that all his emotions were on the outside, for show.

He was a good man, in his way. He took presents for the orphans at Christmas, and he was good to her and the twins. But in all the time she'd known him, she'd never really seen inside his mind. It was like he'd locked it away, and didn't know how to unlock it anymore.

177

Now, with all this talk about moving to London, she knew it was just a matter of time before he left Badgers End. She also knew she couldn't go with him, no matter how much she'd miss him. Much as she loved him, she didn't think he could ever give her the kind of love she needed. She would just have to let him go without her.

The lump in her throat hurt, and she rinsed her hands under the tap and wiped them dry on her apron. It was Christmas, she told herself, and soon her twins would be home. That's all she needed to be happy. Her Lillian and James. Who needed a man? She certainly didn't.

Having convinced herself of that, she opened the silverware drawer and started loading a tray with the polished utensils.

Cecily reached the foyer just as Madeline arrived, wearing a black coat over her flowered cotton frock with Angelina cradled in her arms.

As usual, Madeline's dark hair flowed down her back, though she had caught up a large strand with a small circle of miniature silk daisies. Her cheeks glowed from the bite of the wind, and she hugged the baby, whom she'd wrapped in a soft pink blanket, as she hurried through the main doors. "It's chilly out there today. We could have more snow before long."

"Goodness, I do hope not." Cecily hurried forward to greet her friend and held out her hands to take the baby. "How precious she is. Look, she's smiling!"

"More likely a spot of indigestion." Madeline handed her Angelina and shivered. "I would love a warm fireplace right now."

"Of course." Carrying the child, Cecily headed for the hallway. "Come, we'll go to the library. There's a roaring fire in the fireplace and I'll have crumpets and tea sent there. Baxter is upstairs working in the suite."

Madeline laughed. "I wouldn't mind in the least if he cared to join us."

"Well, I would." Cecily lowered her voice. "I need your help."

Madeline nodded. "I thought perhaps that's why you invited me. After all, I intend to be here tonight for the pantomime. We'll be seeing each other then."

"Ah, but we'll have no chance to talk then."

Still carrying the baby, Cecily led the way to the library where, to her relief, they found it unoccupied. Once inside, Angelina started fussing, and she handed her back to her mother.

After settling them both in a chair by the fireplace, she summoned a maid with the bell rope. "Now," she said, when Angelina was quiet again, "I assume Kevin has told you about Ellie."

"Yes." Madeline lowered her head and pressed her lips against her baby's forehead. "That poor mother. I can't even imagine how she is suffering right now."

"It must be so hard on her." Cecily sighed. "The worst part, of course, is not knowing who did this dreadful thing to her daughter. Knowing that whoever killed her is out there somewhere, free to do the same thing again to someone else's daughter."

"And you want me to tell you who he is."

Startled, Cecily looked at her. "Can you do that?"

"I rather doubt it." Madeline undid her coat and slipped

it off her shoulders. "But that is why you wanted to see me, isn't it?"

"Not entirely." Cecily gave her a guilty smile. "I always enjoy a visit with you."

"It's all right, Cecily. You know I will do my best, but I have to confess, since Angelina came into my life, my powers have somewhat diminished. I'll do what I can, but don't be surprised if I can't be of much help." She sat back, closed her eyes, and was still.

Cecily waited, one anxious eye on the now sleeping baby in case she should wake up and disturb her mother's trance. Madeline was now breathing deeply, her face a mask of concentration. Her eyelids fluttered, then opened. She stared ahead, at something Cecily couldn't see, and now her breathing became more shallow, quickening, while her fingers twitched as if they were reaching for something.

For several long moments Cecily watched in silence, until suddenly Angelina stirred and let out a soft whimper. Madeline was instantly awake, rocking her baby.

Cecily waited in an agony of suspense while Madeline fussed with her daughter, until once more the child was quiet. Madeline laid the blanket on the floor and set Angelina down on it. "I saw Ellie," she said, her voice low and anxious. "I saw her attacker but it was dark. I couldn't see. He had his back to me. I tried to reach him but he kept moving farther away. I'm so sorry."

Disappointed, Cecily nodded. "It's all right. I understand. Is there anything at all you can tell me about him? His voice? His clothes? His hair?"

Madeline shook her head. "Nothing that I can remember.

There is something, though. Something that seems important, though I don't know why it would be."

With a flare of hope, Cecily leaned forward. "Tell me,
what is it?"

"A handkerchief." Madeline frowned, as if she were struggling to see again the elusive article. "A small lace-edged
handkerchief, belonging to a lady."

"A lady?" Cecily sat back. "That can't be. I don't know
how the killer got Ellie's body into the woods, but I doubt a
lady would have had the strength or the fortitude."

"You're quite right. The killer is a man. It was definitely
a lady's handkerchief, however." Madeline shook her head. "I
don't know why it is so significant, but believe me, Cecily,
you would do well to take note."

Feeling defeated, Cecily could only nod. She simply
couldn't imagine what bearing a woman's handkerchief
could possibly have on Ellie's murder. Then again, she had
dealt with such matters often enough to know that anything
and everything was possible.

She'd hoped that Madeline would be able to give her a
little more to go on, but it appeared that once more, she
would have to rely on her wits and a great deal of luck, if she
was to bring a ruthless killer to justice.

"I suppose you didn't tell Mr. Baxter that you were going to
the Fox and Hounds," Samuel said, as he helped Cecily into
the carriage that afternoon.

"Mr. Baxter hasn't returned from his visit to Weller-
combe." Cecily settled herself on the seat and tucked her
hands in her muff. "He is doing some last-minute Christmas

shopping and doesn't expect to be back until later this afternoon. By that time I hope to be home again, Samuel."

"Yes, m'm. I'll do my best." Samuel touched his cap, closed the door, and climbed up into the driver's seat.

The carriage jerked, sending Cecily back against the cold leather. Shivering, she leaned forward again to look at the ocean as they rattled down the Esplanade.

Patches of white froth rode in on the waves, driven by a chill east wind. All along the seafront the stiff arms of the gas lamps were wrapped in holly, the bright red berries adding a splash of color against the dull gray sky.

The latticed windows of the shops lining the street displayed their wares, everything from toy soldiers and red-cheeked dolls to Christmas crackers and decorations of all shapes and sizes—silver stars and white angels, brilliant red and green glass balls twisting on slim cotton thread, colorful paper chains and tiny candles.

A shudder of dread shook her body. She had once almost burned to death in a fire caused by Christmas tree candles. Ever since then she had been unable to view them without a shudder and a feeling of dread.

Shaking off her morbid thoughts, she focused her gaze on the ocean again as Samuel urged the horses into a fast trot. Madeline's words popped into her mind. A handkerchief. How could a woman's handkerchief help her find the killer? Unless it belonged to Ellie. Why hadn't she thought of that before?

With a start she remembered the necklace. Samuel hadn't mentioned it, so she had to assume he hadn't found it. She made a mental note to ask him as soon as they arrived at the Fox and Hounds.

The ride took them over the cliffs and across the Downs. Buffeted by the winds and bouncing along the rutted path, the carriage rocked and bucked until Cecily was quite sure she would lose her front teeth.

She was most thankful when they arrived at last in the courtyard of the Fox and Hounds. Feeling bruised and battered, she climbed down from the carriage before Samuel had a chance to offer her a hand.

"I'm coming in there with you, m'm," Samuel said, without waiting to be asked. "I know Mr. Baxter would want that."

"Thank you, Samuel. But before we do, tell me, did you look for the necklace?"

"I did, m'm. I didn't see it anywhere in the yard, and it was sort of hard to look for it in the coal shed. I shone my torch all over the coals but didn't see nothing. It could have been scooped up in one of the coal scuttles and thrown on the fire."

"I suppose it could have. Well, thank you for looking, anyway, Samuel."

"Yes, m'm." He hesitated, then asked, "Was it really important?"

"I really don't know." She shook her head. "To be honest, Samuel, I don't know what is important and what isn't. Perhaps we shall find out something useful from Barry Collins." With that, she marched across the gravel to the side door, where the publican had his private quarters.

After rapping on the door with the fox's head door knocker, she waited, hoping she wasn't disturbing the publican's afternoon nap. Since the pub had to stay open until eleven p.m., that brief respite when it closed in the afternoon had to be so coveted.

The door opened to reveal a young woman holding a baby. She seemed shocked when she saw her visitor. "Mrs. Baxter! Whatever are you doing here?"

Cecily smiled at the publican's wife. "I'm so very sorry to disturb you at this hour, but I would like to ask your husband some questions. I was hoping he'd have a few minutes to accommodate me."

"Of course, do come in." The woman sent a curious glance at Samuel, who was hovering behind Cecily, his cap crushed in his hands.

"Oh, this is my driver and stable manager, Samuel. I'd like him to accompany me, if he may."

"Of course. Welcome." Mrs. Collins drew back and opened the door wider.

The baby gurgled, and Cecily smiled at him. He was about the same age as Angelina, though a good deal heavier, by the look of him. No doubt his diet wasn't as nutritious as Madeline's meals.

Following the young woman into the parlor, Cecily took a seat by the window, while Samuel stood close by.

"I'll fetch my husband," Mrs. Collins said, and left them alone.

Looking around the familiar room, Cecily could see little change since Barry Collins had taken over the license. Her eldest son had become publican of the Fox and Hounds soon after his father died, and she had spent many hours in this room, listening to Michael's tales about unruly customers and the hard luck stories he'd heard.

Now the pub belonged to someone else, and Michael was on the other side of the world. She rarely heard from him. She thought of him often, but never quite as clearly as she did when in the warm comfort of the Fox and Hounds.

Her thoughts scattered as Barry Collins walked into the room. A tall man with a luxurious mustache and a thick head of blond hair, he seemed more suited to be a musician or artist than a publican charged with keeping a rowdy group of drunkards in order.

He seemed a little disoriented as he greeted her and acknowledged Samuel's presence with a brief nod. "To what do I owe the pleasure of this visit?" he enquired, as he perched on the arm of a comfortable easy chair.

Cecily wasted no time in coming to the point. "I have reason to believe that Mr. Mick Docker visited your establishment three nights ago."

Collins frowned. "Docker? Oh, the roofing chap. Yes, he was here. He came in soon after opening time, if I remember, with that other young fellow. Lenny, his mate."

"They stayed all evening, is that so?"

The publican gave her an odd look. "Well, now, I can't swear to that. I saw them come in, and I saw them leave at closing time, but I can't say if they were here all evening. We had a bit of excitement in here that night, so I wasn't paying much attention as to who was here and who wasn't."

"Excitement?"

The publican looked uneasy. "Look, I don't like telling tales. If this is about the fight between Docker and Stan Whittle all I can tell you is that no one really got hurt. A couple of glasses got smashed but that's all, and we got the mess cleaned up right away."

Cecily sat up. "Mick Docker fought with Stan Whittle? Do you know what the fight was about?"

"Nothing. It was just a couple of chaps letting off steam, that's all. Those two are always going at it over something or other. A Scotsman and an Irishman. What can you expect? They've both got hot tempers. It doesn't take much to set them off. We broke up the fight, Stan left, and . . ." He paused. "Come to think of it, I don't remember seeing Mick for a while after that, but I know he was here at closing time. I chased him out myself."

"So it was possible he could have left and returned without you noticing?"

The publican lifted his hands and let them drop again. "In a place like this, Mrs. Baxter, anything can happen under my nose. There's always something going on, and I don't have eyes in the back of my head." He laughed to soften his words. "I often wish I did."

"So do I, Mr. Collins." Cecily rose to her feet. "So do I."

Frustration was making her snippy, she thought, as she made her way back to the carriage, with Samuel close behind. Every path she took resulted in a dead end. Mick Docker had been telling the truth when he said he spent the evening at the Fox and Hounds. But had he stayed there all night, as he'd proclaimed? It seemed she would have yet another conversation with the slippery roofer.

She had to wonder how much more patience the man would have with her before he refused to answer any more of her questions. Or worse, decided that she was becoming a nuisance, and needed to do something drastic to shut her up.

CHAPTER

❀14❀

Phoebe stood in the wings at the back of the ballroom glowing with pride. The pantomime was almost over, and for once there had been no major disaster. True, the dancers had stumbled on occasion, but they had managed to finish their numbers without knocking down any of the scenery, which was a major victory for her.

There might have been one or two occasions when she'd had to hiss cues at the Ugly Sisters. Unfortunately, the Fairy Godmother had caught her wand up in her net skirts and had to be untangled, but considering past disasters, these were all minor concerns.

Only a few more minutes to go and she could chalk up a successful event for once. The triumph of that moment would be well worth all the hard work and constant irritations she'd been forced to endure during the six weeks of rehearsal.

As always, she was concluding the performance with a pyramid—something the audience anticipated with noticeable glee. The fact that a good many of the male onlookers were expecting to see the young ladies topple to the floor, thus revealing more of their appendages than was seemly, was something Phoebe preferred to ignore.

After all, men would be men, and she lived in hope of her dance troupe holding the pose at least until the curtains were drawn. Something that didn't happen too often.

The orchestra, or rather the string quartet she'd bullied into attending, did their best to rise to a crescendo as Cinderella accepted the prince's proposal and the dancers gathered onstage for the final presentation.

Phoebe crossed her fingers and waited.

One by one the dancers lined up, linking arms to provide the bottom rung of the pyramid. Slowly they bent their knees, allowing three of the remaining women to climb up on their shoulders.

Phoebe held her breath. Only one more to go. She had picked Deirdre, the lightest and skinniest of the young women, to climb to the top of the pyramid. Deirdre was a little dense at times, but she enjoyed the attention, and was willing to risk life and limb to get it.

Not that Phoebe expected anything disastrous to happen to her. At the very most, if she fell, there were plenty of women there to catch her, and it really wasn't that far to the floor. Besides, Deirdre was quite nimble and supple. She had learned how to fall—completely relaxed, with head and knees tucked in ready to roll.

Nevertheless, Phoebe gritted her teeth as Deirdre ran lightly over to the group and began to climb over knees and shoulders to the top. Some of the dancers muttered an "Ouch" or two, but at last, Deirdre wobbled to a full stance. Straightening her back, she stretched out her arms and threw her head back in triumph.

A burst of applause greeted this remarkable feat. Bursting with excitement and relief, Phoebe rushed out onto the stage to take her bow. As she did so, an ear-splitting scream rent the air. Then from somewhere in the audience, another voice joined in, howling as only a baby can.

Crying, "No, no, *no*!" Phoebe turned, just in time to see the pyramid collapse. The young women fell to the floor and lay sprawled all around, some moaning, others convulsed with the giggles.

The audience groaned in unison, until someone in the back sent up a cheer, and once more applause rocked the roof. Phoebe directed her fiercest glare at the front row, then dashed over to see if Deirdre had survived the calamity.

She found the young girl sitting on the floor, making a dreadful noise with her wailing. "Where are you hurt?" Phoebe demanded, trying to draw the girl's skirt down to cover her knees.

Deirdre only shook her head and cried louder. The rest of the dancers picked themselves up and gathered around, offering words of advice.

"She's hysterical," Dora explained. "Here, I'll slap her face. That'll bring her out of it." She stepped forward, her hand raised.

Phoebe lifted her own hand and knocked Dora's arm

away. "If there's any slapping to be done, I'll do it." She looked back at the sobbing girl. "Deirdre, dear, you must tell me where you are hurting."

Again Deirdre shook her head, then waved her hand in the air.

"Who the heck's she waving at?" one of the dancers wanted to know.

"Dunno," someone else answered.

"I told you she was hysterical," Dora declared. "You'll have to slap her face."

Aware of the fascinated audience out front, murmuring and speculating among themselves while the baby continued to screech, Phoebe turned on Dora. This was to have been a rare performance, free of disaster. Once more at the last moment she had been foiled by yet another calamity. Consequently, she was not in the best of moods.

"Since you refuse to keep your silly mouth shut," she snapped, "if I slap anyone's face at all, believe me, it will be yours."

The audience applauded, and someone cheered again.

Deirdre wailed louder, and pointed up over her head.

Phoebe followed the gesture, looking straight up into the rafters. Then she clutched her throat and let out an unearthly shriek, far louder and shriller than Deirdre's howls.

In fact, startled by the noise, Deirdre stopped crying and clutched the skirt of the dancer standing closest to her.

The murmurs of the audience intensified, and the baby howled again, but Phoebe was now past caring. Her shocked gaze was locked on the slowly swinging figure of the woman hanging from the rafters.

*　　*　　*

Cecily wasn't quite sure when she realized something was seriously wrong. She was seated a few rows from the stage, with Baxter on her right, and Madeline on her left. Kevin had charge of the baby next to his wife.

Angelina had been sleeping peacefully throughout most of the performance until the screaming began. The baby awoke and began screeching at the top of her lungs, so loud it actually brought pain to Cecily's ears.

Both Madeline and Kevin tried in vain to calm her, while Cecily looked up anxiously at the stage, wondering if she should go up there to see if anyone was hurt. The sight of the dancers sprawled all over the stage was a familiar one. Phoebe rarely put on an event without something disastrous happening, but it seemed the young woman in the center of the attention was in some kind of distress.

Making up her mind, Cecily leaned toward Baxter, who sat with a pained expression on his face, his shoulders hunched against the noise Angelina was making.

"I'd better go to see if I can do anything," she said, and he immediately rose to his feet.

"I'll go with you."

They had barely reached the end of the aisle when Phoebe's scream echoed throughout the ballroom followed by another bellow of fright from Angelina.

Even then, Cecily thought that Phoebe was simply expressing her outrage. Her friend could be quite vocal when seriously upset. She hurried through the wings with Baxter on her heels, and signaled to the footman in charge of the curtains to bring them down.

He was clinging to the ropes, and looking at her with an odd expression, rather as if he were in a trance. She paused for a moment, puzzled by his attitude. "Bring the curtains down, please," she ordered. "At once."

"Begging your pardon, m'm, but I can't." He glanced back at the stage then turned to her, his movements all in slow motion. "They won't come down."

"What the devil do you mean?" Baxter demanded. "Here, I'll do it."

"You can't." The footman stubbornly held on to the rope. "There's a dead body hanging on the other end."

Cecily felt as if she had just swallowed a large glass of icy water. She heard Baxter utter a curse as he strode past her and out to the stage. For a moment she couldn't seem to move her legs, then she heard him say, "Oh, good Lord."

Forcing herself to move, she rushed out after him. Phoebe was in a dead faint on the floor, surrounded by whispering dancers. Some were looking up at the rafters, while others stood huddled together, looking ready to cry.

Baxter stood with his face upturned, his lips clamped together. She followed his gaze, and clutched her stomach when she saw the limp body of a woman twisting slowly around on the end of a rope.

Taking several deep breaths, she turned to the audience. A few had left their seats and were wandering toward the doors, while the rest stood about, looking as if they weren't quite sure what to do.

"Ladies and gentlemen," Cecily announced, holding up her hand. "I assure you that all is well, here. Just a little mishap, that's all. If you would all care to retire to the library, I will see that refreshments are served in a few minutes."

"We won't be able to keep this quiet," Baxter said, his voice grim.

"Perhaps not." Cecily glanced up again with a shudder. "But we can try, at least for now." She pushed her way through the group of girls to Phoebe's side.

Phoebe was struggling to sit up, one hand holding on to her hat, which had somehow remained stuck to her head. It was a little lopsided, but with great presence of mind, she shoved it back into place. "What happened?"

"You fainted when you saw the body," Dora said helpfully.

Some of the girls whimpered, and Cecily said quickly, "All of you, go back to the dressing room and get out of your costumes. What you see up there is just a dummy. The object of a bad joke, nothing more."

Dora peered up, squinting against light from the gas lamps. "It looks real to me."

"Yes, well, whoever did it was very clever." Cecily gave the woman a forced smile. "Since Mrs. Fortescue is feeling a little under the weather, would you please take charge of the dance troupe? Perhaps you could make sure that they all get dressed and go home?"

Dora gave the body a second look, then shrugged. "All right, everybody, get a move on. Let's get out of here. I'm hungry."

To Cecily's relief the dancers moved off, some still glancing up at the figure above their heads. She waited until both the stage and the ballroom had emptied out, except for Madeline, who stood out front, rocking Angelina back and forth in her arms.

Just as Cecily was about to ask the whereabouts of Kevin, the doctor strode onto the stage. He took one look at the rafters and shook his head. "This is getting to be too much," he muttered.

Cecily heartily endorsed that sentiment. She signaled to the footman, who still held on to the curtain ropes. "Find Samuel and ask him to go up there with you and bring that poor woman down."

The young man gave her a nod, finally let go of the ropes, and disappeared. Baxter started pacing back and forth, while Kevin gazed up at the body. "Do you know who she is?"

Cecily felt perilously close to tears, and had to swallow hard before answering. "Her name is Caroline Danville. She was here on her honeymoon." She reached for Baxter's hand to steady herself. "Someone will have to tell her husband."

Kevin looked around. "So where is he? Why wasn't he with her?"

Cecily looked down at Madeline, who had seated herself in the front row. She was looking down at her baby, whispering something to her.

"He could be looking for her," Cecily said. "I'll see if I can find him. First, though, I'll take Madeline up to the suite. She can wait for you there."

Kevin gave her a nod of approval. "That would be best. Thank you, Cecily. By the way, has anyone sent for P.C. Northcott?"

"Not yet." Cecily sighed. "He won't be pleased to have his Christmas interrupted again."

"Not to mention ours," Baxter put in. "When the blazes is this going to stop? It's obvious Northcott's theory is shot to shreds. Someone out there is going around killing people willy-nilly, and somebody has to stop him." He glared at Cecily. "You have to give that note to Northcott now."

Kevin raised his eyebrows. "Note?"

"Yes," Cecily said hastily. "I'll tell you about it later." She

194

gave Baxter a reproachful look. There had been absolutely no need for him to reprimand her, especially in front of the doctor. In any case, she had specifically asked him not to mention the note. She would have words with him about it later.

She turned back to Kevin. "Right now I really should find Mr. Danville and inform him of his wife's death. It's not something I look forward to, I promise you."

Her husband at least had the grace to look repentant. "If you would rather I—"

"No, thank you. As manager of this establishment, I should take care of it."

"And as a woman, you will do a much better job," Kevin said gently.

She flashed him a smile of gratitude.

Just then, a shout from above them lifted their heads. Samuel peered down at them, his face a white blob among the dark shadows. "We're getting ready to lower her down now," he called out.

"I'll take care of this," Kevin said. "Perhaps you'd like to ring the constabulary, old boy?"

Baxter gave him a stiff nod.

"Use my office," Cecily told him. "It will be more private than the foyer."

"I had intended to, of course," he said, looking offended. "I'm not completely obtuse."

"My apologies." She felt even more like crying. It wasn't often she was at odds with her husband, and it pained her greatly when they were.

She hurried ahead of him, unwilling to exchange any more words with him until they were alone. Madeline looked up as she reached her. "That poor child."

"Yes." Cecily swallowed hard. "All of them. So young. Such a tragedy."

Madeline stood, and Angelina whimpered. "Don't blame yourself, Cecily. It has nothing to do with you. There was nothing you could have done to prevent it."

She shouldn't be surprised that Madeline had read her mind. "I can't help feeling I should have done more before this. Maybe I could have done something. . . ."

Madeline shook her head. "No, Cecily. There was nothing. Please believe me." She pushed the baby toward her. "Here, hold her. She will help ease your mind."

Cecily took the child, who had begun to fuss, and rocked her. She had forgotten how comforting it was to hold a tiny, warm body close to her. She walked toward the door with Madeline at her side. Passing under the kissing bough, she dropped a kiss on the baby's forehead.

Madeline's gasp startled her. "No! Don't do that!"

Clutching Angelina tighter to her bosom, Cecily cried out, "What? What is it? What do you see?"

Madeline's face was a mask of fear. She snatched the baby from Cecily's arms and bent over her as if to shield her from some unspeakable horror. "I don't know," she whispered. "I don't know. Just a . . . feeling . . . I don't know."

Cecily saw Baxter heading their way and grabbed Madeline's arm. "Come. Let us go to the suite. You can rest there until you feel better."

Madeline merely nodded, her lips clamped shut as if she were afraid to speak. Carrying Angelina, she climbed the stairs behind Cecily without saying a word.

A small group of guests stood on the first landing, whispering among each other. When they caught sight of Cecily they stopped talking, and nodded and smiled instead as she and Madeline passed them by.

A small child broke free of the group and ran over to them. "Oh, is that a baby? A real live baby? Let me see! Let me see!"

"Adelaide!" The male voice thundered across the landing and the child shrank back. Turning, she ran back to her father, who took her hand and led her away, with her brother trailing along behind.

Cecily felt sorry for the little girl. Obviously, Lord Millshire was a strict parent. She couldn't imagine Kevin shouting at his child like that.

Opening the door to her suite, she ushered Madeline and the baby inside. "Wait in here for me. I'm going to see if Mr. Danville is in his room. If not, I'll send a footman to look for him. Then I'll come back here."

Madeline nodded, though Cecily couldn't be sure if her friend had really heard the words. She seemed preoccupied, worried. Her obvious distress intensified Cecily's apprehension as she closed the door and started back down the corridor.

The Danvilles' suite was on the same floor, and Cecily saw no one in the hallway as she approached the door. Just before she reached it she saw something white lying on the carpet. She bent over to pick it up, and saw it was a woman's lace-edged handkerchief.

Initials had been embroidered in one corner. An *R* and an *M*. Madeline's words came back to her. *A small lace-edged handkerchief, belonging to a lady.*

Frowning, Cecily tucked it into her sleeve and tapped lightly with her knuckles on the door panel. When there was no response, she turned to leave, then paused. Perhaps he was asleep, having grown tired of waiting for his wife to return. She rapped harder. To her surprise, the door inched open.

Worried now, she put her mouth up to the gap. "Mr. Danville? Are you in there?"

Nothing but silence greeted her.

She hesitated, heart beginning to pound. Something was wrong. She could feel it, like an ugly sense of evil, reaching out to her.

Carefully, she pushed the door open. "Mr. Danville?"

Inside the room, light from an oil lamp flickered across the wall opposite. Cecily caught her breath, prickles of ice attacking her spine. Across the rose-patterned wallpaper she could see letters scribbled in red.

She pushed the door open wider and stepped into the room, her gaze pinned on the message scrawled on the wall. *ALL WHO KISS BENEATH THE BOUGH WILL NOT LIVE TO KISS AGAIN.*

She caught her breath, and turned to leave. As she did so, her glance fell on the bed. Her shocked cry seemed to echo around the silent room.

He was sprawled on his back, his eyes wide open. His neck had been cruelly slashed. She had found Mr. Danville too late to save him. The killer had struck again.

CHAPTER
❀ 15 ❀

"Well, that settles it, dunnit." P.C. Northcott removed his helmet with a flourish and dropped it on the nearest chair. "You've gone and done it this time, Mrs. B. You've got yourself one of them serial killers, that's what."

Standing in front of the dying fire in the library, Cecily eyed the constable with frosty disdain. "I hardly think that any of this can be attributed to anything I might have done."

Northcott looked flustered as he stammered, "Oh, no, no, m'm. I wasn't blaming you, of course. I was merely pointing out that you have a very large problem on your hands."

"So I've noticed. The point is, what are you going to do about it?"

The constable stuck his stubby fingers into the top pocket

of his tunic and pulled out a tattered notebook. He took a great deal of time flipping through it before he found a clean page. Then he fished in his pocket again and pulled out a short pencil. After examining it for a moment or two, he licked the point of it and poised it over the page. "Now, Mrs. B., tell me exactly what you saw in that room."

Cecily clenched her fingers. Where the devil was Baxter? He was so much better than her at intimidating this irritating man. "Sam, I have already told you what I saw. You were in the Danvilles' suite. You saw it for yourself."

"Yes, m'm. You're quite right. I did. Just in case the evidence had been tampered with, however, I need to know what it was you saw when you first entered the room, so that I can compare it to the scene as I saw it." He licked the pencil again and began scribbling. "But first, let us begin with the body of Mrs. Danville. You say it was hanging from the rafters over the stage."

"I've already told you *everything* I saw." Cecily made a supreme effort to keep her voice down. "Meanwhile, a dangerous killer is somewhere in or near this hotel, most likely looking for his next victim."

"I am fully aware of that possibility, Mrs. B." His pencil crawled across the page. "'Owever, it h'is my duty to write down all pertinent information from the witnesses as soon as possible." He squinted at the notebook and held it a little farther away. "You'd be surprised how much people forget after the shock wears off."

To Cecily's immense relief, the door opened and Baxter strode in, his features carved in stone. "What are you still doing in here, man? Why aren't you out there looking for this beastly brute?"

The constable snapped his notebook shut and tucked it in his pocket. After stowing the pencil, he looked at Baxter as if he were a particularly nasty insect. "Not that it's any of your business, sir, but my hands are tied at this moment."

Baxter's eyes turned icy. "Then I suggest you untie them, unless you want another body on your hands."

Northcott drew himself up a half inch. "It is my considered opinion," he said, turning his back on Baxter and addressing Cecily instead, "that as I aforementioned, there is a mass murderer afoot somewhere around here."

Baxter snorted most unbecomingly. "Why didn't we think of that?"

"Sam," Cecily said, ignoring her husband's churlish behavior, "we really need to look for this man now. This moment."

"Yes, well, as I'm trying to establish, I'm afraid I can't do that." Northcott puffed out his chest and rocked back on his heels. "I wouldn't be at all surprised if this murderer is the Mayfair Murderer that Scotland Yard is after. That is a top priority case and calls for a fully fledged investigation by Inspector Cranshaw. He would not thank me for messing about with his case. Oh, no."

Cecily couldn't suppress a shiver at the mention of the inspector's name. "Nonsense. I don't believe it is a serial killer at all. I've been giving this whole situation some thought, and I happen to believe that this all started with Ellie. I believe Charlie saw who killed her and had to be silenced."

Northcott smiled, in an indulgent manner that had Cecily seething. "It's obvious, Mrs. B., that you have no h'experience with such matters. This has all the marks of a serial killer. After all, there are four people dead now, and there's the writing on the wall. That's the killer's way of leaving his signature, so to speak."

"If that is so, then why didn't he leave his signature with the first three bodies? For that matter, why would he kill both men and women?"

Northcott frowned. "I can't see what that has to do with anything."

Baxter, who until now had kept remarkable control of his temper, suddenly uttered a mild curse and strode forward. "How you can be so dense and remain in the constabulary is beyond me," he snapped. "What my wife is trying to say is that a serial killer's victims all share a common trait of some kind. The serial killer usually has an image in mind, connected to someone or something that has deeply and adversely affected him in some way. That's why he kills. He's ridding himself of that perceived evil over and over again."

It was obvious to Cecily, judging from the constable's expression, that he had understood not one word of her husband's comments. Again he addressed Cecily, with a somewhat desperate look that suggested he was losing his authority and couldn't wait to get out of there. "In any case," he announced, "I can't do h'any more until I have reported to the inspector and received his instructions on how to proceed next."

"Then I suggest you do that right now." Baxter strode to the door and flung it open. "You can use the telephone in Mrs. Baxter's office."

"I can't do that." Northcott picked up his helmet and tucked it under his arm.

Baxter roared again. "In God's name, why not?"

"Because," Northcott said, moving warily toward the

door, "the inspector is on holiday in France. He won't be back until after the New Year."

Cecily relaxed her shoulders in relief.

Baxter, however, was not in the least thrilled. "Well, good heavens, man, there has to be someone taking his place while he's away?"

Northcott, having reached the door, edged around him. "Yes, sir, there is. But Inspector Cranshaw is most particular about his cases, and he wouldn't thank me for handing it over to someone else. Oh, no, sir. We shall just have to wait until he returns."

Baxter looked ready to explode into tiny pieces. "And what, pray, are we supposed to do about this dangerous killer in our midst?"

"Well, I suggest you all lock your doors at night." Northcott nodded at Cecily. "Goodnight, m'm. I will be contacting you just as soon as I've heard from the inspector." He exited, leaving Baxter purple in the face.

"One of these days," he said, through gritted teeth, "I'm going to take great pleasure in throttling the life out of that idiot."

"Don't say that!" Cecily shuddered again. "Not even in jest."

"Who's jesting?" Baxter came up to the fireplace, rubbing his hands. Holding them out to the dying embers, he added, "Did you show him that note?"

Cecily gave a guilty start. "No, I didn't. In all the upheaval, I completely forgot about it." Seeing Baxter's skeptical frown, she added, "Since you brought it up, I really didn't appreciate you telling Kevin about it. Or, for that matter, your tone of voice when you mentioned it."

Baxter sighed. "My apologies. I was out of sorts."

"We are all out of sorts, but I manage to remain reasonably civil."

His expression softened. "You are quite right, my dear. I'm sorry." He sighed again. "I seem to be apologizing a lot lately."

"Yes, you do." She eyed him warily. "Are you ready to tell me what it is you have been keeping from me?"

He put an arm about her shoulders and gave her a light squeeze. "All in good time. Right now we have more than enough to worry about. I must say, I am greatly concerned about that note. I really do think we should have given it to Northcott, if only to escape the inspector's wrath should he find out we kept it from the constable."

Appeased by the hug, Cecily leaned into him. "Sam would most likely lose it before it got to Cranshaw. In any case, even if I had given it to him, it wouldn't have changed anything. He would still have insisted on contacting the inspector first."

Baxter sighed. "You're right, I suppose. How that man can call himself a policeman, I don't know."

"I do think he's rather out of his depth this time."

"He's always out of his depth, which is the reason my wife takes extreme risks to ferret out these criminals."

"I'm being very careful, dear."

"That was before these other two deaths."

"I'll still be careful." She moved closer to the fire. "I take it you no longer believe this is the work of the Mayfair Murderer, either."

"I don't know that I ever thought so. I do know that if the chap in room nine wrote the note that Pansy found, he was either clairvoyant or he's the one who stabbed that poor chap in the neck. Just as he said he would."

"There is a problem with that theory."

"How so?"

"The note said he would leave by the window. To do that he would have to leap four floors to the ground."

Baxter pursed his lips. "Unless he had a ladder."

"That's a possibility." She frowned. "I'll have Clive take a look under the window tomorrow. Though I still can't believe a murderer would be foolish enough to write down his plans to kill someone and leave them lying around for anyone to see."

Baxter studied her face. "You don't believe this Mortimer chap is the killer."

"I didn't say that. I just can't imagine why he would kill two members of our staff, and then two guests who have absolutely nothing in common with them."

"The murders certainly don't appear to be connected in any way."

Cecily sighed. "Well, there is the kissing bough and that message on the wall. I happen to know that all four victims at some point in time kissed under that bough. As far as I can see, that's the only connection. Maybe our killer has something against people kissing in public."

"It's certainly a consideration. Though again, why didn't he leave that message with the other bodies?"

"Exactly, which leads me to believe that the message was an afterthought, most likely to throw everyone off track and make it look as if it was the work of the Mayfair Murderer."

"Clever." Baxter frowned. "And utterly cold-blooded. Killing innocent people just to throw the constables off the scent? Diabolical."

Remembering something, Cecily murmured, "I found something else outside the Danvilles' door."

Baxter frowned. "And you neglected to mention it?"

"I forgot about it until now."

"What is it?"

"A lady's handkerchief." She was about to tell him about Madeline's prediction, but thought better of it. Baxter had no time for what he called Madeline's hocus-pocus. She pushed her fingers into her sleeve and, after a moment of hunting, pulled out the handkerchief. "Look, it has the initials R.M. embroidered on it. Who do we know with those initials?"

Baxter frowned in concentration, then after a moment or two, shook his head. "The only one whose last name starts with M is Mortimer. It could belong to his wife."

"Exactly what I was thinking. Though why he would carry around one of his wife's handkerchiefs is beyond me. I must admit, though, he is beginning to look most suspicious. I suppose I should have mentioned all this to Sam Northcott, though he still would have done nothing until his dratted inspector gets back to town."

"We shall just have to try and keep an eye on the chap until this is over. I'll have the footmen keep watch on him from now on."

"As if they don't have enough to do." Cecily sighed. "Has Kevin finished his examinations?"

"Yes. He promised he'd ring tomorrow. He was anxious to get his wife and baby home. The baby was making a horrible noise." He glanced at her. "Are you certain you want the child in the library during the carol singing ceremony? I can't imagine how anyone can possibly sing carols with that racket going on."

"Madeline wants to be there. She's going to be here all day anyway. She's coming in the morning to bring fresh greens for the ballroom decorations, and she has offered to help us get ready for the ceremony. So she'll stay here the rest of the day and Kevin will meet her here tomorrow evening." Cecily headed for the door. "We could certainly use her help, and if that means I have to spend the evening keeping a baby quiet, well, it won't be the first time."

He wore such a soulful expression she felt a pang of remorse, though she wasn't sure why. She paused, looking up at him when he reached her side. "What is it, dear? What did I say?"

"Nothing." To her pleasant surprise he bent his head and kissed her. "It's just that I wish we could have had a child of our own."

She smiled, touched by the sentiment. "We have two wonderful godchildren," she reminded him. "And they will be home tomorrow, so I hope you have finished all your Christmas shopping."

He patted her on the shoulder, then opened the door for her. "You know I always leave it until the last minute. After all, that's why we have Christmas Eve, is it not?"

Cecily shook her head. "You men are incorrigible."

"Which is precisely why you adore us. Come now, let us get to bed. You have a long day tomorrow, and something tells me it won't be a pleasant one."

"Indeed. Four families devastated by loss at Christmastime. How awful. I suppose there's little hope of keeping all this from the rest of the guests."

"Unlikely. We shall just have to reassure them as best we can."

"The only way to do that is to find the killer." Cecily sighed. "And every moment that feat seems to get farther out of reach." She led the way down the hallway, deep in thought. If her theory about the killer proved correct, the best way to prevent more murders would be to advertise the fact that the Mayfair Murderer was responsible, thus leading the killer to believe his ruse had worked, and therefore there would be no need for any more deaths.

The problem with that line of thought was that everyone in the building would think a serial killer was on the loose and they could well be the next victims.

It seemed that whichever way she turned, she was doomed. Christmas Eve was tomorrow. All she could do was see that her guests had the best Christmas she could give them, and hope with all her heart that there would be no more of these ghastly murders.

"So, Gertie," Pansy said, as she stacked the last dish on the pile in the cupboard, "where are you and Dan going tomorrow afternoon?"

Gertie took her time answering. The truth was, she wasn't looking forward to her meeting with Dan as much as she usually did. She had the feeling that they were reaching some kind of turning point in their relationship, and she had the distinct impression that it wasn't going to be in her favor.

She fervently hoped she was wrong, but if she wasn't, she prayed it would happen after the New Year, just in case Dan was planning to break it off and leave her down in the dumps all over Christmas. She'd have to pretend to be happy and cheerful, so as not to spoil everything for the twins.

Sighing, she pulled the plug in the sink and watched the gray soapy water disappear down the drain. How she missed her babies. Though they weren't babies anymore. They were growing so fast she probably wouldn't recognize them when they got back tomorrow.

"Gertie? Are you all right?"

Hearing Pansy's worried voice, Gertie snapped up her head. "'Course I'm all right. I was just thinking about my twins, wasn't I. They'll be home tomorrow night, just in time for the carol singing ceremony. They've always loved that."

"Is Dan coming? Like he did last year?"

Gertie's stomach seemed to drop at the mention of Dan's name. "I expect he will. I haven't asked him yet."

Pansy got a funny look on her face. "Why not?"

Gertie shrugged. "I dunno. I just didn't think about it until now."

"Well, you'd better hurry up. You'll have to ask him tomorrow when you see him."

"Yeah, I will." Gertie wiped her hands on a towel. "I think—" She broke off as the kitchen door flew open and Samuel rushed in, eyes wide and hair mussed. "Gawd, Samuel. What the bloody hell happened to you?"

Pansy let out a cry of dismay and rushed over to him. "Are you all right, Samuel? Are you hurt?"

Samuel shook his head and sat down heavily on one of the kitchen chairs. He started to speak, then shook his head again and sank back.

Gertie stared at him a moment longer then said sharply, "Pansy! Go and get the brandy from the pantry."

She reached for a brandy snifter from the cupboard and set it on the table.

"What's up then, mate? Seen a ghost or something?" Gertie asked him.

"Something," Samuel muttered, as Pansy rushed back with the bottle.

Gertie poured a generous amount in the glass and put it in Samuel's shaking hand.

"Mrs. Chubb will be cross you helped yourself to that," Pansy said, watching Samuel sip at the spirits.

"It's an emergency." Gertie put the stopper back in the bottle. "That's what it's for—emergencies."

Pansy sat down on the chair next to Samuel. "Oh, I thought it was to keep Michel from attacking everyone with a carving knife."

Samuel choked on the brandy, then wiped his mouth on his sleeve. "Don't say that! Don't ever say that!"

Pansy looked startled, then offended. "I was just trying to cheer you up with a joke, that's all."

She looked about to cry, and Samuel muttered something under his breath, then leaned forward to cover her hand with his. "Sorry, luv, but if you'd seen what I've seen you wouldn't make jokes like that, I promise you."

Pansy snatched her hand away. "Whatcha mean?"

Gertie felt cold all over. "Tell us, Samuel. Not someone else killed, is it?"

She felt for the edge of the table for support when Samuel nodded, while Pansy let out a shriek. "It's that Mayfair Murderer! That man in room nine. I told you it was him! Why won't anyone listen to me?"

Samuel grabbed her flailing hand and held on to it. "We don't know that yet," he said, sounding dreadfully tired.

"Yes we do!" Pansy tugged on his hand so hard the brandy

he held in the other hand spilled in his lap. "He wrote a note about it. I gave it to madam but she didn't do nothing about it and he's still lurking about in his room waiting to kill anybody what walks by, I know it."

Samuel stared at her. "What are you talking about?"

Pansy seemed beyond words so Gertie butted in. "Pansy found a note in his room and it said he was going to stab someone in the neck while they were asleep."

Samuel's eyes widened even more. "That's exactly what he did," he said, his voice hushed.

"See? See? I told you!"

Pansy's voice had risen to a shriek again and Samuel held out his glass. "Here. You'd better take some of this."

Gertie stepped forward. "Never mind that. Who the heck got killed?"

Pansy swallowed the brandy and coughed. "I don't think I want to know."

"It's the Danvilles, poor devils," Samuel muttered.

Pansy whimpered, while Gertie stared at him in horror. "The honeymoon couple? Both of them?"

In a tired voice, Samuel described the scene in the ballroom and in the Danvilles' suite. "Horrible," he said, when he was finished. "It felt like dead bodies all over the place."

Pansy's whimpering got louder.

"What's madam doing about it?" Gertie demanded, feeling like crying herself. "I've got my twins coming home tomorrow night. I don't want them here if there's a madman running around stabbing people."

Samuel squared his shoulders and stood up. "I'm sure madam will do her best to find out who did this. She's really good at ferreting out murderers."

"Well," Gertie muttered, reaching for another brandy glass, "I hope she bloody well hurries up or we'll all end up dead." She winced as Pansy howled. "It's all right, I didn't mean it. I was just joking."

"It's no joking matter," Samuel said, frowning. He pulled Pansy toward him and put his arm around her. "It's all right, luv. I'll take care of you. Nothing's going to happen to you while I'm here."

Pansy snuggled up to him and Gertie felt a pang of envy. She and Dan had been like that once. What had happened to them? When did things start going wrong? Picking up the bottle, she poured brandy into the glass. Maybe it was time she had a real heart to heart with Dan. Tomorrow. That's what she'd do. Maybe if she told him a lunatic was running around carving up people he'd want to take care of her, like Samuel and Pansy.

Her lips curved in a bitter smile. Fat bloody hope of that. Closing her eyes, she shot the entire glass of brandy down her throat.

CHAPTER
❀16❀

Mr. Mortimer was a man of habit. For the last three mornings, at precisely half past ten, he had left the building to take a leisurely stroll along the seafront. Cecily knew this because Philip, her sharp-eyed desk clerk, had watched the odd gentleman with great interest, and had been only too eager to share his observations.

Mr. Mortimer had returned each morning after a half hour or so. Having watched him leave through the front door a few minutes earlier, Cecily estimated that she had at least twenty minutes to search his room. She could do it in even less if she hurried.

This was probably the best time to carry out her intention, or at least make the attempt. Baxter would have a fit if he knew what she was about to do, so it was just as well he was occupied for the time being.

She would be taking a risk, of course. Then again, one accomplished very little without taking a risk or two. This was something that must be done, and could only be done by her. Squaring her shoulders she opened her door and marched purposefully down the hallway.

Standing outside the door of room nine, she glanced up and down the corridor. Having satisfied herself that she was quite alone in the hallway, she turned the handle and slid inside the room, gently closing the door behind her.

The dull skies gave her little light from the window, but she resisted the impulse to light the oil lamp. She couldn't afford to leave any evidence of her intrusion.

A quick glance around the room assured her it was empty, and she went to work right away. The first thing she looked for was the wastebasket, which she soon found by the armchair in the corner.

Picking it up, she found it crammed with balls of paper, all with scribbling on them. Frowning, she pulled one out and smoothed out the creases, then took it over to the window. It was in the same hand as the note Pansy had found, just as hard to read and just as cryptic.

Not in the garden. Too obvious. Perhaps behind the windmill.

Heart thumping with anticipation, she crumpled the paper in her hand and set it aside, then drew out another wad of paper and smoothed it out. After reading it quickly, she squished it in her hand and reached for another. Then another, and another, until she opened one and saw a name she recognized.

Unable to believe what she'd seen, she kept opening up

the paper balls, each one confirming what she now knew. Of course.

J. Mortimer. James Mortimer. How could she possibly have missed it.

She threw the last ball back in the wastebasket and set it down carefully by the chair with a hand that shook. She had to tell someone. No, she couldn't tell anyone. Unless, perhaps, Baxter. He would keep it quiet. On tiptoe she crept to the door, peeked outside, then let herself out.

Bursting into her suite moments later, she found Baxter in his usual armchair, buried in the daily newspaper. "I have something absolutely astonishing to tell you!" she cried, causing him to drop the newspaper, which fluttered to the ground.

Leaning over, he picked up the pages and, taking his time, fitted them all together again. "And I," he said, in the pompous voice she hated, "have something to tell you."

Sighing, she sank on a chair. "All right, you tell me first."

He looked at her over the top of the newspaper. "You'll no doubt be less than surprised to know that our killer is not the Mayfair Murderer. That gentleman was caught late last night, in the act of attacking his latest victim."

"Well, I'm very glad to hear it." She paused, then added slowly, "It doesn't change the fact that we still have a mass murderer on our hands."

"Indeed it doesn't. All the more reason to take extra precautions." He looked at her. "What is it that you have to tell me that is so terribly fascinating?"

"Oh." She sank back. "Well, now it isn't quite such a startling revelation. Nevertheless . . ." She leaned forward again. "As you have already pointed out, Mr. Mortimer is not the Mayfair Murderer. Neither is he a serial killer. In fact, he's not a killer at all."

Baxter raised an eyebrow. "And I assume you know this for certain?"

"Absolutely."

"May I ask how?"

She raised her hand in an impatient gesture. "I searched his room."

"Oh, good Lord." Baxter's scowl creased his forehead. "How many times—"

"He had left for his stroll, so I knew I had plenty of time." She dismissed his displeasure with another wave of her hand. "It was quite safe, anyway. Mr. Mortimer is not whom he appears to be."

"I'm not surprised. Normal people don't scribble down plans to commit murder."

"He wasn't planning to commit a murder." She smiled in triumph. "Only to write about one."

Baxter's frown changed from disapproval to puzzlement. "Write about one?"

"Yes. Our Mr. Mortimer is an author. He is here incognito."

Now Baxter had begun to look intrigued. "A famous author?"

"Very."

"So who is it?"

She couldn't resist leading him on a little. "Think about it. Where have you heard the name J. Mortimer before?"

"I can't say I have."

"Then perhaps, James Mortimer?"

He frowned. "It does sound vaguely familiar."

"Think about a hound."

"A hound?" He frowned some more, then sat up. "Good Lord. You don't mean he's—"

"Yes, I do." The words bubbled out in her excitement. "I should have known. J. Mortimer. James Mortimer. It's a character in one of his books. His name appears on the first page of *The Hound of the Baskervilles*."

Baxter's eyebrows shot up. "Are you telling me he's that chap who writes in the *Strand* about that detective fellow . . . ah . . . what *is* his name?"

"Sherlock Holmes! Yes! Mr. Mortimer is Sir Arthur Conan Doyle! I found all sorts of notes in his room, with names and incidents I recognized. He must be working on another book." She clasped her hands to her bosom. "My favorite author. We actually have him staying here at the Pennyfoot. I simply must have his autograph."

Baxter made a choking sound. "Wait just a moment. If he's here under an assumed name, it's quite obvious he doesn't want people to know who he is, which explains the hat over the face and the hiding in his room. He won't thank you for gushing all over him, asking for his autograph and such."

"Gushing?" Cecily folded her arms and gave her husband a hard stare. "I do not gush. I shall simply wait for an opportune moment when we are quite alone and quietly murmur my request. I, of all people, respect the privacy of our guests. You should know that."

Obviously chastened, Baxter nodded. "I do, my dear, I most certainly do. I was merely concerned for the gentleman's privacy and spoke without thinking."

Mollified by his attempt to placate her, Cecily relaxed. "The only problem is that now we can rule out our esteemed guest as a murder suspect, I have to look for another suspect."

Baxter frowned. "But what about the handkerchief? You said you found it outside the Danvilles' suite. If it does belong to Mortimer, or Doyle, whichever it is, what the devil was it doing there?"

"The suite is on the same floor as Sir Arthur's room. He probably dropped it while passing by the room." Cecily gave him another triumphant smile. "I think I know why he's carrying it around. He recently lost his wife, which is most likely why he is here in Badgers End for Christmas. He is getting away from the memories, which can be so awfully painful this time of year. I think the handkerchief belonged to his wife, and he's carrying it to keep her with him." Her smile faded. "In which case, he's probably devastated by its loss."

Baxter's frowned deepened. "There's just one thing I don't understand. If Mortimer is actually Doyle, why would the initials be R.M.?"

It took a moment or two for his words to sink in. Then she let out an explosive sigh of disgust. "Of course, how thoroughly stupid of me. It wouldn't be, of course. I was so caught up in the romance of it all I completely ignored that point." She picked up the handkerchief and studied the embroidery. "Which means I have to find out to whom this handkerchief belongs. It's back to square one."

A sharp tap on the door brought up her head. She hastily tucked the handkerchief in her sleeve as Baxter got up to answer the summons.

She heard Pansy's voice in the hallway and relaxed her

tense muscles. She had half expected a hysterical outburst announcing yet another death.

Baxter closed the door and returned to his chair. "Mrs. Prestwick is here and waiting for you in the library."

"Oh, good heavens. I completely forgot Madeline was bringing fresh greens this morning. This dreadful business is completely muddling my head." Cecily rose and hurried to the door. "Madeline will be joining us for the midday meal, so we'll meet you in the dining room." She waited just long enough for his nod of agreement, then darted out the door and down the hallway.

Reaching the library, she found Madeline busily fastening miniature candlesticks on the Christmas tree among the green and gold glass balls and red heart-shaped sachets.

Upon seeing the tiny candles, Cecily's heart skipped a beat. "What are you doing?"

Madeline turned with a guilty smile. "It just didn't look right without the candles. Don't worry, Cecily dear, we won't light them."

Cecily took a deep breath. "I certainly hope not." She glanced around the room. "Where's the baby?"

"Over there." Madeline nodded at the deep armchair facing the French doors. "She's sleeping, so I thought I'd leave her there while I run into the ballroom and change over the greens. The ones I put in there a few days ago are looking extremely dried up. That's the problem with them being out of water. I wish there were some way to keep them watered while they are hanging on the wall."

"I'll keep watch over Angelina." Cecily glanced at the tree again. "I'll put the rest of the candles on while you're in the ballroom."

Madeline smiled. "That's a very good idea. It will help you overcome that awful phobia you have." Her smile faded. "I don't suppose you found out who killed that lovely honeymoon couple?"

Cecily shook her head. "P.C. Northcott was convinced it was the Mayfair Murderer, but he's been caught now, so I don't know if the constable will decide to continue the investigation or wait for Inspector Cranshaw."

Madeline studied her face. "You're not going to pursue it yourself?"

"I don't know that I can." Cecily picked up a candlestick and fastened it to the branch with unsteady fingers. "I have an idea who it might be but there doesn't seem to be any way to prove it." She frowned. "Yet that little voice that always tells me I know more than I think I do is starting to make a noise in my head. I need to concentrate on what I know. Perhaps I can think of something useful."

"Excellent idea." Madeline picked up the huge basket crammed with holly, cedar, and fir. "Meanwhile I'll get these greens hung up in the ballroom." She flipped her hand in farewell and disappeared through the door.

Sighing, Cecily picked up another candlestick. Somewhere in all the muddle in her head lay the answer. She was sure of that now. All she had to do was go back to the beginning, and try to remember everything that had happened, and all she had learned.

Hopefully, something would jump out at her and she could go from there.

Deep in concentration, she fastened the candlesticks one by one, her mind focused on her conversations with Mick Docker and Stan Whittle. Barry Collins had said that he couldn't remember seeing Mick Docker for a while the night Ellie died. She needed to talk to Mr. Docker one more time. Stan Whittle, too, since he had left the pub well before closing time.

Samuel said he heard Mick Docker arguing with Ellie that night. It was possible, however, that Samuel had mistaken Stan's Scottish accent for Mr. Docker's Irish accent. Then again, how had either one of them been able to get into the Pennyfoot to kill the Danvilles, and why?

Unless her theory was right about wanting to make it look like the work of the Mayfair Murderer. After all, everyone was at the pantomime that night. In that case, it wouldn't have been quite so difficult to enter and leave the building without being seen.

Hearing a slight sound behind her, Cecily turned her head. Thinking Angelina was waking up, she waited to see if the child would cry. She could hear no further sound, however, and turned back to fasten the last candlestick.

What if it wasn't either Mick Docker or Stan Whittle? She had concentrated so much on those two, she really hadn't considered anyone else. Who else would have wanted to kill Ellie? That's what she needed to know, for that's where it had all started. Find the motive behind that murder and she'd find the clues to the rest. She was sure of it.

For some reason, the handkerchief she'd found kept popping into her head. She reached into her sleeve and drew it out again. It was a very pretty handkerchief, edged in fine French lace, with the initials embroidered with a deep purple silk thread.

She raised it to her nose to see if she could detect a fragrance and was rewarded with the smell of rosewater. She was about to unfold the handkerchief, when the door opened and Madeline floated into the room, her floral frock swirling around her bare ankles.

At the same time Cecily felt a distinct draft—more like a blast of cold air. She glanced over at the French doors and was stunned to see them standing open.

Madeline came to a halt, her gaze fixed on the armchair. For a moment she looked like a statue, her face white and set in stone. Then, in a strangled voice Cecily hardly recognized, she spoke one word. "Angelina."

With a harsh cry of disbelief, Cecily rushed across the floor to the armchair. The baby's fluffy pink blanket lay on the seat, with a little pink bonnet lying on top of it. A wave of nausea made Cecily clutch her stomach.

Inconceivable as it seemed, Angelina had disappeared.

Pansy had just begun to lay the tables for the midday meal when Gertie rushed into the dining room, hair flying out from under her lopsided cap. "Quick," she said, breathless and panting, "go and find Samuel." She held out a pink baby's bonnet, the ribbons dangling almost to the floor. "Give him this and tell him to shove it under his dog's nose."

Pansy frowned. Gertie was always playing tricks on her, but this was really stupid, even for her. "What for?"

"Ms. Pengrath . . . I mean Mrs. Prestwick's baby. It's been stolen!"

Still unsure if this was a joke, Pansy shook her head. "Go on with you."

"Pansy, it's true. The baby's gone and madam wants Samuel to look for her. She said the dog might help if it smells the bonnet."

Staring into Gertie's face, Pansy thought she saw tears glistening in her eyes. Gertie never cried. Not even when her husband died. Her heart beginning to pound, Pansy took the bonnet. "All right, I'll find him." She started for the door, then paused. "What about the tables?"

Gertie threw a hand up in the air. "Never mind the flipping tables, just go! Everybody's going out to search for the baby. I have to find Clive and tell him. Come on!" She rushed past Pansy and flew down the hallway faster than Pansy had ever seen her move.

Picking up her skirts, Pansy raced after her. No one was in the foyer when they ran across it, and they both burst out onto the steps together. Gertie went one way, toward the rose garden, while Pansy ran as fast as she could to the stables.

Samuel was cleaning one of the motorcars when she dashed inside. He looked up in surprise as she skidded to a halt. She was so out of breath she couldn't get out the words, and she gulped air into her lungs as she shoved the bonnet into his hand.

He looked down at it as if he expected it to bite him. "What's this?"

"It's Mrs. Prestwick's baby's bonnet." Still gasping for breath, Pansy held on to her side. "Someone stole her. Madam wants you to give it to Tess so she can find the baby."

Samuel looked from the bonnet to her and back again. "Give it to Tess?"

Pansy puffed out her breath. "You know, make her smell it so she can follow the scent."

"Oh!" Samuel nodded. "But if someone is carrying the baby, how can Tess follow the scent?"

Pansy felt like crying. "I don't know! Just try it. That poor little baby is missing and heaven knows where she is and we have to f-find her. . . ." She didn't realize she was crying until tears started rolling down her cheeks.

Samuel dropped the rag he was holding and put his arm about her shoulders. "Hold on, hold on. Oh, God, don't tell me the killer has that little baby. This is real then?"

"Yes, of course it's real!" Pansy sniffed and lowered her voice. "Gertie said everyone is out looking for the poor little thing. Oh, we have to find her, Samuel. Where is Tess?"

Samuel dropped his arm, turned his head, and uttered a shrill whistle. From somewhere outside a rough bark answered him, and a moment later the dog came bounding into the stable.

"Here, girl. Good dog. Come here." Samuel held out his hand and Tess eagerly bounced toward him. He held out the bonnet, and she sniffed, then looked up at him, tail wagging, waiting for further orders.

Samuel looked at Pansy and shrugged. "I don't think it's going to work."

Pansy wiped her nose on her sleeve. "It has to work. Show it to her again."

Samuel bent over and held the bonnet to the end of Tess's nose. "Here, find her, girl. Find the baby, Tess. Let's go and find her."

Excited now, Tess barked and ran out into the yard.

"Come on!" Samuel grabbed Pansy's hand and tugged her almost off her feet. "We have to follow her."

Pansy held back. "I can't go! I have tables to lay."

"What's more important? Laying tables or finding a lost child?" He tugged again. "Come on. Four eyes are better than two. Don't you want to find that little baby?"

Pansy hesitated another second or two, but then Tess barked again, more urgent this time. Putting the tables out of her mind, she followed Samuel out into the chilly air.

CHAPTER
❀ 17 ❀

"It's all my fault." Cecily sank onto a chair in her suite and buried her head in her hands. "I should have been watching. How could someone have come into the library and taken that baby without me hearing? I'll never forgive myself."

"It's all right, Cecily." Madeline's soft voice carried across the room. She stood by the window, peering out at the bowling greens that stretched down to the woods. "Please don't blame yourself. It would have happened just the same had I been there instead of you."

"No, you would have known that someone was in the room." Cecily shook her head. "I should have known."

"Don't worry. Everything will be all right."

Cecily raised her head, brushing tears from her cheek. "How can you be so calm? Your baby is missing!"

"She will be all right." Madeline turned, her face strangely composed. "Please, Cecily. Don't worry."

Cecily gulped. Madeline had to be in some kind of catatonic state, her mind incapable of accepting the reality of what had happened.

Madeline knew about the words scribbled on the wall of Geoffrey Danville's suite. *All who kiss beneath the bough will not live to kiss again.* She had kissed the baby beneath the kissing bough, not once, but twice. And now the baby was gone. She could not, would not, let her mind dwell on what might happen to the child if the murderer had taken her. The consequences were too unbearable to contemplate.

Glancing again at Madeline's unruffled countenance, she couldn't believe that her friend hadn't considered the outcome of this deplorable act. Her baby, the child for whom she had yearned for so many years, was in the hands of a mad killer. How could she not be wailing and howling, or lying in a dead faint?

The door opened at that moment and Dr. Prestwick hurried in, his face drawn in agony. Now here, thought Cecily, was the look of suffering. The dreadful look she expected to see on her friend's face.

Madeline's smile was somewhat fragile as she greeted her husband. He clasped her to him, burying his face on her shoulder. His voice, choked with emotion, brought fresh tears to Cecily's eyes. "How could this have happened? What in God's name have we done to deserve this horrible torture?"

Madeline patted her husband's head. "Hush, dear, try to calm down. I know this is worrying but I'm sure that everything will be all right in the end."

Kevin raised his head, his words raw with his pain. "How can you say that? How can you possibly know that?"

"Because I do."

He drew away from her. "No, you don't. All your devilish visions are not going to return our baby to us. Can't you understand? She's in the hands of a vicious killer."

Madeline flinched, then said softly, "No, I don't believe that."

Kevin turned away and rubbed a hand across his eyes. "She's in shock. May I ask for brandy to be brought up here? She needs something to stimulate her brain."

"Of course." Trembling, Cecily reached for the bellpull. She gave it three tugs and let it go. "Madeline, come and sit down by the fire."

"Thank you, Cecily, but I'm quite all right here."

Cecily exchanged a worried glance with Kevin. "Do you think perhaps it's better to let her go on believing that everything will be all right?"

Kevin shook his head. "It will only make the pain so much worse when she learns the truth. We must force her to accept what is happening, so she can be prepared."

Madeline turned, her voice sharp. "Please don't speak about me as if I am not here. I know you, Kevin, do not believe in my powers, but Cecily, I should have thought you would know better. I am dreadfully concerned about my daughter. Of course I am. But I do not believe that whoever has taken her means her harm. Quite the opposite. So let us all calm down and wait for events to unfold."

Jolted, Cecily stared at her. "Are you sure?"

"Quite sure."

"Do you know where she is?"

Kevin made a guttural sound of disbelief, and Madeline sent him a wary glance. "No, not at present. I only know she is safe."

It was true, Madeline had an uncanny ability to sense certain events and situations, but in this case, Cecily found it difficult to share her friend's faith in Angelina's welfare. She felt more attuned to Kevin's skepticism, and could quite understand his impatience with his wife.

She was about to comment when the door flew open and Baxter strode in. "I've got every footman searching the entire building," he announced. "If that baby is anywhere on the premises we will find her."

Madeline merely nodded and turned back to stare out the window.

Baxter inclined his head toward her and raised his eyebrows at Cecily.

Recognizing her husband's signals, Cecily nodded to assure him Madeline was fine. "Thank you, dear. I've sent Samuel out with his dog, and Gertie went to ask Clive to search the grounds as well."

"Then we have the Pennyfoot covered. I'll notify the constabulary and they can start a search in the village."

He sounded tired, as if he'd already given up. Cecily held out her hand to him, but Madeline spun around, saying, "There's no need to contact the constable. Angelina will be found close by."

"Oh, for heaven's sake, Madeline." Kevin bounded over to her. "We need everyone available out searching for her."

"No, we don't." She faced her husband, defiance flashing in her dark eyes. "I would never risk my daughter's life if for one moment I thought she was in real danger.

Trust me, Kevin. Just this once, have a little faith in my powers."

He narrowed his eyes. "Are you aware of something that you're keeping to yourself?"

"Of course not." She turned away from him. "All I can tell you is that Angelina is somewhere close by and she's safe. I shall be as relieved as you are when she is found."

Kevin turned his back on his wife, shaking his head in defeat.

Baxter cleared his throat. "Ah, perhaps I should wait to call the constabulary?"

"Suit yourself." Kevin strode to the door. "I'll be searching the grounds if anyone needs me." He flung open the door and disappeared.

Baxter patted Cecily's outstretched hand. "I'd better go along and help him." He turned to go, then paused. "Oh, by the way, that photographer chap came by with the photographs from the banquet. I left them in your office."

Cecily nodded absently, her thoughts still with the missing baby. "Thank you, dear."

Just as he reached the door someone rapped on it from outside. Baxter stood back to let the maid pass then rushed out into the hallway.

For a moment Cecily had forgotten why she'd sent for the maid, but then Madeline spoke, coming forward to sit next to her. "I don't need brandy," she said, sounding less confident than she had earlier. "I just need my baby back."

Cecily studied her friend's face, then nodded at the maid. "Have Pansy and Gertie returned yet?"

"No, m'm." The maid looked worried. "They're both missing."

Cecily's stomach lurched, and she made an effort to calm herself. Expecting the worst would not help matters. "They are probably helping in the search. Tell Mrs. Chubb to serve the midday meal as best she can. I'm sure Pansy and Gertie will be back shortly."

"Yes, m'm." The young girl curtsied and quietly left the room.

Cecily looked at Madeline. "They're all right, aren't they?"

Madeline looked down at her hands. "I don't have any signals that tell me otherwise."

Not exactly comforted by that, Cecily had to accept the fact that she could do nothing but wait . . . and pray.

"Where is she going?" Pansy was panting so hard she could barely get the words out. As it was, her voice was carried away by the wind, drowned by the rustling branches. Ahead of her, Samuel was following Tess, but now all Pansy could see of the dog was a flash of white at the tip of her tail as she disappeared in the brush.

Afraid of being left behind, Pansy lifted the hem of her skirt and plunged into the prickly shrubs and grasping weeds. The wind tugged at her cap, and strands of her hair blew across her eyes. She swiped at her face, then yelped as a greedy bramble grabbed her hand and carved a deep scratch across her knuckles.

Samuel must have heard, as he paused and looked back. "What's the matter? Are you all right?"

"Yes," she shouted back. "I'm just trying to keep up with you."

His "Sorry!" floated back to her on the wind, and thankful to see him waiting for her, she lifted her skirts higher and leapt over a clump of blackberry vines.

Samuel held out his hand as she approached. "Come on. Tess has gone in here somewhere."

She looked around, but could see nothing but solid, gnarled tree trunks, low-hanging branches, and undergrowth thick with ferns, thistles, and scratchy brambles. "Is she lost?"

Samuel took hold of her hand and led her into the damp shadows of the woods. It smelled of decaying leaves and wet earth. She felt cold and frightened, trying not to imagine the lifeless body of that little baby.

What would she do if they found the baby lying dead on the ground? Faint, that's what she'd do. Samuel would have to bring the baby back. She couldn't touch the baby, not if her life depended on it. She felt sick at the thought, and hastily directed her mind to think of the ocean and the sands, and summer walks along the beach.

Samuel whistled, the shrill sound making her jump. An answering bark made her nerves tighten. Tess sounded urgent. Could she have found something?

"Tess?" Samuel quickened his pace, moving toward the direction of the dog's barking.

Stumbling after him, Pansy prayed as she'd never prayed before. Head down, she bumped into Samuel as he stopped short, holding up his hand.

"Shhsh! Wait a minute."

It took all her courage to peek around him. She caught her breath when she saw Tess, a few yards ahead of them, digging frantically in the soft earth, dirt flying from her paws.

Pansy gasped and clutched Samuel's coat. "You don't think it's . . ." She gulped, unable to say the words.

Samuel stretched his hand out behind him and found hers. "Let's hope not."

Tess paused to snuffle in the ground, then started digging again, spraying clods of earth in the air. Samuel started to creep forward, but Pansy tugged her hand loose, unable to move from the spot.

Samuel had covered about half the distance when Tess suddenly stopped digging and backed away, tail wagging and a proud look on her face. He hurried over to her, while Pansy clutched her stomach and prayed she wouldn't be sick.

Samuel paused, looking down at the hole Tess had dug. Then he squatted, reaching down with his hand.

Pansy moaned and shut her eyes.

She heard Samuel's voice, and he sounded relieved. "Look, it's all right. It's only a bone."

She forced her eyelids up just a bit and saw Samuel still squatting by the hole, holding up a very dirty bone. "She must have buried it here some time ago," Samuel said, getting to his feet. "It's amazing what dogs can remember."

Feeling weak in the knees, Pansy stumbled toward him. "Thank goodness it wasn't the baby," she said, when she reached him.

"Yeah." Sam threw the bone to Tess, who sniffed it, then promptly walked away. "But now we have to go on looking for her."

Pansy grabbed his hand for comfort. "Let's just hope we find her alive."

Samuel nodded. "God willing, we will."

*　　*　　*

"I'm coming with you." Gertie jutted out her chin and stared up at Clive. "Just try and stop me."

Clive's lips twitched in a reluctant smile. "I've got no intention of trying to stop you from doing anything. I know my limitations."

Gertie wasn't quite sure what that meant, but she rather liked the way he said it. "Well, all right then. Let's go and look for that baby."

Without another word, Clive turned and strode off across the lawns toward the woods.

Following behind the big man, Gertie had trouble keeping up. She was not exactly dainty herself. In fact, she was taller and bigger than most other women she came across, but the man charging across the grass ahead of her managed to make her feel strangely weak and fragile.

It was not a familiar feeling for Gertie, and she wasn't quite sure how she felt about it. She was used to taking care of herself. And her twins, come to that. Her first marriage had turned out not to be a marriage at all, since Ian was already married—something he hadn't bothered to tell her until his real wife had spilled the beans.

Her second marriage was cut short by Ross's death, leaving her alone again. Everything that had happened to her in her life had given her the stamina and fortitude to get through anything, and she was proud of that. Much as she loved Dan, she knew that if she had to, she could manage quite well without him.

Yet whenever she was with Clive, she felt like surrendering all that stamina and control, and just letting herself be protected and guided by him. He was a quiet man, never said much, but she could feel the power of him, that hidden strength that made her want to lean on him and trust that he would make things right for her.

Her thoughts startled her. She could never think of Clive that way. Not like her and Dan. Yet she had to admit, whenever she was with Clive, she felt an inner peace, as if she could stop trying to be in charge of the world and just allow him to take over.

He had reached the edge of the woods, and stood waiting for her to catch up to him. "I don't know where to start looking," he said, as they started walking down the trail side by side. "I can't imagine anyone bringing a baby in here, unless he intended to harm her."

"Don't say that." Gertie shivered, and pulled her shawl tight about her shoulders. "Madam wanted us to search the grounds, and we've looked everywhere else. The woods is the last place to look."

"What I don't understand, is why take a baby at all." Clive shoved a low-hanging branch out of her way, holding it until she was safely past it. "I mean, he's already killed four people. Why would he want to kill a tiny baby? It doesn't make sense."

"None of it makes sense." Gertie lifted her skirt to step over a fallen tree. "Why kill all those people, anyway? We thought it was the Mayfair Murderer. After all, he was going around killing people all over the place, but Mrs. Chubb said she heard he'd been caught. So it can't be him."

"This doesn't look like the work of a serial killer." Clive paused to help her down a steep slope. "They usually pick victims that all look alike in some way."

"That's what I thought." Gertie hesitated, then put her

hand in his. His fingers felt warm and really strong. Unsettled by the contact, she skipped down the slope and pulled her hand free. "So why is this lunatic killing men and women who look nothing alike and have nothing in common?"

"That's something we'll only find out when he's caught." Clive halted and held up his hand. "Listen. Can you hear what I hear?"

Gertie paused, straining her ears. "It sounds like someone laughing. A child laughing."

Clive nodded. "Come, I have an idea." He took off at an angle, charging through the undergrowth without regard for the brambles snagging his hair.

Stumbling after him, Gertie was surprised when they reached a trail that looked familiar. "This is the way to the tree house," she said, as Clive set off down the narrow path.

"We took a shortcut."

His words were tossed over his shoulder, and she had to run to catch up with him. She could hear the laughter now, closer and more clearly. There were at least two of them as far as she could tell. Who were they, and what were they doing in her twins' tree house?

Clive had built it for the twins' Christmas present the previous year. She could still see their faces the first time they'd caught sight of it. James had climbed up there immediately and refused to leave. She'd had to threaten all kinds of horrible punishments. All of which were ignored. It was Clive who had finally persuaded him to climb down.

The twins had spent most of the summer playing in that tree house. They would not be happy to find out other kids had taken it over.

Clive had reached the clearing and was standing still, apparently listening. She crept up to his side, and listened, too. She could hear them talking, but couldn't make out what they said. Then she heard another sound that took her breath away. The quiet whimper of a baby.

She looked up at Clive and met his triumphant gaze. "I think," he said softly, "we have found Angelina Prestwick."

CHAPTER
✿ 18 ✿

Sitting by the fireside in her suite, Cecily struggled to keep up a decidedly one-sided conversation. Madeline was preoccupied with her thoughts, and Cecily could hardly blame her. She couldn't imagine how she would have felt had someone stolen away one of her babies.

Even now, with both her sons grown men and living in a foreign country, she worried when she didn't receive word from them. One never stopped worrying about one's offspring, no matter how old they were.

Nevertheless, she felt compelled to keep Madeline's mind off her troubles, or at least distract her for a while. "Are you quite sure you don't want to summon the constable to organize a search party?"

Madeline shook her head. "I don't want to cause unnecessary trouble."

"Unnecessary?" Cecily stared at her, totally unable to comprehend her friend's thinking. "I don't like to disagree with you, Madeline, but I can't help feeling you are making a grave mistake. How can you be so certain your baby is safe?"

Madeline sighed. "I didn't say I was certain. I simply have a very strong feeling that if I raise a hue and cry about this, an innocent person will be greatly harmed. I have to trust my instincts, Cecily. I have to have faith in my powers."

"And if your powers are wrong this time?"

A brief spasm of pain crossed Madeline's face. "Then I shall lose faith in everything."

Cecily blinked back a tear. "Oh, Madeline. I pray you are right. I hope—" She broke off as a timid summons on the door brought her to her feet.

Madeline looked up, hope flaring in her face. She uttered not a word as Cecily hurried over to the door and opened it.

The young maid who stood there looked frightened, as well she might. The events of the last few days were not exactly in keeping with the festivities of the season. "You have visitors, m'm," she said, dropping a deep curtsey. "Colonel Frederick Fortescue and his wife request to call on you."

Cecily heard Madeline muttering behind her. She could guess the general content of her comments. Although she confessed to being fond of Phoebe Fortescue, Madeline was often irritated by the capricious woman, and could be quite biting toward her when her mood was low. Cecily could not imagine her mood being much lower than it was at present,

240

which did not bode well for any interaction with Phoebe, much less her bombastic husband.

Between the two of them, the Fortescues could be exhausting, and Cecily was quite sure that Madeline would not be in a suitable frame of mind to handle such turmoil.

She was about to inform the maid to give Phoebe her regrets when Madeline called out, "Oh, for heaven's sake, Cecily, invite them up here. They will help take my mind off things. After all, one can never dwell on private matters when Phoebe is in full gusto."

It didn't matter how many times Madeline read her mind, Cecily could never get accustomed to the jolt it gave her. She instructed the maid to send up the couple, though she had the distinct feeling it was not the wise thing to do.

Closing the door, she looked across the room at Madeline, who was gazing into the fire, her chin propped on her hands. "Are you quite sure you want to be in such . . . ah . . . invigorating company right now?"

Madeline sat up, smoothing her long hair away from her face. "Of course not, but you were dithering about for so long I felt someone had to make a decision. I could hardly tell you to send them away, now could I?"

Cecily sighed. "I'm sorry, Madeline. I know this isn't the best time, but Phoebe is most likely here to prepare the library for her musicians. The carol singing ceremony is tonight, remember?"

"Yes, of course I remember." Madeline got up from her chair and wandered over to the window. "What on earth is taking them so long?"

"Well, they do have to walk all the way up three flights of stairs."

"No, I don't mean the Fortescues. I mean the people searching for Angelina. Someone should have found her by now. She's cold. She doesn't have her blanket." She turned suddenly, her face pale and drawn. "Oh, Cecily, what if I *am* wrong? What if—"

"Don't even say it!" Cecily rose swiftly and hurried over to her. "You've never been wrong before. I shouldn't have questioned you. I've put doubts in your mind—"

A loud rapping on the door made them both jump. Cecily raised her eyebrows at her friend, silently asking if she was ready to receive the visitors.

Madeline gave her a brief nod, then moved back to the window.

Calling out, "Do come in!" Cecily walked toward the door to greet her friends.

Phoebe entered first, carrying an umbrella, her skirts rustling as she walked. As always, she looked spectacular, dressed in a pale green tea gown, covered with a navy blue coat and a massive dark blue hat perched sideways on her head. Green ostrich feathers curled over the brim, which was heavily adorned with holly and frosted red berries.

"Cecily, dearest!" she cried, as she swept across the carpet. "I've been hearing such dreadful stories! As if that poor girl wasn't enough. I can't close my eyes without seeing her swinging from the rafters. Now I hear that her husband is dead and Madeline's poor little baby is missing." She grasped Cecily's hands in her gloved fingers, tears gushing from her eyes. "Please tell me it isn't true."

"It's quite true."

Madeline had spoken from her spot by the window, and Phoebe spun around so fast she almost lost her balance.

"Dear heaven, Madeline! I didn't see you there. Oh, you poor thing. How can you possibly bear it?"

"I'm bearing up quite well, thank you." Madeline came forward and suffered a hug from Phoebe before drawing back. "Nice of you to ask, though."

"Of course. I—"

Phoebe's next words were drowned out by a deep, booming voice at the door. "Blast it, woman, do you have to walk so fast? I'm out of breath trying to keep up with you."

The gentleman who entered wore a tweed hacking jacket and carried a matching tweed hat. The lower half of his face was hidden behind a mass of white whiskers and his nose glowed viciously red, suggesting a recent bout with a large bottle of brandy.

"Freddie, dear, do come in and shut that door. There's such a dreadful draft." Phoebe shivered and tucked her hands in her muff. "I simply can't get warm these days."

"It must be old age creeping on," Madeline said, moving closer to the fireplace. "Come and sit down, Phoebe. It's warm by the fire."

Phoebe gave her a suspicious look, then, apparently deciding Madeline meant well, delicately lowered herself onto the armchair. "So do tell me all about it. Where did you find that poor dead man? How long has the baby been missing?"

Cecily was about to loudly change the subject when Colonel Fortescue did it for her.

"Reminds me of when I was on a tour of duty for the British army in India, old girl." He'd pronounced it *Inja*, thrusting out his chest and tucking his thumbs into the top pockets of his waistcoat. Standing with his back to the fire, he rocked back and forth on his heels. "Ah, yes, I remember it well."

"Oh, Freddie, do please be quiet." Phoebe gave him a fierce frown then turned back to Madeline. "As I was saying—"

The colonel, as usual, completely ignored his wife's reprimand. "Middle of the desert, hot as blazes, and we were all dying of thirst. I was riding ahead of the troops on a blasted elephant. Dashed awkward beasts to ride. Much prefer a horse. All that wriggling around was playing havoc with my—"

Phoebe sat up straight. "Freddie!"

The colonel coughed. "Ah . . . ahem, yes. Anyway, my batman spotted a pile of rags up ahead. He—"

"Frederick!" Phoebe glared at him. "No one is the least bit interested in your interminable war stories. Please cease and desist this minute."

Normally Cecily would have been in full agreement. Knowing, however, that Phoebe was intent on learning every detail of the murders and the missing baby, the colonel's tales were vastly preferable. "It's quite all right, Phoebe. Do go on, Colonel. Your story is quite fascinating."

Madeline sent her a grateful look, while Phoebe stared at her as if she'd lost her mind. After all, Cecily was always the first one to cut off the Colonel's hair-raising accounts.

Fortescue needed no further bidding. "Well, anyway, that pesky bundle of rags turned out to be a child. Must have been abandoned by her tribe. Half dead she was, and skinny as a gutted rabbit."

Cecily winced, while Phoebe shuddered. "Don't say I didn't warn you," she muttered.

Oblivious to the appalled reaction to his story, the colonel blithely continued. "Chalky, my batman, suggested we put her on the elephant with me and take her into town. Well, of course, we had to put the dratted thing on its knees to get her up there. Got it down all right, managed to get some water down the child's throat, and tied her to the harness so she wouldn't slide off." He paused, staring at the clock on the mantelpiece. "I say, is that the time? I'm late for my midday snifter."

Phoebe looked relieved. "So you are. Run along, then, Freddie. I'll catch up to you later."

The colonel blinked at her, as if he didn't understand a word she'd said. "Right ho. Now, where was I? Ah, yes. Well, the elephant started to get up before I was ready. I slid right off the blasted thing. Fell right down on my—"

"Freddie!"

Fortescue scowled. "Tailbone. Couldn't sit down for a week. Had to eat standing up. Dashed awkward that. Especially at the regimental dinner. Dribbled gravy all down my uniform. Still hurts in the rear if I sit down too hard."

Phoebe rose from her chair, quivering with indignation. "Frederick Fortescue. I insist that you either be quiet or leave. This instant."

The colonel looked surprised. "No need to shout. I'm on my way." He turned to Cecily and bowed. "Good to see you, old bean. Looking forward to the carol singing tonight. Should raise the roof, what? What?"

"Indeed, Colonel. We look forward to enjoying your participation."

Phoebe grunted something under her breath, while the colonel reached for Madeline's hand. "Don't worry, my dear," he said gruffly. "All will be well. I feel it in my bones."

Madeline smiled. "So do I, Colonel. Thank you."

Phoebe waited until the door had closed behind her husband before exploding with wrath. "That man can be so insufferable, I really don't know—" A loud rapping on the door interrupted her. "Well! If that's Frederick again I'll—"

She never got the chance to say what she would do. Without waiting for permission, Gertie had bounced into the room, words tumbling from her mouth so fast it was difficult to understand her.

"We found her. She's all right. It was the Millshire youngsters. Found them in the tree house. Laughing like hyenas they were. Clive climbed up the tree and got her. He's—" She looked over her shoulder. "Clive? Come on! Bring her in here, then!"

Madeline was already halfway across the room. As Clive's bulky body filled the doorway, the baby in his arms, Madeline let out a cry so desperate, only then did Cecily realize just how well her friend had hidden her torment.

Madeline snatched the baby from the maintenance man and held her close, rocking her while murmuring soft words in her ear.

Cecily got up and patted Gertie on the shoulder. "Well done."

"Yes, m'm, but it was Clive that found her." Gertie's face was flushed with excitement. "It was the little girl, Adelaide. She said she wanted to play with a real live baby. I don't think she understands what she did." Gertie glanced at Madeline. "She took really good care of her, Mrs. Prestwick. The baby's all wrapped up in Lady Millshire's shawl, and she wasn't crying all that much."

Madeline buried her face in the soft folds of the shawl for

a moment, then looked up at Clive. "Thank you," she whispered. "Thank you both. I will give you both a special gift for this. Something precious to last a lifetime."

"Completely unnecessary, m'm," Clive said, looking bashful. "I just did my job, that's all."

"And me. I'm just glad the baby is all right." Gertie glanced at Cecily. "I suppose I should go and help Pansy. She's in the dining room. I'm afraid the midday meal is taking a bit longer to serve up."

"That's all right, Gertie. I think we can be forgiven for that this once."

"Yes, m'm." Gertie grinned and bent her knees in a slight curtsey.

Cecily turned to Clive. "Would you see if you can find my husband and Dr. Prestwick? Tell them we will meet them in the dining room."

"Yes, m'm. I do believe they went up to the roof garden. I'll find them."

He turned to leave, then paused, waiting for Gertie to go ahead of him.

"I'll be going then." Gertie nudged Clive in the arm as she passed him by, and he followed her out the door.

Phoebe rose from her chair. "Well, thank goodness that's over. Let me look at the little precious." She cooed for a moment over the baby, who now appeared to be sleeping.

"Would you and the colonel care to join us in the dining room?" Cecily asked, ignoring Madeline's rolling eyes.

"Oh, no thank you." Phoebe reached for her umbrella. "Freddie is probably drinking his meal, and I have too much to do to waste time eating. I'll take advantage of the fact that everyone is in the dining room. It will give me time to make my preparations for tonight." She bustled over to the door. "Thank you, Cecily, and Madeline, I'm so happy your little one is safe." She blew a kiss, and left.

Cecily walked over to Madeline and patted the baby's head. "Did you know that the little girl had taken Angelina?"

"No." Madeline looked down at her sleeping baby. "I just knew that it would be a mistake to call in the constables. I knew that whoever had her meant her no harm."

"Still, it was a terrible thing to do. The child must be made to realize—" She broke off as yet another tap on the door interrupted her. "Really," she murmured, as she crossed the room, "we are most popular today. The whole world is calling on us."

The woman standing outside had obviously been crying. In fact, the moment she started to speak, more tears poured down her cheeks. Recognizing her, Cecily opened the door wider. "Do come in, Lady Millshire."

"I was told Mrs. Prestwick is with you," the other woman said, gulping back a sob. "I would like a word with her."

"Yes, she's in here." Cecily stood back, and Lady Millshire entered, dabbing at her eyes with a small white handkerchief.

Cecily decided to leave. Obviously the woman had come to apologize to Madeline, something that would be difficult enough for her to do without having to suffer an audience.

"I will meet you in the dining room," she told Madeline, and left them alone to have their discussion in peace.

Instead of going straight to the dining room, she stopped by the office to take a peek at the banquet pictures left by the photographer.

She found them lying on her desk and quickly shuffled

through them. She found one of herself and Baxter that she particularly liked, and put it to one side. It was a shame that someone hadn't yet perfected colored photography, she thought, as she gazed at the images of elegantly dressed guests enjoying the feast. The pretty gowns lost some of their luster in the sepia shades.

She put the photographs down, and as she did so, she had an odd sensation of recognition. She knew the feeling well. It meant she was aware of something that hadn't yet registered in her mind.

Could it be something in the photographs? She picked them up and studied each one for several moments. There was nothing she could see that had any bearing on the murders. Frustrated, she glanced at the clock. Right now she was supposed to be meeting Madeline and her husband, and it would be most rude of her to be late. Leaving the photographs on her desk, she left the office and hurried along the corridor to the dining room.

CHAPTER
❀ 19 ❀

Gertie stood by the dumbwaiter outside the dining room, fidgeting in a fever of impatience. The delay in starting the midday meal had cost her valuable time. Right now she was supposed to be on the seafront, meeting Dan under their favorite lamppost by the Punch and Judy stand. That's if he bothered to turn up.

Tapping her foot, she waited for the waiter to rise, her arms aching from holding the tray weighed down with dirty dishes. In order to save time she'd overloaded it, and now she was in danger of dropping the bloody lot on the floor.

The rope jerked, then started threading downward, which meant the platform was on its way up. About flipping time, too.

She barely waited long enough to secure it before dumping the tray on it, then lowered it rapidly to the floor below.

A loud clattering of china echoed up the chamber, and she flinched. Maybe she'd done it a little too fast. As if to agree with her, an irate voice floated up to her. "Here! Flipping watch it up there, will you!"

"Sorry!" Gertie shook her head and rushed back to the dining room. Pansy was just coming out the doors with another loaded tray, and Gertie had to skip sideways to avoid crashing into her.

"Blimey." Pansy stared at her. "That was close."

Gertie gritted her teeth to prevent a curse from escaping. "I just hope Dan's there waiting for me, that's all."

Pansy sighed. "Look, why don't you go on and meet him. I can finish up here. I can get one of the other maids to help me."

Gertie felt like hugging her. "You will?"

"You did it for me when I was meeting Samuel." Pansy grinned. "Remember? You said I could do it for you some day. Looks like this is the day."

"You're a good sort." Gertie slapped her on the shoulder, rattling the tray in Pansy's hands. "Ta, ever so." Wasting no more time, she tore off down the hallway, dragging her apron off as she went.

Ten minutes later she was running down the Esplanade, praying that Dan would be there. After the flipping row they'd had at the cottage, he might have decided to forget about her. Or maybe he'd got there and waited so long he'd thought she wasn't coming.

It was already getting dark, and the lamplighter had started his rounds. As Gertie rushed past him, he nodded and smiled, then reached up with his long pole to light the gas lamp above his head.

Farther down, to her immense relief, she saw a tall figure leaning against their lamppost. Gasping for breath, she slowed her step and patted her hair. He was there. He'd waited. That's all that mattered. She had an hour and a half to spare before she had to get back. The twins would be arriving on the evening train. They'd be home just in time to go to the carol singing ceremony.

A twinge of doubt attacked her stomach. What if he couldn't come to the ceremony? He was always busy on Christmas Eve, taking toys to the orphans. Once she'd even managed to get away from her duties to help him.

Tonight he'd have to go on his own. Tonight belonged to her twins. They'd been gone over a week, and she couldn't wait to see them again. Still, that was later. He'd still have time to come carol singing before he left for the orphanage.

She drew closer, close enough to see Dan's grin as he waved at her. A rush of warmth almost overwhelmed her. She loved this man. If only she knew how he really felt about her. If only she could trust him.

For some reason a vision of Clive popped in her head. Impatient with herself, she pushed the thought away. Clive was a good friend, but she could never think of him in that way. Only Dan could make her knees weak and her heart beat so fast she could hardly breathe.

She reached him, and he held out his arms. She went straight into them, regardless of who might see her. After all the worrying, the relief was like a warm blanket, wrapping itself around her and shutting out all the cold and darkness.

"How's my sweetheart?" Dan murmured in her ear.

He always greeted her that way, and she never got tired of hearing it. Tonight, however, she needed more. She pulled back, tilting her chin up so she could see his face. "Am I your sweetheart? Really?"

"Of course you are." He pulled her close, and would have kissed her, except she turned her face away. "What's the matter?" He sounded irritated and the warm feeling melted away. "Are you still angry at me?"

"No." Without the comfort of his arms the cold seemed to seep into her bones. She hunched her shoulders against the wind.

"It's just that I never really know if you mean it or not."

"Of course I mean it."

He tugged at her arm, but she kept the space between them, wary of being swayed by his soft words. Deep down she knew they were at some kind of crossroads, and what was said in the next few minutes could change everything.

Dan let her go, and turned away. He took a few steps away from her, and for a frightening moment she thought he was leaving, but then he halted, and walked back to her.

"Look, Gertie, I'm sorry about what happened in the cottage. I was wrong to pressure you. I know that. If I didn't care so much about you it never would have happened. It's because I think so much of you that I got carried away. I'm sorry. It won't happen again."

He still hadn't said he loved her. He couldn't say it, she told herself, because he didn't feel it. He never had really loved her. Pride made her lift her chin and look him in the eye.

"I think perhaps I should go home. My twins will

be arriving soon and I want to be there when they get home."

"The train isn't due for another two hours." Dan's face was grave when he looked at her. "Besides, I rather wanted to be there with you when they came home."

He'd surprised her. She looked down at her feet and drew a circle on the pavement with her shoe. "What for?"

He didn't answer right away, and when he finally spoke, his voice sounded strange. "Gertie, I was going to do this later, but I think this might be a better time."

In utter disbelief, she watched him kneel down in front of her. "Gertie McBride, would you do me the honor of becoming my wife? I promise to take care of you and the twins, and try to be the best husband and father I can."

Her mouth hung open so long her tongue froze. She tried to speak, but only a squeak came out.

Dan tilted his head to one side and peered up at her. "What was that?"

Gertie took a deep breath. "Bloody hell."

Dan looked anxious. "Is that a yes or no?"

"Yes!" Gertie choked and cleared her throat. "I'd love to marry you."

"Well, thank goodness that's settled." Dan got to his feet, grabbed hold of her, and soundly kissed her.

A burst of applause drew them apart. The lamplighter stood just a few feet away, his pole propped against his shoulder. "Congratulations!" he called out, and pulled off his cap to wave it at them.

Gertie felt as if the entire Esplanade was rocking under her feet. All the lamps along the seafront twinkled in the dusk, bathing their garlands of holly and berries in a warm glow. Gertie drew her hands to her face, still trying to believe what had just happened. Dan had asked her to marry him. Now it was really Christmas.

Cecily stood next to Baxter by the library door, hoping she'd put enough pins in her hair to keep it securely fastened all evening. Having been kept busy all afternoon, she'd barely had time to breathe, much less get herself dressed for the carol singing ceremony.

Inside the room, Phoebe was darting about, giving last-minute instructions to the fidgety schoolgirls who were opening the evening with the first carol. Behind them, the pianist and violinist were quietly arguing about an arrangement, while the other two members of the quartet sat on their chairs looking bored.

The colored glass balls on the Christmas tree slowly rotated in the draft, sparkling in the light from the chandelier above. Flames leapt in the fireplace, and above it boughs of holly and fir covered the mantelpiece, tied together with bright red and white ribbons. Holly wreaths clung to the wood paneling and Madeline had hung little golden bells among the prickly leaves. Satisfied that the room looked its best, Cecily prepared to greet her first guests.

Sir Walter arrived first, looking resplendent in a black morning coat. His wife, dressed in a gorgeous pink lace gown, clung to his arm as if afraid to lose him.

"You look utterly ravishing this evening, Mrs. Baxter," Sir Walter murmured, as he raised her gloved hand to his lips.

Cecily felt a telltale warmth creep over her cheeks. "You are too kind, sir."

"I speak the truth." He turned to Baxter, who looked as if he'd swallowed a sour lemon. "Do I not, old chap?"

"If you say so, then it must be true," Baxter said, his voice as stiff as his face.

Cecily hurriedly turned to Sir Walter's wife. "Such a pleasure to see you, Lady Esmeralda."

"And you, Mrs. Baxter." She gave Cecily a gracious smile. "The library looks so festive. A perfect setting for singing carols."

"Thank you." Cecily turned to look into the room. "I was just thinking, it's a shame I didn't have the photographer come back this evening. He took such lovely photographs at the banquet. I must say, however, that Mrs. Prestwick surpassed herself this year decorating the library, and it would have been lovely to have photographs to keep."

Lady Esmeralda nodded. "It would, indeed. I must confess, I'm anxious to see the photographs of the banquet. Walter and I don't have that many photographs taken."

"Ah, well, I left them in my office." Cecily smiled. "I'll have them all on display in the library tomorrow."

"Splendid!" Lady Esmeralda took hold of her husband's arm again. "Shall we, then?"

"Of course, my dear."

"I do hope you will enjoy the evening," Cecily said, giving her own husband a nudge.

Baxter coughed. "Yes, yes, do have a nice evening."

"We'll certainly try." Lady Esmeralda sighed. "We almost didn't come down. My husband has such a dreadful headache." She sent him an anxious look. "He's had far too many headaches lately."

Cecily took a closer look at Sir Walter's face. He did seem

drawn and pale. "I'm so sorry. Can I get you a powder? Mrs. Chubb always keeps some in the kitchen for emergencies."

Sir Walter shook his head and winced. "Thank you, no. A glass of your good brandy will soon chase it away."

"That always makes him feel better," Lady Esmeralda said. "He'll be in good spirits once he joins in the singing. Though I must confess, it's rather hard to feel festive when one is in fear of being murdered in one's bed."

Cecily felt a pang of dismay. Apparently word had spread faster than she'd thought. "We are taking every precaution to see that doesn't happen," she said, and received a questioning look from her husband, which she duly ignored. "I'm hoping the soothing effects of the carols will help take our minds off the tragedies."

"Ah, yes. The carols. We adore carol singers, don't we, Walter?"

"Positively, my dear." Sir Walter patted the hand clutching his arm. "We always had them call on us at Rosewood. This is our first Christmas away from home. We would have missed the carol singing had we not been fortunate enough to enjoy it tonight. After all, it wouldn't be Christmas without carols, is that not so?"

"Quite so, and I'm happy you were able to join us." Cecily waved a hand at the door. "Please, go in and make yourselves comfortable."

The couple glided into the room, and Cecily turned to her husband. She was about to make a comment about Sir Walter's sickly appearance, but just then the Millshires arrived, minus their children, much to Cecily's relief. From all accounts, the Millshires' offspring could be quite disruptive.

She had no time to dwell on her thoughts after that. The

rest of the guests arrived in groups, and by the time every-one was settled the schoolgirls were about to start singing the first carol.

As the clear voices rose to the high ceiling, the beautiful chords of "It Came Upon the Midnight Clear" accompanied them, filling the room with the lyrical music.

Cecily wished that Madeline had been there to hear it. She loved Christmas carols. She had decided not to come to the ceremony after all. Apart from the fact that Angelina had tasted more than her share of adventure that day, the trauma had taken a toll on Madeline, and all she'd wanted to do was take her baby home and watch over her.

It was a shame, really. The carols were such an important part of the season. The story of the birth of Christ, and the meaning of the true spirit of Christmas. As Sir Walter had said, it wouldn't be Christmas without carols.

Something clicked in her mind, and she frowned. There it was again. That odd sensation. Something Sir Walter had said. . . . She caught her breath. Surely not. She struggled with her thoughts for several minutes, while the singing rose and fell all around her. Of course. Now it all made sense. All she had to do was find the proof.

The platform was deserted when Gertie arrived at the train station. Although the wind had turned even colder, and flakes of snow drifted sideways across the tracks, Gertie was warm with excitement.

She'd intended to have one of the footmen fetch the twins in a carriage, but Dan had insisted on driving her to the station. The twins would be thrilled to have a ride in the motorcar. She hugged herself as she gazed along the empty tracks into the darkness. She couldn't wait to see them.

"It should be here any minute," Dan said, glancing up at the large clock swinging above his head.

As if to confirm his comment, the station master appeared, a large oil lamp swinging in his hand. He walked to the end of the platform and put the lamp down at his feet.

In the distance Gertie heard a faint whistle. Grabbing Dan's sleeve, she gave it a tug. "They're coming!"

Dan laughed, and put an arm around her. "All this excitement just to see the twins come home! Just wait until we all move up to London. You'll be so excited then you'll forget how to talk."

A sharp stab of cold shot through Gertie's stomach. How could she have forgotten what it would mean to marry this man?

She would have to leave Badgers End again, and everyone she knew and loved at the Pennyfoot.

She couldn't seem to breathe, and her vision blurred, so that the oncoming train seemed to fade into the cloud of steam. She could hear the clatter of the wheels now, and the whistle, much louder, shattering in her ears. *Not now*, she told herself, pushing away the fear. *Don't think about it now. Just enjoy the twins' homecoming. Worry about it all later.*

The engine roared into the station, then screeched and rattled to a stop. Steam hissed from the chimney, and Gertie wrinkled her nose as the musty coal fumes filled her lungs.

Only three of the train's doors opened, spilling out its passengers. At the far end of the train, Gertie saw two small figures jumping down the steps and onto the platform.

"There they are!" Without waiting for Dan, she flew toward the twins, arms outstretched.

Lillian was the first to see her. Her scream echoed all the way down the platform. She rushed forward, followed closely by James, while Daisy, dragging a large portmanteau behind her, brought up the rear.

Gertie stooped to hug the twins, who smothered her with kisses. By the time she had untangled herself from their arms, Dan had taken the bag from Daisy and was walking her back to the motorcar.

James talked nonstop, his tongue tripping over the words in his excitement. Lillian tried to get a word in now and then, but with all the jumping up and down she was doing she had no breath to compete with her brother.

Basking in the warmth of their affection, Gertie forgot all about her troubles with Dan. It was Christmas Eve, and her twins were home. That was all that mattered for now.

Cecily found it hard to concentrate on the carol singers. She had one eye on the clock, wondering how soon she could leave without attracting attention. The schoolgirls came to the end of their rendition, and polite applause followed. Phoebe signaled the quartet and they began to play "We Three Kings."

Some of the guests got up to stand around the Christmas tree, while others moved closer to the piano. Voices began singing a hesitant chorus of the carol, somewhat out of tune and unusually sedate.

No doubt the news of the recent murders had dampened their spirits. She would have to think of something to lighten the mood.

This was the one night of the year when the staff was invited to join the guests in the singing, though few of them took advantage of the offer.

Cecily noticed Clive standing over by the window, and Mrs. Chubb next to him. Neither Pansy nor Gertie were visible, much to Cecily's surprise. Gertie always enjoyed the ceremony, and she was supposed to bring the twins. Cecily was really looking forward to seeing her godchildren, and although Baxter would be the last one to admit it, she knew he was anxious to see them as well.

Deciding that perhaps the train was late, Cecily looked around for her husband. Baxter was standing near the door, talking to one of the guests. She was rather hoping to slip away for a few minutes and return before he noticed her absence.

"Cecily! Why aren't you singing?"

Startled, Cecily turned to find Phoebe staring at her with an offended look on her face. "I was singing," she said, steering Phoebe away from a couple of guests. "I simply forgot the words, that's all. I'm afraid this isn't one of my favorite carols."

"Well then, what is your favorite carol? I'll have the musicians play it for you."

Cecily shook her head. "Really, Phoebe, there's no need. Actually I like all the carols. I just know some better than others. I will sing the next one, I promise."

Looking only slightly appeased, Phoebe cast a stern glance around the room. "Really, I don't know what's the matter with these people tonight. No one seems to want to sing. By the way, where are Madeline and the good doctor? I thought they were coming tonight."

"Madeline decided to take little Angelina home. The poor little thing has had quite enough excitement for one day."

Phoebe nodded, sending wisps of ostrich feathers floating to the floor. "She has, indeed.. Dreadful children to do such a thing." She glared in the direction of the Millshires, who were singing with obvious reluctance. "They are little savages, those two. I had to chase them out of here this afternoon. They were trying to crawl under the branches of the Christmas tree. Can you imagine? All those glass balls rattling back and forth. I was quite sure they would all be broken." She fanned her face with her gloved hand. "Thank goodness they didn't bring the little monsters—"

She broke off with a gasp of horror. "Goodness, there's Frederick. I told him to stay in the bar. Once he starts drinking he thinks he's the world's greatest tenor. I'd better get over there before he starts tormenting everyone's eardrums." She darted off toward the door, where the colonel was apparently regaling his captive audience with his war stories.

Cecily was pleased to see that Baxter had made his escape and was now over by the fireplace, talking to a seemingly enchanted young lady hanging onto his every word. Deciding that this was a good time to disappear for a while, she edged over to the door, trying to be as inconspicuous as possible.

Across the room, Lady Esmeralda was in an animated discussion with another woman, while her husband gazed around the room with a bored expression. For an instant his gaze met hers; then, as if unaware of the contact, he turned away.

Cecily drew a deep breath, opened the door, and slipped outside into the hallway.

CHAPTER

❀ 20 ❀

Gertie had no chance to speak to Dan on the way home from the station. The twins, bursting with excitement, bombarded her with questions about Father Christmas and the carol singing ceremony, and Daisy, when she could get a word in, filled Gertie in on everything they'd seen and done while in London.

Dan sat behind the wheel of his motorcar and didn't say a word while he drove back to the Pennyfoot. Seated next to him in the front seat, Gertie gave short answers to the twins, and paid scant attention to Daisy's long-winded accounts.

Her mind kept going back to Dan's proposal and what it would mean to them all. What would happen to Daisy? Would she be able to come with them? How would the twins feel about having a new nanny at this stage in their lives?

How would they adapt to living in the city, going to a new school, having to make new friends? They were bound to miss the Pennyfoot, and the people they had come to know as family. Though probably not half as much as she would.

"Mama! *Mama!* You're not listening to me!"

Gertie jumped, staring back at the small face glaring at her. "I'm sorry, James, I was thinking of something else."

"Well, I want to know if Father Christmas is going to bring me a puppy."

Gertie sighed. James had been asking for a puppy for the past three years. Each time she'd had to tell him they couldn't keep a puppy in the hotel. "I'm sorry, James, I don't think Father Christmas can bring puppies."

"Why *not?*"

"Because he can't carry them on his sled. They'd fall right off."

"They can't go down the chimney, neither, silly," Lillian piped up.

James sounded close to tears. "But I *want* one."

Gertie rolled her eyes. She'd been through this argument before, and knew it would be a long, drawn-out battle. Then she had an idea. "Well, I have some news for you. Samuel has a dog now. Her name is Tess and she lives in the stables. If you ask him, I'm sure he'll let you play with her sometimes."

James sat up. "Really? Is she a big dog?"

"Really big. You'll both love her."

Both twins let out squeals of excitement. Gertie felt Lillian's hand creep into hers. "Mama? This is going to be the best Christmas ever! I'm so happy we live in the Pennyfoot, aren't you?"

Gertie swallowed hard. "Very." She turned her head to watch the gas lamps flash by as they turned onto the Esplanade.

Beyond them she could just see the glow of golden sand before it disappeared into the shadows.

It was too dark to see the ocean, but she knew it was there, washing ashore. Once she left Badgers End, there'd be no more walks along the Esplanade, no more donkey rides along the sands, no more watching the twins laughing at Punch and Judy, no more band concerts to listen to, *no more Pennyfoot*. She and the twins would be giving up a lot to marry Dan and live with him in London.

She jerked forward as the motorcar came to a halt. "We're home!" the twins shouted, and waited impatiently for Daisy to get out so they could scramble out after her.

Gertie leaned out the door. "Daisy, take the children inside and get them dressed for the carol singing. I've laid out their clothes. I'll be there in just a minute or two."

Daisy nodded, grasped the twins' hands, and led them up the front steps of the club.

Dan switched off the engine and turned to open the door.

"Wait!" Gertie closed the door, then tugged at the collar of her coat and unfastened the top button. She felt hot and cold all at the same time. "I have to talk to you," she said, "before we go in there."

He must have heard something in her voice, because he gave her a long look before answering. "All right. What's this all about?"

She took a deep breath but it didn't seem to help. Her chest hurt, and an ache cut her so deep she hugged her stomach.

Kate Kingsbury

"It's about you and me."

His face was shadowed, with just enough light from the gas lamps to see his set expression. "What about you and me?"

She looked away, because it hurt too much to look at him. Her voice trembled so badly she could hardly get out the words. "I can't marry you."

She heard his sharp intake of breath and squeezed her eyes shut tight so she wouldn't cry.

"Why not? I thought that was what you wanted."

"I did." She gulped. "I do. But I can't drag my children away from their home and everyone they know."

"Children that age are adaptable. They'll soon forget all about this place once they settle down. There is so much more to do in the city. Visits to the park and the zoo, boat rides on the Thames, museums and historical places to explore. They will love it there."

"But it won't be home. They've just spent a week or so in London, and look how excited they were to be home. They'll miss the people, and the life here. They'll be miserable and lonely in the city."

He was silent so long she was afraid he was never going to answer her. Just when the silence became unbearable, he spoke.

"What you really mean is that *you* don't want to leave here and move to London."

She thought about it for several seconds, then sighed. "Yes, I suppose that's what I mean."

"I'm sorry, Gertie. I wish I could tell you I'd stay here, but I can't. My life is in the city. That's where I belong."

She hadn't realized how much she'd been nursing that

small hope. "I understand, Dan. I really do. That's why I can't marry you."

She stole a look at him. He sat staring straight ahead, and she couldn't see his expression, but she could guess from the set of his shoulders.

When he spoke again, his voice was gruff. "Very well. Then I suppose this is good-bye."

The pain cut deeper and she blinked. Hard. "Good-bye, Dan. I wish you lots of luck in London."

He nodded. "You, too."

She turned quickly and scrambled out. She didn't wait for him to crank the engine and leave. Without looking back she fled around the corner and into the kitchen yard.

Shutting the gate behind her, she leaned against it, listening to the engine turn over until at last it caught and roared to life.

His motorcar door slammed, and it was like a door slamming on her life. She'd turned down the chance of a future with a man she'd loved with all her heart. Probably the last chance she'd ever have of marriage and a home of her own. Perhaps tomorrow she'd feel better about it. Perhaps tomorrow she'd know she'd made the right decision.

Right now, however, it felt as if she was the biggest fool on earth. And still she didn't cry.

The quartet began playing the opening chords of "God Rest Ye Merry, Gentlemen" as Cecily quietly closed the library door. She could hear Colonel Fortescue's voice booming out above the rest. Apparently the deaths of four people had little effect on him. Phoebe, no doubt, was at this very moment doing her best to shut him up.

Cecily hurried along the corridor until she reached her office. Once inside, she felt for the matches on her desk and quickly lit the oil lamp. The photographs were where she'd left them, and she picked them up, thumbing through them until she found the one she wanted.

Now she was convinced she knew who had killed Ellie Tidwell and most likely the other three victims. As for the motive, she could only guess right now. What she needed was proof, and there was only one way to get that.

To do so meant being elsewhere far longer than was prudent. Baxter, at least, was bound to notice her absence, but that couldn't be helped. He would understand if she found what she expected to find. Wasting no more time, she dropped the photographs back onto her desk, picked up her oil lamp, and left the room.

She encountered no one on her way upstairs, and reached Sir Walter Hayesbury's suite without being seen. It took only a moment to unlock the door with her master key, and slip inside the room.

Placing the lamp on the bedside table she headed for the wardrobe. She had learned long ago that if someone wanted to hide something, the wardrobe was usually the first choice.

Opening the door, she quickly rummaged through the contents, searching pockets, feeling along shelves, and tipping boots upside down to make sure nothing had been hidden inside them. She had almost given up when she found it. A rolled-up cravat, with something solid inside it.

Carrying it over to the lamp she opened it up. As she

did so, a white bow tie fell to the floor. She barely noticed, her gaze focused on the glitter of gold that sparkled in her hand. With a feeling of triumph, she held up the broken necklace.

Stopping to pick up the tie, she saw at once the smeared bloodstain. That's why Sir Walter couldn't wear it the first night at the banquet. Why he'd borrowed one from Baxter. He must have had blood on his fingers from the cut on Ellie's neck when he tore the necklace from her.

Quickly she wrapped the tie and necklace back in the cravat and tucked it into her sleeve. Then she picked up the lamp and left the room.

P.C. Northcott would not be pleased with her for summoning him on Christmas Eve, but she had no choice. The man had in all probability committed four murders, and once he realized she had uncovered evidence to the fact he would most likely do everything in his power to see that it didn't reach the constable.

Again she passed no one on her way back to her office. Once inside, she went straight to her desk, lifted the telephone off its hook, and held it to her ear.

The operator's voice asked, "Number, please?"

Cecily was about to answer when she heard a slight sound behind her. She spun around, dropping the phone onto the desk with a clatter.

Moving toward her, a wicked-looking knife gleaming in his hand, was Sir Walter Hayesbury.

"Where's madam? I can't see her anywhere." Gertie held on to the hands of Lillian and James, just in case they got too close to the Christmas tree. It wasn't often they were allowed in the library, and now that it was transformed into a Christmas wonderland, their excitement had them jumping all over the place.

Gertie had visions of them crashing into the tree and sending it to the ground. She'd never live that one down.

Looking over at the window, she saw Mrs. Chubb and Clive. They'd know where madam was. Pulling the twins with her, she edged over to them.

The housekeeper held out her arms the minute she saw them and hugged the children. "Where have you been? I thought you would have been here ages ago."

The children ran to Clive, and he wrapped his arms around both of them.

"I was talking to Dan," Gertie said, her attention on her daughter, who was clinging to Clive's arm.

Mrs. Chubb gazed around the room. "Where is he? Didn't he come with you?"

"No, he didn't." She hesitated, aching to tell someone, yet knowing this was not the right time.

She had underestimated Mrs. Chubb's perception. The housekeeper leaned forward, asking softly, "What happened, Gertie? You can tell me."

Gertie shrugged. "Dan asked me to marry him."

Mrs. Chubb clasped her hands together with a loud gasp, while Clive uttered a slight choking sound, then coughed. "I think I'll be off, now," he said, immediately invoking a chorus of protests from the twins.

"Oh, no, Uncle Clive, don't go," Lillian pleaded. "We just got here."

"Gertie!" Mrs. Chubb threw her arms around Gertie's shoulders. "I'm so happy for you!"

"I turned him down."

Gertie pinched her lips together as both Clive and the housekeeper stared at her.

Mrs. Chubb was the first to speak. "What did you do that for? I thought you were so in love with him!"

"Shhsh!" Gertie glanced around to make sure no one had overheard. "I don't want the whole world to know."

"I'm sorry." The housekeeper lowered her voice. "Gertie, what happened?"

"He wanted us to move to London."

"Oh." Mrs. Chubb looked up at Clive for help.

Gertie met his gaze and looked away. He was looking at her so intently, he made her nervous.

"Would that be such a terrible thing?"

He'd spoken so quietly she'd barely heard the words. "I don't know." She looked down at her daughter's face. "I just didn't want to leave everyone we know and go to a strange place where we don't know anybody. James and Lillian's friends are all here, and I—" She broke off, appalled to hear the catch in her voice.

Mrs. Chubb patted her on the shoulder. "It's all right, dear. You don't have to talk about it now. You're upset, I can see that. Perhaps you'd feel better if you went and lay down for a while. I can keep an eye on the kiddies."

Gertie shook her head. "No, we came to sing carols, didn't we, loves?"

The twins nodded, each of them holding one of Clive's big hands.

Gertie looked over at the quartet, which was gamely

struggling through their rendition of "O Holy Night." She could never understand why Phoebe hired the aging musicians every year. They sounded terrible, though most of the time the guests were singing so loud they drowned out the missed chords and fumbled notes.

Tonight, however, everyone seemed subdued. She could understand why, what with all the terrible things that had been happening at the Pennyfoot lately. Surely madam would be able to find out who did it and see the bugger put away. She was so good at doing that.

Gertie turned back to Mrs. Chubb. "Where did madam go? I can see Mr. Baxter over there, but I can't see madam anywhere."

"She was here a few minutes ago." Mrs. Chubb looked around, too. "I don't see her now. That's strange. It's not like her to leave her guests, especially tonight. The carol singing is her favorite night of the whole Christmas season."

"I'll see if I can find her." Clive gently disengaged himself from the twins' grasps. "I'll be back as soon as I can, little ones," he promised them. Looking at Gertie, he added, "Don't go away."

She watched him skirt the guests, sliding along the wall until he reached the door. Then he was gone, the door closing behind him.

She shivered as an odd sensation chased down her back. His words had unsettled her, but even more so, the look he'd given her as he'd said them. Shaking her head, she banished the thoughts from her mind. She'd had enough of men and their confusing behavior.

Dan had been hurt when she'd told him she couldn't marry him. She hadn't been prepared for that. It had been too hard to explain why she couldn't drag her children to London, where their lives would be so utterly different. Or why she couldn't tear herself away from everyone she loved.

She'd done it once before, when she'd married Ross and moved all the way to Scotland. She'd been so miserable, and deep down she knew the reason Ross had given up his business to come back to work at the Pennyfoot was because of her heartache over leaving Badgers End.

Dan wasn't like Ross. He would never come back to Badgers End for her. That small hope that she'd been nursing, the chance that if he knew how much it meant to her, he wouldn't leave, had been crushed tonight.

No, if she wanted him, she and her children would have to be the ones to uproot their lives and go with him. She might have been able to do that, but for one thing. For the one thing she hadn't told him, or anyone else for that matter, the biggest reason she had refused to marry him, was the fact that in all the time they'd been together, not once had he told her he loved her. Not once. Not even when he'd asked her to marry him.

She wasn't even sure why he'd asked her. Perhaps for companionship. Perhaps he felt responsible for her and the twins. Whatever the reason, it wasn't enough.

Gertie Brown McBride simply couldn't give up everything she knew and loved to marry a man who couldn't love her. Not for all the money and posh living in the world. That's all there was to it.

CHAPTER
❀ 21 ❀

Cecily mentally cursed herself for being so careless. Sir Walter was well aware that she was investigating the murders.

She should have known he would realize the photographs would incriminate him in a lie, thus leading her to her conclusions.

He was between her and the door. Her only chance of escape was to keep him talking and hope that Baxter would soon come looking for her.

"Is there something I can do for you, Sir Walter?" Thankful for her measured tone, she carefully backed around her desk.

Fear gripped her throat, however, when he moved forward, the knife poised to strike. "You should have left well enough alone, Mrs. Baxter. Look where your meddling has led you. I really, truly dislike having to silence you, but I have no choice."

"I could promise not to say a word to anyone about what I know," Cecily suggested hopefully.

Sir Walter's face darkened. "I am in no mood for frivolity. I—" He broke off, passing a hand across his forehead as if in great pain.

"I'm so sorry, you still have your headache. I really think I should fetch a powder for you." She reached for the bell rope. "Let me ring for the housekeeper."

"Let go of that this instant!" He brandished the knife in her face and she backed away, out of reach of the rope. "I'm not relishing this moment. I wish you had just minded your own business, then none of this would be at all necessary."

He really didn't want to kill her, she realized. Maybe she could take advantage of that. "I'm really sorry. I've never been able to resist a puzzle, and you were so clever in everything you did. I greatly admire your fortitude."

He scowled. "I'm afraid it's a little too late for sweet words. I must do what I have to do, to preserve the good name of both my wife and myself. The scandal would kill her."

He moved closer to the desk, forcing her to back up to the wall. Now she had nowhere to go. "I would like to know just one thing." She edged sideways, one hand supporting herself on the back of her chair. "I would like to know why you went to all the trouble of killing all those people."

"I was under the impression you knew the reason."

She shook her head. "I really don't, and it's puzzling me greatly. I do know that Ellie worked for you when she was in London. Her mother mentioned that she worked at Rosewood Manor. It was your wife's handkerchief I found outside the Danvilles' suite. I realized that the R.M. stood for Rosewood Manor."

"Ah." He moved closer. "I wondered where that handkerchief had gone. My wife gave it to me to wrap around a cut on my finger. I'd tucked it in my pocket and forgotten it."

Strange that she hadn't seen any blood on the handkerchief, Cecily thought. Then again, she hadn't unfolded it. "A cut on your finger? Or was it, perhaps, blood from Ellie's neck when you tore the necklace from her?"

Sir Walter's face darkened. "That ungrateful little libertine. I gave her that necklace, and she had the audacity to refuse my favors. She left my house without a word to me. Just simply disappeared."

"So you came here looking for her."

Anger flashed in his eyes. "I did not! I had all but forgotten the little guttersnipe. My wife and I had heard good things about the Pennyfoot Country Club. We decided to spend our Christmas here for a change. I had not the faintest inkling that *she* would be here. I couldn't believe my eyes when I saw that trollop engaging in a disgusting display of lust right under my nose."

"Is that why you killed Charlie?"

He frowned. "Charlie?"

"The footman. You were jealous of him?"

He uttered a short, contemptuous laugh. "Jealous? Great heavens, no. That evening, after the banquet, I saw Ellie Tidwell again crossing the yard. I followed her, intending to have it out with her. She was quite insolent, arousing my temper. That was a mistake. I saw the necklace she wore, *my* necklace, and snatched it from her neck. She clawed at me, screaming at the top of her voice. I had to silence her. Before I knew it, my hands were at her throat."

He was having difficulty reliving the incident. She could see the sweat standing out on his forehead, which was still creased in pain.

She moved just a fraction of an inch, but he saw her and jerked the knife. "I can't possibly let you leave. You must realize that."

Her heart pounded so hard she thought she would faint. Her chest hurt with the effort to keep her voice calm and quiet. "I don't understand why you killed Charlie, too."

"He saw me, that's why." Again Sir Walter drew the back of his hand across his forehead. "When I realized what I had done, I dragged the body into the coal shed. I was going to leave it under the coal, and hope that no one would find it until long after I had gone back to town."

"And Charlie saw you?"

"Yes. I had to move the body again. Silly young man. He tried to blackmail me. Said he would say nothing if I paid him five thousand pounds." He shook his head. "I knew it wouldn't stop there. That young man was shrewd. He would have bled me dry. I arranged to meet him an hour later in the rose garden. I told him I would bring him the money then. He should have known I couldn't get my hands on that much money in such a short time."

"So you went up on the roof and dropped the gargoyle on his head."

"Yes." He nodded at her. "You have a unique little garden up there on the roof. I discovered it the first afternoon we arrived. Those steps leading up through the attic make it so easy to get up there. Very nice view." He blinked, as if he'd lost track of what he'd been saying.

Cecily made a mental note to keep the attic door locked in future. That's if she survived. Where was Baxter? Why wasn't he looking for her? Surely her office would be the first place he looked?

"We're wasting time," Sir Walter said, reading her mind. "I really do regret having to do this, Mrs. Baxter. You have been a most charming host, and under any other circumstances our relationship could have been most pleasant. I cannot allow you to repeat what I have told you, however, though I must admit, it has been quite a relief to tell someone about it. It has all been weighing heavily on my mind. I do have to thank you for that."

"There's just one more thing," Cecily said quickly. She edged sideways again. On the top of her filing cabinet stood a large glass paperweight in the shape of a pyramid. If she could just reach it and throw it at his head, it would most likely do enough damage to allow her to escape. "Tell me, why did you kill the Danvilles?"

Sir Walter sighed. "That was also regrettable. Mrs. Danville was such a pretty little thing. She struggled so hard I almost couldn't go through with it, but once I'd started there didn't seem any way to stop."

Cecily's stomach heaved, and she had to take several deep breaths. Another inch or so and she could reach the paperweight. "But why did you find it necessary to kill her?"

He smiled, an evil smile that chilled her to the bone. "Actually, Mrs. Baxter, you gave me the idea."

She stared at him in horror. "I? How is that possible?"

"You were in the dining room, seated at the next table to

me, and you were talking to your husband about the serial killer. It seemed that more than one person thought that the deaths were the work of the Mayfair Murderer. I decided to foster that assumption. He had apparently left London. He made the perfect scapegoat. According to your husband, however, I needed some kind of signature to leave behind. Something to tie them all together." Once more he paused, this time pressing his fingers to his forehead.

"Your headache seems to be getting worse." Taking advantage of the fact that his eyes were closed, Cecily slid sideways again. Now the paperweight was within reach. How much time would she have to grasp it and throw before he struck with the knife?

She knew the answer to that. Not much. Nevertheless, it was the only chance she had. She jumped when Sir Walter spoke again.

"I remembered the kissing bough in the ballroom. I had seen Ellie with that foolish young man beneath it, and I had seen the Danville couple beneath it as well. It wasn't much, but it was enough. I decided to make the kissing bough my signature to leave behind, which meant the Danvilles had to die, too." Once again he brandished the knife. "And now, regrettably, it is your turn. I'm sure you must have kissed someone under that thing. Your death, as with the others, will be attributed to the infamous Mayfair Murderer."

"There is just one flaw to that plan, Sir Walter. The Mayfair Murderer has been captured."

"Oh. Well, then, the deaths will be attributed to some other serial killer. No one will suspect a respected baronet of such dastardly deeds."

Deciding to try one last time to reason with him, Cecily

held up her hand. "I'm afraid it's too late for that now. I have sent for the constable. It will only be a matter of time before he arrives to arrest you. He will be far more kindly toward you if you give yourself up, so why don't you just give me the knife and we'll go to meet him together. I will tell him how you spared my life and I know he will take that into consideration."

Sir Walter laughed—a most unpleasant sound. "I don't think so. The constable is not coming, my dear. You were about to ring him, if I'm not mistaken." He leaned forward to pick up the telephone. "You never had the chance to talk to him."

All hope gone, Cecily moved swiftly and grasped the paperweight.

Anticipating her move, Sir Walter jerked backward.

Cecily threw with all her might, and just missed his head by a fraction of an inch. Horrified, she instinctively ducked down behind the desk just as the paperweight crashed into the door.

She heard Sir Walter utter a vicious curse, and braced herself for the cruel slice of the knife.

Then without warning, the door crashed open. There were sounds of scuffling, voices shouting, and a heavy thud, followed by silence.

Her knees trembled so badly she couldn't seem to get up. She felt strong arms reach for her, and her husband's desperate voice uttered her name, over and over. She clung to him as he raised her, then crushed her to him.

"Are you all right?" he asked hoarsely, and she nodded.

"I'm not hurt, only scared." She glanced across the desk to where Sir Walter stood with head down, looking dazed and unsteady on his feet. P.C. Northcott was fastening the killer's hands behind his back, while Kevin Prestwick looked on. Standing behind them, Clive was rubbing his knuckles.

"Come," Baxter said, leading her out from behind her desk. "I will take you back to the suite and we will talk there."

"No." She held back, anxious to know what was happening. "I need to go back to the library. I hope the guests know nothing of this?"

"Not as far as we know."

"I'll be taking this fellow here down to the police station," P.C. Northcott said, looking at the doctor. "That's if you will take us in your carriage, Dr. Prestwick?"

"My pleasure." Kevin Prestwick looked grim. "I'm happy he will be getting exactly what he deserves."

"I think you will be needing this," Cecily said, pulling the cravat from her sleeve. "You will find Sir Walter's tie inside, and the necklace he tore from Ellie's neck."

"Oh, well done." Dr. Prestwick glanced over at Cecily. "Are you sure you are not feeling out of sorts? I can give you a sedative. You might not be able to sleep well after this."

"I will be quite all right, thank you." Cecily gave him a wobbly smile. "I really must get back to my guests."

"Very well." The doctor waited for the others to leave, then followed them out the door.

The moment the door closed behind them, Baxter drew his wife close again. "I thought he'd killed you," he muttered, and rested his forehead against hers. "When I rushed in here and didn't see you I thought—"

She pulled back and laid a finger against his lips. "You should know it would take a far more clever man than Sir Walter to be rid of me."

He stared into her eyes for a moment, then smiled. "I suppose that means I am encumbered with you forever."

She returned the smile. "Indubitably, my dear husband."

Gertie picked up the last silver platter and stacked it on the tray. One final look around the library and she could take the dishes down to the kitchen. The rest of the evening, what was left of it, would be hers. Hers and the twins.

She looked up as the door opened and smiled at Clive as he walked toward her.

"Here." He held out his hand. "Let me take that down for you. You must be anxious to get back to the children."

She pulled a face. "I don't know about anxious. They're so wild with excitement it will take them hours to settle down to sleep."

He grinned. "Just tell them Father Christmas won't come until they fall asleep."

"I usually do." She handed him the tray. "Doesn't always work."

"They'll grow up so fast. You'll miss these days."

"Yeah, I know." She looked up at him. "You like children, don't you?"

"Yes, very much." He gave her one of his disturbing looks. "Children are what make life worthwhile."

"Did you never get married?"

"I was married once."

"Oh, I'm sorry."

"So am I."

She wanted to ask him if he had children, but was afraid it might upset him. Deciding it was time to change the subject, she said quickly, "Madam must be so grateful to you."

Now he looked wary. "Why?"

"She told Mrs. Chubb what happened, and Chubby told me. She said you rushed in her office and punched the daylights out of that horrible man. He would have killed her if you hadn't been there."

Clive shrugged. "I just happened to get there first. Mr. Baxter and the doctor were right behind me, and the constable was there, too."

"Well, I'm proud to know you, Clive Russell." She looked up at him. "Thank you for being so good to my twins. They really like you."

"I like them, too." He looked at her for a long moment, then carried the tray over to the door.

"Here, I'll open it for you." She hurried over to him and opened the door. "Thanks for taking the tray down."

"My pleasure." He inclined his head, gesturing for her to go first.

She brushed past him, and stepped out into the corridor. "Happy Christmas, Clive."

He nodded at her. "Happy Christmas, Gertie."

She was halfway down the hallway when he called out after her. "What about you?"

She stopped and looked back. "What about me?"

"You said the twins like me."

His grin brought a glow in her cheeks. "I like you, too, Clive."

A few moments later she opened the door of her room to find the twins waiting for her. Her heart still ached for Dan, and probably would for a long time to come. In another week he would be gone, and she would be alone again.

Well, not quite alone. She had her babies, and the Pennyfoot family. The memory of Clive's shy smile warmed her again. Maybe it wasn't such a bad Christmas after all.

"That was a very narrow escape tonight," Baxter said, sternly, as he closed the door to their suite. "Much too close for comfort."

Cecily had to agree. Seated in front of her dresser, her legs still trembled every time she thought about that knife in Sir Walter's hand. "Kevin said he thinks Sir Walter has a brain tumor. It makes people do all sorts of things they'd never dream of doing normally."

"Including mass murders?"

Cecily sighed. "I must admit, it was rather extreme. I feel so sorry for Lady Esmeralda. I saw her leave with Sam Northcott. I could tell she was in a state of supreme shock." She stared at her husband's image in the mirror. "Speaking of Sam, how did the constable come to be here tonight?"

"The operator rang him."

"Operator?"

"Yes. Apparently you took the telephone off its hook to ring someone, and didn't put it back until some time later. The operator was listening to the conversation, realized something was wrong, and rang for Northcott."

"Good heavens. There are some advantages to having a meddlesome operator after all."

"Yes, well, Northcott rang Prestwick and asked him to

bring him over in the carriage. He thought it would take too long on his bicycle."

"Ah, so that's why Kevin was here. But what about Clive? How did he happen to be there at just the right moment?"

"He was looking for you when he saw Northcott arrive. He came and told me and we reached your office just in time to hear the crash on your door. Northcott and Prestwick were farther down the hallway, but we all made a dash for the door. Clive was the first one to go in and he took the blighter down."

"How very courageous of him. He saved my life."

Baxter looked offended. "I would have done the same had I arrived there first."

"I know you would, dear." Cecily smiled at him. "It wouldn't be the first time you've saved me from the hands of a killer."

"Well, I certainly hope it's the last." He walked over to her and sat down beside her on the stool. "So what made you suspect Sir Walter?"

"Remember the handkerchief I found?"

"With the R.M. initials?"

Cecily nodded. "His wife must have noticed blood on his finger. He told her he cut it, and she gave him her handkerchief to cover it. The initials stand for Rosewood Manor. Ellie's mother told me that Ellie worked there when she was in London.

"Sir Walter mentioned Rosewood when he was talking about the carol singers. That's when I realized that Sir Walter must have been well acquainted with Ellie."

"That wouldn't necessarily mean he killed her."

"No, of course not, but then I started thinking about the photographs."

Baxter looked puzzled. "What do they have to do with anything?"

Cecily removed the string of pearls from her neck and laid them in their velvet-lined box. "Sir Walter told you his valet had forgot to pack his white tie, which is why he asked to borrow one of yours for the ball."

"Yes, I remember."

"Well, I knew he had to be wearing a white tie the night before at the banquet. I surely would have noticed if he hadn't.

"Which made me wonder what had happened to that tie. Just to make sure, I looked at the photographs. There is a very clear image of him wearing a white bow tie. There had to be a reason why he lied about it."

Baxter's frown deepened. "Why *did* he lie about it?"

"He couldn't wear his own tie because there was a bloodstain on it. He had blood on his hand after tearing Ellie's necklace from her neck, and must have touched his tie. It's a silk tie, and he knew he wouldn't be able to remove the stains, so he asked to borrow one from you."

"How did you know all that?"

"I didn't." Cecily began unpinning her hair. "I knew there had to be a good reason why he wasn't wearing his own tie, so I thought if I could find it, I might find evidence that would convict him. So I searched his room."

Baxter closed his eyes with a groan. "I might have guessed. So that's where you found the tie and the necklace. Still, it wasn't much for you to take such a chance. After all, he could have simply mislaid the tie."

"Perhaps, but I also remembered that Samuel had a nasty streak of black on his coat. He said he got it from cleaning one of the cars. He also mentioned that the car was extremely dirty. I realized it could have been coal dust from Ellie's body. Whoever killed her would have had to find some way of taking her into the woods."

"How did you know it was Sir Walter's car?"

She smiled. "A simple process of elimination. There are only three cars in the stables. One belongs to Mr. Mortimer, or rather, Sir Arthur Conan Doyle—" She broke off with a gasp. "I really must get his autograph before he leaves."

"The Millshires' car is also in the stables."

"True. I considered him for an instant, but there again, there was the handkerchief, and the fact that Ellie had worked for Sir Walter." She was tempted to tell him about Madeline's prediction, but quickly shunned the idea. "With everything put together, I was convinced I had the killer. All I had to do was prove it."

"And, as has happened so many times before, you almost died in the process." He shook his head, his grave glance meeting hers. "When, Cecily? When are you going to give up all this nonsense and live a normal life?"

She sighed. "I don't go looking for these situations. They come to me."

"Yes, I know." He stared down at his hands. "I'm beginning to believe in the Christmas curse. Either the Pennyfoot is cursed or you are."

She laughed. "I suppose we'll never know exactly which one it is."

"There's one way to find out." He looked up again, his expression giving her cause to worry. "You could leave."

The cold feeling in her chest spread rapidly. "We tried that once. We were miserable."

"*You* were miserable. I was unhappy because I knew you were." He drew such a deep breath she saw his chest rise and fall. "Cecily, I have had an offer from a very influential businessman. He purchases properties in foreign lands and turns them into hotels. He wants me to go to these places, oversee the renovations, then hire and train the personnel to run them."

She stared at him, eyes wide, not knowing quite how she felt. "Bax, darling, that would be so wonderful for you! Seeing all those exotic countries and meeting the people, what an exciting career!" The familiar lump rose in her throat and she swallowed. "Oh, but how I should miss you. I imagine you would be gone months at a time."

He nodded, his face a mask of wariness. "Months."

"Well," she swallowed again, "you must take it, of course. You can't possibly allow such a wonderful opportunity to slip by. I'll manage somehow, and we'll make up for lost time when you are home."

"He wants you to come with me."

Now she felt as if all the breath had been knocked out of her body. "What?"

Baxter nodded. "When I told him about your experience with hotel management, he thought we would make a wonderful partnership. I would oversee the renovations, while you train the staff." He turned her toward him and grasped her hands. "Think of it, my love, being together in places like China, India, Australia, Jamaica. We could meet up with your sons, and see the world together. Can you imagine how exciting that would be? You wouldn't have time to be miserable."

Yes, she thought. Exciting. But how could she bear to leave Badgers End and the Pennyfoot again?

He must have known what she was thinking. "Just promise me one thing."

"All right."

"Promise me you will think about it."

She let out her breath on a long sigh. She'd probably be thinking of nothing else from now on. "I will."

He leaned forward to kiss her and she clung to him. How could she take this opportunity away from him? Then again, how could she leave the Pennyfoot again after all these years?

"Happy Christmas, my love."

She drew back to look at him. "Happy Christmas, darling."

She would put away the decision for now. For no matter what she decided, or what happened in the future, nothing would ever change her love for her husband. That was all that really mattered.